BLOODY IS THE NIGHT

Bloody is the Night

ROBIN JEFFREY

Bloody is the Night

TRADEMARK ACKNOWLEDGEMENTS

The author acknowledges the trademarked status of the following wordmarks mentioned in this work of fiction:

Skid Row Coffee
Maserati
Honda
Louis Vuitton
Armani
Recuerdo
Escalade
Chateau Marmont
U-Haul
Sine Qua Non Patine Syrah

All wordmarks are property of their respective trademark owners.

BOOKS BY ROBIN JEFFREY

The Cadence Turing Mystery Series
.exe: A Cadence Turing Mystery (Book 1)
R.A.T.: A Cadence Turing Mystery (Book 2)
LOS: A Cadence Turing Mystery (Book 3)
The Night Series
Hungry is the Night (Book 1)
Bloody is the Night (Book 2)
Lonely is the Night (Book 3)

To Philip Allen
You have & will forever be
home to me.

CONTENTS

~ 1 ~

CHAPTER 1

Andy

Hidden behind the spires, smog and sprawl of Los Angeles, the sun was struggling to rise. I looked around my feet at what was left of a human being, what was now various scraps of meat and pools of blood and other fluids too vile to name. Putrescence filled my keen nose and drowned out all other scents. I took a tentative step farther into the midst of the massacre. It was a circle of destruction about thirty feet wide, more if you counted what had made it onto the walls and ceiling. The lights were muted and glowed brown beneath the dried blood. I flipped over a chunk of flesh with the toe of my shoe before crouching down to take a closer look. A bicep with part of a tattoo on it; the top half of a cloudy crescent moon. The bottom half was either somewhere in this mess or in someone's stomach. I rubbed my forehead with my fingertips, exhaling through my nose.

This was a hell of a way to start the weekend. Even in this town.

"So, what do you think?" A cheery voice above me queried. "Was this one of yours?"

I looked up into the face of the ruddy cheeked police officer who was supposed to be at the cordon, making sure the second floor of the California Plaza Parking Garage was clear of any early morning looky-loos. To my chagrin, I recognized him. A human, a perennial patrol officer, uninterested in moving up in rank because it took him farther away from the streets on which he wielded an inordinate amount of power. I sighed and turned my attention back to the bloody mess in front of me, placing my arms akimbo on my hips. "Yeah."

"Jesus." The cop hooked his thumbs into his utility belt and flashed me a toothy grin, his white teeth in stark contrast to his pasty skin and flaming red hair. "What the fuck did the poor guy do? See something he wasn't supposed to?"

That was the real question, wasn't it? Why? Why would a wolf do this? It's what the head of our den had tasked me with finding out. Why I was standing here, a few hours fresh off my own final transformation for the month. Why, and maybe even more importantly, who?

But all that was a few steps above this gringo's paygrade. He was low-level, not a part of the den, not even trusted with knowing the truth about the people he took money from. He didn't know about the sacrament. He didn't know that the hands he shook didn't belong to human beings.

He thought werewolves could only be found on the studio backlots.

Lucky guy.

I rolled my sore shoulders back. The three nights of the full moon had taken its toll on me this time. I was tired. But I had a job to do. And Rick Gregory wasn't making it any easier.

"Aren't you guys usually less...flashy than this?" The cop continued to chatter on, gesturing around at the horror show we stood in the midst of. "This is going to take a hell of a lot of cash spread around to make disappear, even if he was just a bum."

I stood and moved to the opposite side of what was left of one of the corpse's arms, careful to avoid any viscera as I walked. "Yeah."

Gregory gave an annoyed grunt, crossing his arms over his chest. "Always love talking with you, Vazquez. Can always count on you for some friendly conversation."

I fixed the cop with a bored stare, letting the uncomfortable silence stretch between us until it threatened to snap. Then I shrugged, shaking my head. "What do you want from me, man? I'm working. Like you should be, Gregory."

The toothy grin returned to his face, and he moved to stand next to me. "Working. Sure."

I glanced at him from the corner of my eye. I often wondered what people like him thought Sangre Sagrada actually was – who did they think they were in bed with? A drug cartel? Another street gang? LA was full of them, everyone wanting their piece of the city. The thought that we were an organization of werewolves, powerful enough to influence the city at every level, that there were more creatures like us in every city across the country, hell, really all around the world? No, that thought would never occur to him. Even when faced with something like this.

The carnage... we'd have to use our influence to get any reports of it wiped from city records. But word would spread. You couldn't keep a lid on wanton violence like this.

Gregory shivered beside me, his upper lip pulled away from his teeth in a grimace. "How can you stand looking at this, man? It's disgusting."

Blood and viscera glistened under the garage's unforgiving fluorescent lights. If you stared long enough, you could almost believe the mess was moving, undulating, trying to pull itself back together into what was at one point a human being. I shook away the mirage, rubbing my eyebrow with my thumb. "I don't know. Strong stomach, I guess."

Gregory clicked his tongue off the top of his mouth. "Goddamn. I thought all you Latinos were supposed to be real hot blooded, fly-off the handle types – but you, Vazquez? You're cold as ice, aren't you?"

In my pocket, my free hand curled into a fist. But my tone remained flat and unaffected as I looked over at him. "I can't dance for shit either. And you don't want to eat my cooking."

Gregory laughed and nudged me with his elbow, leaning forward and miming breasts over his uniform. "Bet you still have a way with the little chicas though, don't you?"

I slapped on a shit-eating grin. "I don't know," I said, walking behind him and tapping his wedding ring with my knuckles as I passed. "Why don't you ask your wife?"

The dig landed hard across his face, his pale cheeks turning a flaming red that rivaled the color of his hair. Sputtering and cursing, the man scrambled to loosen his collapsible baton from his belt, expanding it with a snap of his wrist. "Son of a bitch–!"

He swung at me, wide and wild, with brute strength and no skill. I swayed backwards, dodging the baton with ease, before throwing myself forward, grabbing hold of his wrist with one hand and his shoulder with the other, using the momentum of his attack to force him to spin around. A well-placed kick to the inside of his left knee sent him hurtling down to the ground, and I fell with him, landing hard on top of him with my own knee jabbing into his kidney like a fist. The impact of us hitting the ground knocked the breath out of his lungs and the baton out of his hand. I moved quickly with my free arm to lean against his neck, pressing against his carotid artery and doubtless causing stars to dance in front of his eyes. When his squirming began to lessen, I lowered my mouth to the side of his head.

"Don't forget who pays for your coke habit, Gregory," I hissed into the shell of his ear. I pressed my knee harder into his kidney. "Try some shit like that again and you'll find out what your balls taste like. Okay?"

Blood dribbling from his nose and mouth, the cop beneath me gave a grunt of acknowledgement. Letting go, I pushed myself away from him. Standing, I brushed off my clothes, leaving Gregory to struggle to his feet alone.

When I saw he was standing on his own two feet, albeit a little unsteadily, I reached over and slapped him hard upside the head before pushing him back towards the cordon. "Now do your job and make sure nobody comes near here."

He shuffled off, wiping blood from his face with one hand and picking up his lost baton with the other. He risked a glare at me, but that was that. Men like him were always more bark than bite.

I checked the time on my watch and was about to return to my examination of the carnage when a buzz in my pocket drew my attention. I fished out my phone and saw a text from Caleb, requesting I join him in the security guard's booth.

Walking down the ramp to the entrance of the parking garage, I slid my hands into my pockets, attempting to reign in my temper. Rick Gregory was an idiot. But it wasn't really him I was mad at. It was me. Why did I agree to take this on? If I couldn't figure this out... If I failed Doña Sangre again...

A freezing pool formed in the pit of my stomach at the thought. I was born a werewolf. I'd never known life outside of the den, never known an existence without the support of the Sangre Sagrada. It sounded like hell.

Of course, one man's hell...

Caleb Beck, the only denless wolf I'd ever met, stood in the doorway to the security booth, waiting for me. As far as I knew, Caleb had never been a member of a den – not once in all of his seven-hundred-plus years of existence. I was tempted then, as I approached the far older wolf, to ask him why, even though I knew he wouldn't answer. Instead, the question that left my mouth was a simple one. "What's up?"

"You'll want to see this," he replied, pushing away from the doorframe on which he had been leaning.

The security booth was painfully well-lit, the fluorescent bulbs burning their imprint onto my retinas as I stepped out of the dim parking garage and into the cramped kiosk. Caleb sat down in a tall rolling chair and pulled himself up to the desk, upon which an ancient computer and several screens sat.

"Find something on the cameras?" I asked, resting my hand flat against the rickety desk, scanning the three computer screens for anything that might help us.

"Maybe." Caleb wiggled his head from side to side, his eyes narrowed. He poked his finger at the haphazard grid of live footage intermixed with blank static. "Most of them don't work – and whoever it was avoided the ones that did. But look at this."

He pulled a file window over to the middle screen and maximized it, so it covered all three screens, double clicking on the image to set it moving. It was the parking garage and the timestamp at the bottom of the footage indicated that it was from 2am last night. We were watching from inside the mouth of the main entrance, somewhere near the ramp that led up to the higher levels.

Brow furrowed, I watched as a figure tumbled down the ramp from the second level, rolling end over end several times, bouncing as they went, light, hooded jacket ripping off them as they fell.

"There's footage of her entering too," said Caleb, running the footage forward a few minutes. "She must have heard something from the street. Came in to see what it was."

After that fall, she must have been scraped up all to hell, but she didn't pause to assess her physical state. When she stopped rolling, she immediately scrambled to her feet and started running, throwing glances over her shoulder as she went.

"Well, well, well…" My eyes followed the fleeing figure from one screen and onto the next. "Who are you?" As the woman looked behind her, the terror on her face was clear even in the grainy security camera footage. I tapped at the screen. "And what are you running from?"

~ 2 ~

CHAPTER 2

Shaye

I didn't stop running until the sun rose. The muscles in my legs screamed at me, my lungs felt like they were going to burst into flames, my heart wanted to explode in my chest – but still, I kept running until I felt the first sweet rays of sunlight hit my face.

I felt safer with the sun up. There was something about what I had seen, something about what had happened to Jason that felt like it could only have existed in the dark. After all, the vision of what would happen to Jason had come to me in the night, sneaking up on me in the dark. After ten years of nothing, after I had come to believe that I was free of the gift, the curse, whatever the hell it was – even after I'd dreamt of Jason's death, I had thought it was nothing more than a nightmare.

Hoped that it was nothing more than a nightmare.

But some part of me must have known otherwise. Some part of me dragged me out of my sleeping bag and into the heart of the city in the middle of the night to watch Jason die. Just as I had dreamed it would happen.

Once the morning broke, I found my feet leading me back towards the California Plaza Parking Garage, sweat-soaked clothes sticking to my body, shivering not just from the cool ocean breeze, but with fear that I was going to find that I hadn't been hallucinating; that what I had seen last night was real; that Jason was dead.

Keeping close to the buildings on the corner of Fourth, I stared down the street. A cold numbness rippled through my chest as I watched the uniformed LAPD officers mill around their police cars, parked in front of the entrance to the garage, blocking all comings and goings from the space. I glanced up towards the second floor. Yellow police tape fluttered in and out of view and the flashing lights of what must have been even more police cruisers reflected off the concrete.

I stayed there like that, peering around the corner at the garage for almost five minutes, confident that I would go unobserved. As I watched, a group of men in business suits walked past the police cars, heads craning on their necks as they attempted to see what was going on inside. A cop soon came over and waved them off but exchanged a few words with them all the same as he sent them on their way. I moved over to their side of the street and sank down into a sitting position on the corner, careful to keep my eyes fixed on the ground as they passed.

"...Angeles keeps getting worse and worse," said one as they strolled by.

"Think it was a gang thing?" said another.

"Who knows?" said the first. "Sounds like he was just some homeless guy."

"Fucking bums, they're everywhere lately..."

I stayed there for a long time after they had gone. I didn't know that I could move.

Jason was dead. He was really dead. What I had dreamed had come true, again. And I had watched my friend die.

What the hell was I going to do?

The whoop of a police siren shook me out of my stupor. I jerked up, heart in my throat, to see one of the cruisers pulling away and heading up the street towards me. Scrambling to my feet, I started walking, turning the corner and heading towards Hope Street without having a clear idea of where I was going.

Before I knew it, my feet had taken me where I always went when I was in trouble. The Richard J. Riordan Central Library, also known as the Los Angeles Central Library, was a work of art as much as it was a place of refuge for me. It was built like a cathedral and right then it felt like the closest I was going to get to the grace of God. I stared up at the words carved over the South Hope Street entrance, my fingers wound tight around the bars of the wrought iron gate that separated me from the doors: "BOOKS INVITE ALL. THEY CONSTRAIN NONE".

I shook the gate. Locked. I dug my cellphone out of my pocket and blinked at the cracked screen. It was 7:30 in the morning. Too early for the library to be open yet.

Tears sprung to my eyes with a ferociousness that stole my breath away. I wept openly for the first time in what felt like years, crumpling down into a heap in front of the library. I crawled away from the gate and propped myself up against the beige stairwell wall, curling in on myself as I sobbed like a child, shaking.

I was too late. Again.

Would I always be too late?

Jason. He was going to get out. He'd heard from his aunt up in Portland; the one he'd told me about the first night we met, the one I encouraged him to reach out to. The woman said she had a place for him if he could make his way up there. Jason was working hard, saving money for the trip. He almost had enough. I remembered the smile on his acne scarred face when he told me the good news – God, was that only yesterday morning?

"I'm proud of you, kid," I said to him, mouth half full of a knock off Little Debbie honey bun. "Portland isn't going to know what hit it when you get there."

We sat outside my tent on Angel's Knoll, sharing a cup of coffee, watching the sun come up over the city. He leaned back on his spindly arm, red hair loose around his face. "I hear it's a cool place. That I can be myself there, you know? There's a big trans community."

"I'm going to miss you," I said, knocking his shoulder with my own.

"You could come with me!" Grinning, he handed over the coffee. "Do you have enough stashed for a train ticket?"

"Nah, not nearly." I shook my head and ruffled his hair with my free hand. "Don't you worry about me, Jace. I'm just glad you're getting out of here."

"'Me too." He sighed, excitement and happiness rolling off him like cologne. "No more creepy old dudes in their crappy cars. Sleeping in a real bed again. I can't wait."

The squeal of metal against metal yanked me out of my memories and into the present moment. I jerked up, ready to run, when I saw one of the librarians, Cheryl, pushing their way out of the gate, a cup of coffee in their hands. She looked down at me and paused.

"You okay, Shaye?" asked Cheryl, half in and half out of the gate behind which the library entrance sat.

"Uh…" I sucked up a nose full of snot and quickly and ineffectually wiped my face dry with my sleeves. Quickly realizing the futility of my actions, I collapsed a little further in on myself. "No." I shook my head, hating how pathetic I sounded. "No, not really."

Without hesitation, Cheryl pushed the gate the rest of the way open. She walked to me, mug in one hand, and dug into her purple cardigan's pocket with the other, removing a hastily thrown together pile of tissues and waving them at me.

She must have been watching me cry for a while. I took the wad of tissues from her with a pained half-smile. "Thanks, Cher."

Blowing my nose, I looked over at Cheryl as she plopped down beside me, my eyebrow quirked upward in a question. "You're not open yet, right?"

She nodded, pulling her sweater out from under herself so she could sit more comfortably. "Right."

I stuffed the dirty tissue into my coat pocket. "Then, what–?"

"Come on. I couldn't let you sit out here all alone." Cheryl leaned her head back against the beige stairwell wall, her loose bun of tight braids cushioning the impact. She was careful not to look at me when she asked, "Do you want to talk about it?"

Taking in a deep, shaky breath, I rubbed at the outside corner of my eyes with my middle fingers, the rest of my hands spidering against my cheeks. "I don't even know how to talk about it," I admitted. Sniffing again, my nose still stuffed up beyond all reason, I pulled my arms tight around myself. "Would it be alright if we just... sat here for a while?"

She nodded, her lips pulled down in an exaggerated frown. "Sure." Then, looking at it as if she'd forgotten she was holding it, Cheryl passed me the multi-colored mug in her hand. "Here; you look like you need this more than me."

I examined the mug – it was hand painted, a collage of different colored cats. It looked like something a child might do. I wondered if Cheryl had kids. We never talked about personal stuff like that, even though we'd known each other for years. You just didn't ask personal questions like that when you were someone like me. And she knew better than to ask the same of me. We all had our reasons for living on the streets, but family was at the heart of ninety-nine percent of them.

I took a large puddle of hot liquid into my mouth before I could dwell any more on these thoughts and was immediately distracted by the sudden, vile taste that assaulted me. I swallowed, even though I wanted to spit, and immediately gagged aloud.

"Oh my god," I shouted through the coughs and sputtering.

"Sorry," said Cheryl automatically, laughing behind her hand.

Face screwed up in sheer horror, I gestured between the librarian and the cup of what I had assumed was coffee in my hand. "Cheryl, this... this is coffee?"

"I know," she crowed, shaking her head, still laughing.

I took another miniscule sip and recoiled violently. "Ugh, oh God – I've never tasted anything like this." Smacking my lips, I tried to identify the cacophony of nastiness that was taking place inside my mouth. "It tastes like pencils!"

"That might be the mug more than the coffee, in my defense," she said, brown eyes narrowed in a wince. "It had pencils in it." She threw her hands up at my sudden burst of laughter, insisting, "But I washed it out real good!"

Still laughing, I brought the mug back up to my mouth without thinking. "Christ! This is homeless abuse," I said, before taking in another mouthful. I managed to gag it down before exclaiming with a smile, "Oh God, why do I keep drinking it?"

"I don't know!" managed Cheryl through laughter of her own.

The respite was only momentary. As soon as our laughter ebbed, reality closed back in on me. I shook my head, mouth going dry as I thought of how I would never hear Jason laugh again. How he'd never make it to Portland.

"Shaye," started Cheryl, her hands folding themselves in her lap. "If you need to talk to someone…if something happened to you and you need help, you know we can connect you with people who will be there for you, right?"

I put the mug down between us and rubbed my hands together. "Yeah. Yeah, I know."

There was another pregnant pause and then, Cheryl leaned down, her face turned upward to look into mine. "Are you in some kind of trouble, Shaye?"

The muscles in my cheek twitched as my lip pulled back from my teeth in a grimace. "Maybe?" I swallowed down the lump that had suddenly formed in my throat, burying my hands in my messy, cropped hair. "Jason is… do you know Jason?"

Cheryl's brown eyes widened. "I think so…little stick of a kid, bright orange hair?" Nodding, she straightened, rolling her shoulders back against the unforgiving wall. "He stops in here every once and a while. Not a regular like you, but I think I'd be able to pick him out of a crowd."

"He's–" The tears welled in my eyes again. *He's dead. Just say it. He's dead.* "He's not going to be coming around anymore."

"Oh?"

"He got…" *Torn to fucking pieces.* "…hurt and…" *I was a coward.* I pulled at my hair, biting hard into my bottom lip. "I couldn't do anything to help him." Shaking myself, I rocketed to my feet, walking away from Cheryl, my impotence galling me to the point of explosion. "I–I just sat there. Fuck! What the hell was I thinking?! Why didn't I help him?!"

"Could you have done anything?" asked Cheryl simply from behind me.

"I–!" I closed my eyes.

In the darkness behind my lids, I was there. Back in the parking garage, peering around a pillar, watching as that thing destroyed Jason with its bare fucking hands. It had almost looked like a man at first, especially the eyes – would I ever be able to forget those eyes? – but that was crazy. What man could turn into…that? No, no man could do what that thing had done. With its teeth. Jason had screamed, and screamed, and screamed, screaming like a child, like a wild animal himself, sounds I didn't know could come from a human being. Until that thing, the monster had put his head in its gigantic mouth, snapping Jason's neck free from his torso like my grandmother used to snap the ends off asparagus.

"No," I said quietly.

"Would you have gotten hurt if you tried to do something?" pressed Cheryl, her voice calm.

Thick, lump-filled blood dripped down the creature's face as it turned – as it looked right at me with those human eyes. And I saw it. Really saw it for the first time. And it saw me. And I knew I would be dead if I didn't run.

I opened my eyes. Cheryl watched me closely. I nodded. "Yes."

"Then you did the right thing." Cheryl swallowed hard. "Jason would say so too." She shook her head and looked down at her hands, flexing and turning them as if she were seeing them for the first time. "We have to take care of each other out here, that's true – but we can't do that if we don't take care of ourselves first."

I leaned against the beige stairwell wall, letting the back of my head thud against the hard stone. "Every time I think I've hit rock bottom," I muttered, holding on to myself as if I would fall to pieces if I let go. "Every single time...I peek over the edge and there's further down to go."

"Life is a bitch," said Cheryl, grunting as she struggled to her feet. "I don't have to tell you that." She turned away to head back inside, her hand on the handle of the black wrought iron fence, and then stopped, looking over her shoulder at me. "But we don't have to go through it alone, Shaye." Opening the gate, she stepped through it, closing it behind her with a clang. "No matter how it may seem, you're not alone."

~ 3 ~

CHAPTER 3

Andy

Closing my eyes behind my sunglasses, I tilted my head back until my face was lifted to the cloud speckled sky, taking deep breaths through my mouth in a failed attempt to avoid taking in the smell of the encampment across the street. Leaning against my car, my arms crossed high over my chest, I waited while Caleb picked his way through the sixth homeless encampment we had visited that morning, showing the grainy photograph we had to anyone who would talk to him for more than thirty seconds.

I brought my watch up to my face and sighed, gritting my teeth together. This was taking too long. Doña Sangre had given me just two days to get a handle on this situation and it was becoming rapidly apparent that two days was nowhere near enough time.

But I couldn't exactly tell Doña Sangre that. Not after everything she'd done for me. Not after what I owed her.

Closing my eyes once more, my mind drifted to how differently my morning had started.

Driving up into the hills of Bel Air for the first time in over a year, my car hugging the curving asphalt lanes, my mind was awash with anxiety and exhaustion. The last night of the full moon was always a particularly tiring one for me. Coming out of the change to find a message from the head of the den, from Doña Sangre herself, summoning me to the den house, had only frazzled me further. I ran my hand over the stubble on my jaw as the car climbed past twenty-million-dollar mansions.

What had I done this time?

I pulled up to the gate and identified myself via voice print and fingerprint to the security guards inside the acre-sized compound. After a moment, the gate soundlessly slid open, and I guided my car as close to the house as I dared.

Parking in an empty spot in the driveway, I took a moment to steady my nerves, my fingers flexing around the steering wheel. The last time I had been here, I had nearly been excommunicated. Things couldn't get any worse than that. Could they?

Before my anxiety could get the better of me, I stepped out of my car, walking down the moss and tile drive towards the twelve-foot-tall door, open wide to let in the fresh sea air.

Between fifteen and twenty wolves stayed on at the den house full time, though they rotated through with a fair amount of frequency based on Doña Sangre's mood, which had proved mercurial over the last year. I avoided the stares and ignored the whispers of the few that had already made it down into the shared living spaces this morning as I trotted through the massive sitting rooms. There were those who blamed me for la Doña's change in demeanor – that said it was my lawless behavior that had caused her to grow sullen and spiteful.

They may have been right about that.

As I climbed the sweeping white oak staircase to the second floor of the Retreat, I let my fingers trail along the topiary growing from the wall itself, releasing the sweet, subtle scents of the mosses and flowers as I went. I had not seen Doña Sangre in over a year, and I had missed this house. I had missed her. After all, she and I had grown up here together. Before she had become Doña Sangre, before she had become the leader of our family, she had been nothing more and nothing less than my friend, Emilia. Part of me would always think of her as that awkward, shy little girl she had been and struggle to reconcile those memories with the graceful, outspoken woman she had become.

I was stopped at the top of the stairs by Sangre Sagrada Security, who proceeded to pat me down without a word. Finding nothing objectionable on my person, they let me pass, one of the men indicating the furthest bedroom at the end of the hall. I gave a nod in return and headed that way, shoes tapping against the hardwood. I stopped just in front of the door, my hand outstretched towards the handle, when I heard a familiar voice call my name. "Andy!"

Looking up, I searched out the source of the voice, and found the wolf with ease. Folding a newspaper closed and placing it under his arm, Lazlo Cabral strode down the hallway towards me. His white-blond hair, pulled back from his face in a tight ponytail, was unmistakable, standing out against his deeply tanned skin.

Lazlo had been the right-hand wolf to Emilia's father and had continued in that exalted position after the den patriarch had passed the torch to his daughter. Lazlo had often been put in charge of keeping Emilia and I out of trouble as children, though he just as often helped us get into scrapes as got us out of them. Last I'd heard, Emilia had sent him out of the country on a goodwill tour of the non-U.S. dens in an attempt to shore up allies internationally.

"Lazlo," I said with surprise, turning to face him fully. I reached out a hand in friendship, brows high over my eyes as I smiled. "Didn't realize you were back in LA."

He took my hand, shaking it once and then returning it to me. "Wanted to catch you before you spoke with Emilia. Do you have a minute?"

I gave a snort of a laugh. "You keep her calendar, tío, you tell me."

His eyes crinkled at the corners as his lips twitched into a smile. With one hand at my shoulder, Lazlo guided me back up the hall, towards the opposite end, as far from the Sangre Sagrada security as we could go. There was a tension in his shoulders, a lack of levity in his expression, which sobered me. I tried to look him in the face, bobbing my head as I pressed, "Lazlo, is everything alright? I was surprised to hear from Emilia."

Lazlo turned on his heel, smoothing back his hair with one hand as he avoided my probing gaze. "Well...no. It's not. We have a problem."

Nodding, I knit my brow. "Okay. What is it?"

He shook his head, almost to himself, letting loose a thready sigh from between his teeth before speaking again. "I'll let Emilia fill you in on the details – wouldn't want to step on her toes – but I wanted to make sure you were up to speed on what's been going on here. Within the den." He looked at me at last, his soft eyes full of sympathy. "You've been out of the inner circle for a while, hijo."

"Not by choice," I started, defensively.

"But by your actions," he countered, his hand rising and falling. "But let's not get into all that right now." He placed his hand on my shoulder and squeezed, his volume lowering even further. "Emilia won't listen to me, but she might listen to you. She needs to be careful. She's making enemies."

I felt the hair on the back of my neck prickle and rise. "Enemies? How? What are you talking about?"

Lazlo cast a furtive glance around us, the tip of his tongue coming out to wet his lips. "She has big plans for the Sangre Sagrada. Always has. Modernizing us, bringing us kicking and screaming into the modern world in her words." He met my eyes from under his brow, jaw clenched. "She's pushing for an end to the sacrament. Opening of the den to half-breeds. An increasing acceptance of the bitten."

Extreme changes for Sangre Sagrada indeed. But ones Emilia had been talking about since we were teenagers. "That's...good. Isn't it?"

A shrug was Lazlo's immediate response. "Good, bad, it's what she wants. But not everyone agrees with her." He gave a rough, low chuckle. "But you know Emilia. She's stubborn. Hears 'no' and thinks the solution is to push harder for 'yes'."

I rolled my eyes, nodding. I had experienced that more than once myself. To say that Emilia was confident and strong-willed was kindness – someone less fond of her might characterize her as arrogant and obstinate. But she was seldom wrong, and her uncanny ability to back the right horse time and time again had earned her the admiration of the den, and her eventual ascension to its head.

Lazlo's hand fell from my shoulder to his side, and he sighed again. "I'm glad she's bringing you back on board, Andy. I think she needs you right now. To look out for her in ways I can't."

I felt my face begin to flush. "I'll... do what I can, tío."

"Bueno. That's all I can ask." Stepping back, Lazlo smiled weakly. "I won't keep you any longer. Come find me when you're done, okay?"

I nodded again and watched him move swiftly back up the hall, disappearing down the stairs. Mind full of all he'd told me, I returned to Emilia's suite, opened the door, and stepped inside.

When I entered her rooms, the scent of her overwhelmed me, coming from seemingly everywhere all at once. My eyes

searched the room for her, and found her quickly, standing in front of the wide-open patio doors, the cool ocean
breeze curling in her long brown hair and blowing through
her open robe, sending the floor length black silk dancing.

Muscle memory took over. I knelt, my head bowed, my
heart tight in my chest. "Doña Sangre," I managed after a
moment. "How may I serve you?"

No answer. I glanced up from under my lashes to find
her watching me in the reflection of the patio door, and the
knowledge that her eyes were on me sent a shiver through
me.

"Andoni, mi querido." Her blood red lips curled into a
smile that was half hidden by her long brown hair. "How
was your night?"

"Long, Emilia." I kept my eyes low as she crossed the
room towards me, her bare feet sinking into the dark blue
rug on which I knelt, her long silk robe trailing behind her,
rustling against the ground like leaves in a breeze. "Very
long."

"And lonely, I imagine." She stopped in front of me, and
I heard her chuckle. Her fingertips were soft against my
cheek, and she cupped my face in her hand, gently lifting
my chin until I was looking into her eyes. Her smile was unwavering, but it had, I thought, taken on an edge of sadness.
"You are always welcome to run with me, Andoni. You know
I would enjoy your company."

I carefully and gently removed her hand from my cheek,
brushing a dry kiss against the back of it before returning

the wandering appendage to her. "It's an honor I'm not worthy of Doña Sangre."

Humming, she shook her head, her smile losing none of its brightness, but gaining more ruefulness. "So formal." She swallowed, shaking her head contemplatively as she turned and walked away from me. "Always so formal."

I risked lifting my head a little more to follow her progress across the room. With sharp, jerky movements, Emilia pulled her robe around herself, cinching the silk shut with an ornate lace tie. Nudity wasn't a social taboo amongst wolves, but I found my muscles untensing when her body was finally hidden from view.

She lowered herself into a high back leather chair behind a stylized glass and cherry wood desk. Crossing her long legs over each other, she settled into the leather like it was a second skin. "Andoni," she said. "You have been a loyal member of this den for more moons than I can remember. More than that, you have been my friend. I know I can depend on you – I know it like I know the beating of my own heart. And I need you now more than ever."

Her tone set the hairs on the back of my neck bristling. Rising to my feet, I followed her to the desk, standing at attention in front of it. "Emilia?"

Watching me for a long moment, she finally nodded and reached down towards the bottom right drawer. Snapping it open, she reached inside, and I heard the beep of a fingerprint scanner. A panel on the top of the desk popped open with a click. Face growing grim, Doña Sangre reached inside the secret compartment and pulled out a thick brown file folder. She shook the contents out over the desk, sending forth a flurry of battered photographs, scraps of papers, and folded reports.

I looked from the pile to her with a raised brow. She stared back at me, her expression almost identical.

Not knowing what else to do, I reached forward and began pawing through the debris. As I did so, Emilia leaned in, watching me piece together what she had worked so carefully over the past four months to keep hidden.

I looked at bodies that were barely recognizable as bodies. Pieces of flesh in seas of blood splattered across seemingly every corner of Los Angeles. John and Jane Does, most of them, although occasionally a name would be put to the body parts: *Olivia Yutz, Ron Kincaid, Alex Kim...*

I skimmed through autopsy reports that called out teeth impressions on bones and claw marks through flesh. Witness reports were vague and unhelpful when they existed at all. Police reports with nonsensical notes scrawled in the margins: *wild animal attack??*, said one, *ritual sacrifice??*, said another.

Each document with a date. Each date corresponding to a night I had spent prowling through the deserts outside the city, fur keeping me warm on the chilly night.

"Four months," Emilia said eventually. "Twelve deaths. One every night of the full moon. The latest reported at first light, a few hours ago."

"A wolf?" I jerked my head up to stare at her, wide eyed. "One of us?"

She nodded, her brows low, her lips pursed. "Killing for sport. For pleasure." She spat the word out as if it were the pit of a cherry. "Openly hunting in my city. We've done what we can to suppress word of what is happening, but..." Gesturing to the photographs and documents spread over the desk in front of us with both hands, her shoulders high, Emilia shook her head from side to side. "I can't have this right now, Andoni. I can't. Things have been unsettled enough with the changes I've been trying to implement, moving us away from the Sacrament. On top of that, the Nameless will be here soon to discuss the state of our joint west coast operations." She collapsed back in her chair, long fingers digging into the side of her temple in small, tight circles. "Since Kassandra Arnaud took over the den last year they've been expanding – aggressively. They've already taken over the territory east of the cascades. They've reached an arrangement with the Red Rose den from Portland which has essentially put them in control of that area and now... now it seems they've turned their eye south."

The carnage on display was breathtaking. I pulled my eyes free of the photographs, turning instead to one of the police reports, flipping through it without really reading it. "You don't think one of them– one of the Nameless–?"

"It's possible," said Emilia, letting out a long breath through her nose. "But I don't think they'd be so bold." She straightened in her chair, pointer finger pressing into the top of her desk. "However, if they find out that someone in our den, that one of the Sangre Sagrada, is risking the exposure of our world – is threatening all we've worked so hard to build? They'll tear us to pieces. And no one will come to our defense. It will be the end of us. Forever."

I dropped the papers at last, crossing my arms, my gaze returning again and again to the mangled human flesh on display in the photographs splayed across Emilia's desk. "We have wolves on the LAPD. Isn't this what they're for?"

She snorted. "Idiotas. All of them. They've had four months to handle this." She rose, sweeping around the desk like a hurricane of silk, her finger now pointed at my chest. "I want you to take care of it, Andoni. You're the only one I can trust with this; you're the only one who understands what's really at stake."

I opened my mouth to argue with her but shut it when she closed the distance between us, her outstretched hand moving up to my face. She looked into my eyes with undisguised affection and shook her head.

"Please," she pleaded, her fingernails trailing along the edge of my jaw and making my skin prickle. "For the den. For me?"

"Of course, Doña Sangre." I hit the ground hard in a one-kneed bow, staring at the floor. "It would be my pleasure."

Her hand felt warm on the back of my head, her fingers working their way into my thick hair. "Find the wolf responsible for these deaths, Andoni. Bring them to me." She tugged at my scalp, and I had little choice but to look up at her. Her face was a mask of rage as she growled, "Alive."

Rubbing the tender top of my head as I made my way back downstairs, one question throbbed within me, still unanswered and at the forefront of my mind.

Why me? It's true, there had been a time when my loyalty to the den had been beyond question – but surely after the events of last year, those times were long gone. Was Emilia trying to give me an opportunity to win my way back into her favor? Or was this a test? If I failed, would it mean my excommunication from the den?

I stopped at the bottom of the stairs, swallowing hard at the thought. I had been born a wolf, and to be denless was spoken of as a fate worse than a silver bullet. All my life I'd heard horror stories about what it was like on the outside. The dangers – the loneliness – it was how wolves went mad.

Staring at the floor, I shook myself and continued through the house, cutting through one of the large living rooms, looking for Lazlo. No, it wouldn't come to that. I could do this. But how? Where would I start?

I found my mentor in a small drawing room, sitting in a highbacked, antique chair, sipping an iced tea languidly. He stood when I entered the room, tossing his head towards the ceiling as he gave a rueful smirk. "So...Emilia's filled you in on our little... situation now?"

I looked behind me in the direction of the bedroom I had just left. "Yeah." I shook my head, frowning. "Don't know what she thinks I can do that will be any different than what our people in the LAPD can."

Lazlo threw an arm around my shoulders and pulled me tight against him, moving me out of the center of the room and towards the open side of the house that led to the lawn and pool. He patted my chest with the palm of his hand. "Well, mi hijo, you have worked miracles for her before."

I ruffled my fingers through my hair, groaning. "Yeah, well, that's the thing about miracles, tío–" Dropping my hand to my side I shrugged. "They're once in a lifetime."

"Come now," said the older wolf, shaking me a little as he chuckled. "You should give yourself more credit!" Coming to a stop, he released me, turning to face me as he said quietly, "And, you should see this as the opportunity it is. A chance to make amends and put some doubts to rest."

I drew back, a little surprised at this line of talk from someone I considered family. "I don't need to prove anything to anyone."

"Don't you?" Lazlo's hand squeezed my shoulder, and he leveled a disapproving look at me from under his brow. "Andoni, you risked everything. For all of us. And for what? A woman?" He scoffed aloud, even more disdain entering his voice as he said, "A human?"

I swallowed hard and shook my head. "It's done. Tied off."

"No thanks to you." Casting one last glance at me, he dropped his hand to his side and turned away, walking the last few steps out onto the lawn, pausing in the open framework of the house. "There's a lot of ill will about the whole business, Andy, and right or wrong that's aimed at you. Doing this, helping Emilia, helping the den – it would go a long way to fixing things."

I followed him outside, moving to stand just in front of him. Slinging his hands in his pockets, Lazlo took in a deep breath, eyes fixed on the blue sky above us. "You know Emilia is very fond of you."

"I know," I answered, my shoulders hunched. "Believe me, tío, I know. And I love her like a sister. I'd do anything for her."

"Well," said Lazlo, shrugging. "Here's your chance to prove it."

Careful to keep my voice low, mindful always of ears perked and ready to hear things that were of no concern to them, I asked, "When are the Nameless supposed to get here, exactly?"

"We're throwing a big party for them in two days," said Lazlo, kicking at the grass coming up between the flat white stones that led out onto the lawn proper.

"Ah, mierda." I gritted my teeth and rubbed my thigh. "I'm going to need some help."

His smirk returned. "I thought you might say that."

I tilted my head to one side, my brow furrowing in confusion. Lazlo answered by nodding over my shoulder. I turned to see what or who he was indicating, and my mouth fell open in shock.

Crouching at the edge of the infinity pool, his fingers trailing in the carefully temperature-controlled water, was a wolf I had not seen in over fifty years. He was at least a half a foot taller than me, broad chested and muscular. His swept back silver hair was the only thing hinting at his true age, everything else about his body looking in its prime. Feeling eyes on him, he turned, the sun behind him making his expression unreadable. Standing, he shook the water off his fingertips, attention clearly fixed on us.

"Is that–?" I started, but before I could finish the wolf in question was crossing the yard, closing the distance between us with a few large strides.

Caleb Beck was a wolf old enough to remember a time before the dens formed. Never comfortable inside the hierarchy of a family, preferring to answer to no one but himself as he traveled the world in search of a way to break his curse, he'd become known to most of the major dens as "the mad mercenary" – a dangerous wolf on a crazy mission, but one who was better to have on your payroll than on the side of your enemy.

I'd worked with Caleb before, back in the forties, when things had been less stable for the den; hell, when things had been a lot less stable for the entire world. We'd been through the wringer together and then some, and I had found him to be not just a reliable soldier, but a good fighter and a better friend.

"Andy," said the large man, looking down at me with a smile. "Good to see you again."

"Caleb Beck." I pumped his hand twice and then slapped his right arm hard for good measure. "Thought you'd be dead by now."

"That's the one thing I can't seem to manage to do," Caleb said, shrugging with one shoulder.

I stepped back from him, looking him up and down assessingly. "Didn't know you were in these parts."

He shook his head. "Wasn't."

I frowned, drawing back and turning to Lazlo for further explanation.

"Doña Sangre had me reach out to Mr. Beck when she told me her plan to pass our problem on to you." Lazlo leaned back on his heels, beaming at us. He offered me his hand in farewell. "Between the two of you, I trust this matter will be resolved quickly."

I shook the older wolf's hand again, smiling. "I appreciate it, Lazlo."

"Good luck." He gave a small chuckle, his brown eyes sparkling as he headed back inside. "You're going to need it."

Luck. That was one thing that hadn't been on my side in what felt like a very long time.

A sound from somewhere in front of me, loud and insistent, shook me back to reality. I startled back to the present moment, eyes shooting open, blinking at the bright sky above me even from behind my dark lenses. Bringing my chin down, I found Caleb standing in front of me, watching me with concern, one hand in his trouser pocket, the other still holding the unknown woman's photograph.

"Andy," said Caleb, for what was clearly not the first time. "You still with us?"

"Yeah," I rolled my shoulders back against my car and pushed myself up onto my feet. "What's up, you got something?"

Caleb narrowed his eyes at me suspiciously, but nodded all the same, licking his lips as he moved his glare from me to the sun beating down on us. "I'm out three hundred bucks, but, yeah, I got something." Smiling, he moved his arms akimbo. "We have an expense account for this little project?"

I shot him a cold stare from behind my sunglasses. "The den's good for it, old man – you'll get your retirement money back."

He flicked the photograph we'd been showing around at me, and I caught it with a swipe of my hand as he spoke. "Her name is Shaye Cassidy. Been on the street a long time, but nobody is quite sure where she makes camp at night. Not a shelter user, not a regular one anyway, so she must have a home base, or a couple, maybe, throughout the city."

"So, our homeless woman is also transient." I turned the photograph around in my hand, shrugging. "Not hearing anything that's worth three hundred dollars, Caleb."

"Hey, nobody might know where she sleeps, but they know where she likes to spend her days." He broke out into a rueful grin and started to walk around the car towards the passenger side door. "When was the last time you read a book, smartass?"

CHAPTER 4

Shaye

I spent the entire day in the library. It was easy to do – as a kid, I'd been a voracious reader, and the books on offer at the LA Central Library were an eclectic bunch. There was even a little coffee shop in the courtyard, Skid Row Coffee, where I had worked on and off during my time in the city. They didn't mind that I was homeless. They welcomed everyone, just like the library itself.

Loitering in the International Languages section about an hour before closing, I meandered towards the information desk where I knew Cheryl would be stationed. I was curious if they had a copy of Don Quixote in Spanish, and if so, where exactly I might find it. Nearing the end of the stacks, I saw that she was already helping two other patrons. Not minding waiting, I began to step out, when something in Cheryl's face made me stop.

"–don't think I can help," she was saying, frowning deeply. "We get a lot of different folks in here every day."

The slighter of the two men nodded, reaching into his inner jacket pocket. "We understand. But some of the other street people–" he said, leaning his hand flat against the reference desk.

Cheryl cut him off before he could get any further, her eyes narrowed. "I don't think they like to be called that."

The dark-haired man took Cheryl's obvious offense in stride, his passive face unchanging. "Okay," he said, shaking his head a little. "So, what do they like to be called?"

Unimpressed, Cheryl leaned her weight onto her back foot, crossing her arms high over her chest and looking the man up and down. "I think people would be a good start. Just people."

The second man, larger with silver-hair, nodded, his hands splayed out before him in a posture of supplication. "Of course. Like my colleague was saying: some of the folks in the area said this woman frequented the library here."

The first man slid an eight by ten glossy, the size most commonly used by aspiring actors, onto the reference desk. But this was no glamor shot of a fresh-faced kid from Minnesota trying to make it big – this was a cleaned-up frame of security camera video footage. It might have been taken at any number of parking garages. It might have been taken on any number of evenings. But the figure in the center of the frame, running out of the garage entrance – that was unmistakably me. Which meant it was a photo from the Plaza parking garage last night.

Fuck. I hadn't even thought about the security cameras. I did my best to keep quiet, hidden in the shadow of the bookshelves, scared to move lest I draw the men's attention to me.

Cheryl drew the picture towards herself, glanced at it, and then, with a wrinkling of her nose, pushed it away with the tips of her fingers. "Never seen her."

Now the dark-haired man's face shifted, a tired smile sliding over his ruddy lips. "Really? Huh." He picked up my picture and turned it towards himself, shrugging. "Because we asked one of the gentlemen shelving books upstairs, and he said he sees her around here a lot."

Letting out an exasperated grunt, Cheryl hugged herself tighter, her glare returning. "Then, why–?"

"He sees her talking a lot with you," he interrupted, his eyes still fixed on my picture.

Cheryl swallowed whatever words she was about to say with a soft, sharp inhale, her expression growing darker. I had practically stopped breathing by that point. I felt like my eyes were bulging out of my head as I ogled the stranger holding my image in his hand. He was looking at it like he could divine my entire essence from that one, blurred-at-the-edges moment in time.

Could he feel the pounding of my heart against my chest as I ran? Could he feel the tears rolling down my cheeks, flying off my face in the dark?

Could he smell the blood?

He looked up at Cheryl at last, flipping my picture towards her with the tips of his fingers. "Do you want to take a look at the picture again?"

Cheryl let out a deep breath, keeping her eyes locked on the dark-haired man's face. "Are you with the LAPD or something?"

He dropped the picture to his side. "We're assisting the police in some inquiries."

She lifted a brow and then scoffed aloud. "So that's a no then?"

Tongue clicking off the top of his mouth, his brows falling hard over his eyes, the man shifted forward, one hand slicing out towards Cheryl as he growled, "Listen–"

"I'm sorry," the silver-haired man cut in, his large hand falling heavy on the shoulder of his slight companion and pulling him back. He smiled, his green eyes dancing over Cheryl until they reached her name tag. "I feel like we may have gotten off on the wrong foot here, uh, Cheryl." He stepped in front of the other man, stopping just shy of physically pushing him out of the way, his free hand pressing into his chest. "My name is Caleb Beck, and this is Andy Vazquez. We're community liaisons with the LAPD. There was an incident last night, a death, and we have reason to believe Ms. Cassidy was in the area when it happened." He shook his head, adopting an expression of sincere concern. "We're not looking to get anyone in trouble – we just need to make sure she's okay."

The tip of Cheryl's tongue came out to wet her lips. She shook her head. "You're telling me that the LAPD suddenly cares about the wellbeing of people experiencing homelessness in this city?"

Caleb blinked at her, and his smile returned, a touch shakier than it had been before. "As I said before, ma'am, we're not LAPD. We're community liaisons."

Cheryl, moving slowly, uncrossed her arms. "I work in a library, Mr. Beck." Hands flat on the reference desk, she leaned forward, eyebrows lifted high over her wide eyes. "A *library*. Where words mean things. Words like 'right to privacy', 'best interests of all members of the community', and 'safe haven for all.'"

"I didn't mean–" started Caleb, but Cheryl didn't let him obfuscate, barreling on as she straightened up, jabbing her pointer finger back towards Andy.

"If – *if* I see this young woman, I will never let you know. Because her being here is none of your business. If that bothers you or the LAPD, I suggest that they – as the police – come back with a warrant." And then, with that tone of voice that most people reserve for telling others to get fucked, Cheryl said, "Have a good rest of your day, gentlemen."

Andy started forward, his mouth open, but Caleb stepped in again, pulling him back and away from the reference desk. "Thank you for your time," he said coolly, seemingly more concerned with his companion's temper than the brush off they'd just received from Cheryl.

Andy allowed himself to be led away from the desk, casting an irritated glare back in Cheryl's direction before doing so. I tucked myself further back in the stacks as they passed, even going so far as to turn my back and pretend to be looking for a book somewhere on the far end of the shelves. I waited until I couldn't hear their footsteps anymore. Poking my head out from between the stacks like a rabbit out of a warren, I scurried across the large room towards Cheryl. "Cher," I said, moving towards her, casting furtive glances in the direction the two men had exited. "Are you okay?"

"I'm fine." She took a deep breath and then looked at me, her face growing concerned when she intuited what I was doing. "You going?"

I nodded, crooking my head to one side. "I think that's probably a good idea, don't you?"

"Not through the main entrance, I don't," she said. Looking around us, she took a sharp breath in through her nose and took me by the arm, jerking her head back towards the stacks from which I had just emerged. "Come on, there's a staff door back through here."

Following her without another word, we wound our way across the library, through the shelves and into the harshly lit work rooms and offices of the people who made the whole magnificent institution keep working. There were a few curious glances from people at desks as we walked by, but no one stopped Cheryl as she escorted me towards a keypad secured wooden door at the end of a short hallway. She swiped an ID badge against the pad and the door popped open inward. Stepping back, she nudged it open the rest of her way with her foot, holding it open with her hip and gesturing me through it.

"You should be good," she said, sighing a little as her head fell to one side.

I stepped sideways through the beat-up wooden door, pulling my baggy short sleeve shirt back up on my shoulder. "Thanks, Cher," I said as I passed, keeping my gaze on the ground, more out of habit than anything else.

The sun was lowering in the sky, but was far from gone, its rays still stingingly hot against my exposed skin. I winced in the sudden natural light, lifting my hand to shield my eyes, but I kept walking out towards the corner of West 5th Street – the only way out of this mess was forward.

"Shaye," called Cher from behind me.

I stopped, turning to look back at her. Cheryl's chest rose and fell with a deep breath. Her mouth hinged open, and I saw in her eyes all the things she wished she could do for me, and that if only thinking about them could make them so, she would.

But there was nothing she could do, and she knew it. In the end, she simply lifted a hand in parting and nodded, her lips a thin, grim line. "Try and take care of yourself, okay?"

I gave a curt nod before heading out onto the street. Behind me, the door closed with a thud.

Alone again.

Pausing on the sidewalk, I tried to keep close to the buildings as I got my bearings. I had stepped out onto West 5th Street, so to get back to my place, I'd have to–

I'm not sure what drew my attention to him. If it was the weight of his gaze, if there was some sound that cut through the general cacophony of a busy Los Angeles thoroughfare that pulled my eyes down from the street sign and across the road to his face. But there he was. Standing half in, half out of the driver's side of an immaculate black Maserati, whose hazard lights were blinking as if he had just skidded to a halt.

The dark-haired man from the library stared at me, his mouth a grim line. I stared back, frozen in place like a lizard on a sunny rock.

He stepped fully out of his car.

I ran.

Thoughts raced through my mind faster than my feet were carrying me. Would he chase me? He couldn't leave the car in the middle of the road. He'd have to drive after me. I needed to get off the street, get inside, somewhere he wouldn't think I'd have ducked in, somewhere I couldn't possibly be...

I ran two blocks down South Grand Avenue before turning right on Wilshire Boulevard, dodging pedestrians with practiced ease as I went. About a block down Wilshire, I saw the building I was looking for – on the bottom floor of a towering apartment complex, a boarded-up retail space with a faded and graffiti covered FOR LEASE sign in the window. The place had been empty for the better part of two years and, unless the property company had fixed it...

I ducked down and pressed against the wooden sheet that covered the bottom panel of one of the glass double doors. It swung up as if on a hinge and I rolled inside.

The floor was covered in dust, a large puff of dirt billowing into the air as I hit the ground and popped up to keep running. A pile of rags in the far corner stirred and I felt eyes watching my progress, but the person didn't seem threatened enough by my ignominious passage through their place to shout or chase after me. I crashed through an unlocked EMPLOYEE ONLY door and into an unused stock room, shelves empty and leaning on each other. Spiderwebs lashed at my face and arms as I ran, but I shook them off without care, bursting out the back door and into the small alleyway outside.

I ran up the narrow alley and then skidded to a halt outside the fire door of my final destination. I shook the grime out of my hair, wiped the sweat off my face with my shirt and took a deep breath. Then, with my face screwed up in a wince, I carefully pulled the door open, ready for the alarm to blare and force me to take off running once more.

Nothing.

I slid inside as fast as I could and shut the door behind me.

Crisp, air-conditioned air hit me full blast in the face, and I gulped down a huge breath of the icy stuff, my lungs burning at the sensation. Leaning back against the door, I let my eyes adjust to the low light, relying for a few moments entirely on my senses of touch and hearing.

The alcove I stood in was a popular place for the bartenders and dishwashers to take their smoke breaks, so I knew I had to move quickly. Starting forward, I turned down the hallway to the left, heading for the front of house and away from the employee-only areas of the Sha Sha Club.

The Sha Sha Club was a retro style bar and dance venue, a melding of old and new in a way only Los Angeles seemed able to pull off without seeming kitschy. If a 1930s dance hall and a contemporary club had a baby, it would be the Sha Sha club. The space itself was two levels, the lighting low and sepia toned, except for over the dance floor, where primary-colored lights swung and flashed. Even at this relatively early hour of the evening, the trendy venue was crowded, and I had to fight my way towards the tall tables at the back, behind the dance area.

I lucked into an empty table, an unoccupied four-seater. I perched myself down on the plush bluish green stool, careful to keep my shoulders hunched, my profile low lest someone realize that I wasn't exactly dressed for clubbing and question how I gained entrance to the exclusive venue in the first place. I twisted around to glance towards the front of the club, but soon gave up any idea of watching people come in or out of the space. I didn't have an unobstructed view of the main doors from my table – which had, after all, been kind of the point. I relaxed my shoulders and let out a huff. They'd never think to look for me in a place like this anyway. I was safe.

I faced forward and froze.

Sitting on the stool across the table was the slim man from the library. He looked me over with an unimpressed glaze to his eyes, leaning against the table, his breathing somewhat labored.

"Shaye Cassidy?" he said casually, as if we had arranged to meet here on a blind date.

I pushed away from the table, my eyes widening. "Shit–!"

Two massive hands clamped onto my shoulders. I tried to twist around, to twist out of their grip, but I might as well have been trying to squirm out of handcuffs. "Stay awhile," said the silver-haired man behind me, pressing me down into the stool, squeezing hard, but not hard enough to be painful.

Heart in my throat, pounding against my skin like it was trying to escape, I watched as the dark-haired man slid himself on top of the plush green seat across from me, reaching forward and picking up a few pieces of hard-shelled candy out of the bowl as he settled himself. "How did you even get into a place like this?" he asked, an amused quirk to the corner of his mouth that set me on edge.

Even in the midst of the chaotic bar, his voice was deep, cool, and clear, like water from a mountain river. I watched as he threw the candy into his mouth piece by piece, and he returned my stare, his brows lifting over his dark eyes.

My tongue darted out to wet my suddenly dry lips. I cleared my throat. "Are you going to hurt me?"

His lips twitched up into a lightning strike smile that was gone almost as soon as it appeared. "No." Tongue probing the inside of his cheek, he leaned forward across the table, so he didn't have to shout. "Are you going to answer my question?"

His calmness grated on my raw nerves. I rolled my eyes and gestured towards the back of the club, past the dance floor. "Fire door alarm around the back is busted. Has been for almost a year." As I shifted my weight on my seat, the man's grip on my shoulders remained steady and firm. I grimaced at the pressure. "I noticed it when they hired me for a day to wash some dishes."

The man looked in the direction I indicated and gave a harrumph, his shoulders rising and falling. He returned his attention to me, nodding. "Clever."

Frowning, I gripped the edge of the table tightly. "I'm homeless, not blind." I looked around. No one seemed to notice that I was under duress. If I started screaming, what would happen? What would anyone do? I decided not to risk it, sighing and staring at the man across from me instead. "I'm not stupid either. You're Andy Vazquez, right?"

His calm facade cracked, if only slightly. This time he actually looked impressed, his eyes widening slightly, faint surprise clear in the opening of his mouth. "Ah, yeah."

"What do you want?" I demanded.

"I thought you said you weren't stupid." He smiled, his eyes narrowing. "What would someone like me want with someone like you?"

"I don't know," I answered with unusual honesty, throwing one hand into the air. "I don't even know who you are; not really. Just that you're looking for me. You and the LAPD." Looking him over more closely, a thought occurred to me. "Is that it? Are you a cop? Like a detective or something?"

As soon as the question was out of my mouth, I knew the answer was no. Getting a closer look at him, he couldn't have been dressed less like a police officer. A part of my brain I had not used in a long time recognized the deceptively plain white dress shirt he was wearing as Louis Vuitton, meaning it cost somewhere close to a thousand dollars. The pants they were tucked into? Armani, over a thousand. The jacket? Even at this distance, I could tell: a single-breasted affair in virgin wool and silk – two thousand at least.

But it wasn't just the clothes. It was the way he wore them.

Like they were strictly temporary.

I blinked several times and looked back up at his face. Dark, hickory brown eyes met mine and I wondered, for just a moment, if I could see all that just by looking at him, what was he seeing looking at me?

Andy's smile broadened. "A cop? Very much no."

I started to lift my hand to push my hair out of my eyes, but the movement was hindered by the heavy weight of the man behind me. Letting out a sharp huff of air, I ran my tongue along the back of my teeth. "Could you tell this guy to get off me? I don't like being manhandled."

Andy reached forward to grab another handful of candy, shrugging. "Tell him yourself; he's not deaf."

Craning my head back on my neck, I looked up into pale green eyes and lifted my brows in question. Caleb dropped his hands to his sides, releasing me. "You run," he said, still standing so close I could feel the rumble in his chest as he spoke. "I chase you. You don't want that."

"Understood," I answered, swallowing down a cheeky response in the face of his sour expression. Returning my attention to the man across from me, I shook my bangs out of my face. "So?" I said, feeling a bit more relaxed now that there wasn't someone physically holding me in place. "Who are you?"

Andy dusted off his hands, all traces of amusement leaving his face. "Someone who can help you."

I lifted my eyebrows. "If you're with the Salvation Army they need to seriously rethink their recruitment policies."

"Funny," he said, in that tone that people use when they want you to know just how extremely unamused they really are. He took a deep breath and leaned in across the table, his elbow sliding over the smooth marble tabletop. "Shaye, I know what you saw last night."

Sweat began to bead at the back of my neck. I swallowed a fist sized lump in my throat and looked away from him, staring at the table as I growled, "You don't know shit about me."

"I can smell the fear coming off you in waves," he said, seemingly unbothered by my vitriol. "And so can the wolf you saw kill that man in the garage."

Hearing someone else say it out loud made my stomach roil, my heart jumping up into my throat and making me choke. That is what I had seen, wasn't it? A man got killed right in front of me. A human being ripped to pieces. I was there. I saw it. And I ran.

"Jason." The tabletop swam in front of my eyes. "His name was Jason." I tried to blink the tears back behind my eyes but only succeeded in sending them tumbling down my cheeks. "And he wasn't a man. He was a kid. He was a sweet, kind kid. Barely seventeen. And I should have done something." Glaring up at Andy, my lips twisted into a sneer. "But I bet you didn't bother to find any of that out, did you?"

I was surprised to find Andy watching me, not with open contempt or boredom, but pain-filled eyes of his own. He swallowed hard and looked away from me, clearing his throat and pushing his hand back through his hair. He shook his head, as if clearing it, before returning his gaze to me, his voice soft as he said, "Jason isn't my primary concern right now."

A thin laugh escaped me. I rubbed my cheeks dry. "Right. Why would he be?"

Andy let a sharp breath out through his nose, rapping his knuckles on the table. "Do you want to die, Shaye?"

I gave the question more consideration than I thought he was expecting. "No."

"Then you need me," he stressed every word. "The wolf you saw–"

I threw my hands up and slapped them back down on the table, causing the whole thing to shake. "I didn't see any-thing–!"

He reached forward, grabbing hold of both my wrists and squeezing. "Don't fucking lie to me." His hands were smooth and hot against my skin. I jerked at the touch, unused to the feeling of someone else's flesh pressed against my own. But his grip was unbreakable, and he held me still, staring me down. "The wolf you saw will find you and they will kill you. Unless you come with me, now."

"What I saw–" I looked straight back into his dark brown eyes. "–was not a wolf."

The intensity of his glare dimmed, and he let go of me. "No – no it wasn't, was it?" Andy scratched the underside of his jaw, wincing and looking away from me for the first time since he'd sat across from me. "It was a werewolf."

I stared at him and waited for the rest of the joke.

He looked back at me. He swallowed hard, his Adam's apple bobbing. "Aren't you going to say anything?"

Blinking, I shook my head. I let out a breathy laugh. "So...okay." Rolling my lips under my teeth, I widened my eyes. "You're a crazy person. Okay. Yeah. That, that tracks, actually."

Letting out a sharp breath through his nose, Andy checked the face of the expensive Rolex wrapped around his wrist. He shook his head, glancing around us furtively and mumbling. "We don't have time for this shit..."

"Andy, here?" said Caleb, and the edge in his voice made the hairs on the back of my neck stand to attention.

"Do we want her help or not?" snapped Andy, placing his hands flat on the tabletop. "Shit, I hate doing this..."

The change was subtle at first, so subtle I didn't even realize there was a change. From one blink to the next, as if it were a trick of the light, his hair looked...longer? The stubble on his chin...thicker? I looked away from his face, pulling my eyes away from the bright lights behind him, thinking that would help, but then I saw his hands.

His fingernails had definitely *not* been that long before. Or sharp. Or...not so much like fingernails, but...

Tongue fat and dry in my mouth I jerked up from the table, but Caleb forced me back down in my seat with one push of his massive hand. My eyes met Andy's once more and I watched as he stretched his neck, as muscles that hadn't been there before writhed beneath his skin, as his jaw widened to make room for a handful of extra teeth that weren't human, but the fangs of a wild animal.

He looked at me, brown eyes bright in the darkness of the club. "Satisfied?" he asked, with a mouth still full of too many teeth.

In a dizzying spiral of horror, the puzzle pieces snapped into place, one after the other. The creature I had seen ripping into Jason last night; the man-not-man sitting across from me now; his words about smelling my fear echoed in my ear like screams in a canyon; the gleam of the full moon against the skyscrapers as I ran through the night.

Werewolves.

"Oh shit." I felt my head begin to spin and my stomach with it. "Oh, holy shit." My feet touched back down onto solid ground, but my stomach continued to churn and lurch. I clapped my hand over my mouth. "Shit. I'm going to be sick."

Andy rolled his eyes and scoffed, but the sound stuck in his throat when I gagged aloud. His eyes went wide, and he scrambled to his feet. "Wait, seriously?"

I nodded vigorously, one hand still over my mouth, the other clutching at my gut. "Seriously, you want me to do it all over you?"

Caleb took a large step back and gestured to a hallway that snaked behind the bar. "Bathroom is that way–"

I stood up and ran for the bathroom, not knowing or caring if either of them were following me or not. When I shouldered my way into the restroom, I had a brief flash of gratitude that it was momentarily empty before my stomach heaved and I had to lunge for the nearest unoccupied stall and wretch into the toilet.

The little I'd eaten that day came up easily, but my body wasn't content with that. I kept gagging and vomiting until I was down to water and bile and even then, my stomach clenched and squirmed painfully inside my abdomen. I collapsed against the porcelain bowl, my shaking legs no longer able to hold my weight and forced ragged breaths in and out of my lungs when I could, tears streaming down my face.

As the sickness subsided, I became vaguely aware that I was not alone in the open stall. I glanced down and looked beside me to see a pair of expensive handmade shoes. I waited for him to speak, but when he didn't, I looked up at him.

Leaning against the stall with one hand in his pocket, he held out a wrapped-up wad of toilet paper towards me with the other. His brows were knitted in concern, but he kept his gaze high almost as if he didn't want to embarrass me by watching me puke. With a stutter of hesitation, I took the toilet paper from him, cleaning off my face.

"Thanks," I said cautiously, throwing the soiled paper into the bowl and flushing.

Andy glanced down at me with an awkward grimace twisting his lips. "It's, uh, it's no problem."

Lifting myself up on unsteady legs, I tried not to stare at him as I wiped the back of my hand across my mouth. Nothing had changed from my first assessment of him. He was the same man – expensively dressed, slim and dark-haired, with eyes that radiated warmth like a heated pool on a cool California night.

Except he wasn't a man, was he? He was a wolf. A monster. The same thing that had torn Jason to pieces.

And he was less than a foot from me.

Claustrophobia hit me suddenly and it took all my self-control not to bolt from the stall. He wasn't human. But he must have been once, right? That's how it worked, at least in the movies. I closed my eyes, twisting my fist into my stomach at the thought. How dumb could I be? I lived in LA, where everyone knew the movies were full of shit.

"You okay?" he asked, still too close for comfort.

"No," I sputtered out.

He shrugged and rubbed the back of his neck. "Right. Well, that makes sense." Taking in a deep breath, he fumbled his hands into his jacket pockets, hunching his shoulders. "Listen, I know it's a lot. But I'm really not here to screw you. I'm here to help."

I leaned back against the stall's graffiti covered metal wall. "Why? Why do you want to help me?"

"I need to find this werewolf who killed your friend." He slumped against the opposite wall, shaking his finger at me. "Right now, you're my only lead."

"Great," I breathed out the word in a sigh, running the palm of my hand across my sweat slicked forehead. "Listen, I don't know what you expect me to be able to do. Do you want me to describe what I saw to a sketch artist or something? Cause it looked like a big fucking monster tearing a person to pieces."

"I don't think you understand," pressed Andy. "They have your scent now. It's not safe for you to be out on the street."

"My *scent*?" I stressed the word and my stomach roiled at the thought of that thing being able to track me by smell, like some kind of bloodhound from hell. "Sweet Jesus, what the hell even is–" I held up my hands and shimmied past him and out to the sinks which lined the far wall of the restroom. "Know what? Never mind, I don't want to know. This is all so fucked up."

"Can't argue with that," I heard him mutter under his breath behind me.

I turned the cold water tap all the way on, sending out a blast of not-quite-cold-enough liquid into the bowl of the sink. I washed my hands, splashed my face, and tried in vain to get a grip. This was real. This was happening. I needed to deal with it.

A thought occurred to me. I reached over to the paper towel dispenser and rubbed my face dry with the scratchy paper, shaking my head.

"But–" I spoke between swipes of the towel. "–I should be good for another month, right? Full moon and all that stuff?"

He leaned his backside against the sink to my left. "You're only human. I don't think this particular wolf is picky about killing people in or out of form."

I gripped the lip of the sink, leaning over it, trying desperately to stop from shaking. "Shit. This can't be happening." Looking up into my own reflection, I shook my head. "Why does this weird shit always happen to me?"

"Look, the way I see it, you have two choices: go it alone and die or help me and live." The bottom of his handcrafted shoes tapped against the linoleum floor as he moved behind me. I looked at him in the mirror, and he met my eyes there. "What's it going to be?"

~ 5 ~

CHAPTER 5

Andy

I don't know what I had expected.

That was a lie.

I knew *exactly* what I had expected. I had expected some lice-ridden, half-psychotic druggie who could barely string a coherent sentence together. Stinking and pathetic and pitiful, someone that would make my skin crawl just to be near them.

I hadn't expected... her.

I watched her as we walked out of the Sha Sha Club and down the street to where Caleb had parked my car. Caleb, ever the gentleman, opened the front passenger door for her, opting to cram himself into the none too roomy back-seat. Maybe he just didn't trust her alone back there. It was probably as much a tactical consideration as a social one, but the girl still seemed to appreciate it, even asking if he was sure once or twice before getting in.

As they climbed in and settled themselves inside the car, I pulled my phone out of my pocket, pausing on the sidewalk as I dialed Lazlo's number.

"¿Andy, qué tal?" The older wolf's voice came down the line crisp and clear, the sound of the ocean soft but audible in the background.

"We have a lead," I said, lifting my face to the sun, eyes narrowing even behind my sunglasses.

"Already?" Lazlo let out a pleased, surprised huff. "Andy, that's wonderful. Háblame."

"It's a human. A witness. They saw last night's attack go down, or at least the last part of it."

"A human," drawled Lazlo, doing nothing to hide his distaste in the very concept. "Hm. Do you think you'll be able to track them down?"

"Already done."

There was a beat of silence, and I was about to move the phone away to check that we had not been disconnected when Lazlo sputtered, "What?"

I smiled, turning away from the car and slipping my sunglasses off of my face. "Hey. Miracle worker, remember?" Folding the glasses with one hand, I slipped them into my lapel pocket. "I'm bringing them to one of our safe houses. I figured—"

"No," Lazlo broke in sharply. "No, bring them to the den house."

"To the Retreat?" I felt my brows draw to a point. Casting a glance over my shoulder, I pressed, "Lazlo, are you sure that's–?"

"We're better equipped to question them there and make sure nobody else gets their hands on them," explained Lazlo, his words clipped and terse. "I'm sure." A long sigh and then a chuckle echoed down the line. "Besides, when we're done with them, we can use them in the next hunt. Estará bien."

I stared at the passenger side door of my car, my stomach flipping inside out. I should have known the den would have no intention of keeping Shaye alive. I should've known better than to promise her safety.

I should have known from experience how little a human life meant to my family.

Nodding mechanically, my voice echoed in my ears as if from far away. "Right. Okay. We— we're heading that way now."

"We'll see you soon," said Lazlo. "Oh, and Andy?"

I swallowed past the lump in my throat. "Yes?"

"Good work."

Wincing as the call went dead, I took in a large breath of heavy, smog choked air. The taste was acrid and burned my nostrils. With a shake of my head, I moved around the car, sliding the phone back into my pocket and getting into the car while trying my hardest to put everything that I'd just said and heard out of my mind.

"Who knew being a werewolf paid so well?" Shaye quipped at me as I joined her in the car. She ran her fingers over the lip of the seat. "This real leather?"

"This is a Maserati," I replied, not even looking at her as the car thrummed to life beneath us. "Of course, it's real leather."

"Fuck, okay, no need to get uppity about it," she said, scowling. "You know, you have a real bad attitude, Andy."

"I get touchy when someone leads me on a foot chase in this heat," I shot back, pulling away from the curb and into traffic.

Shaye harrumphed, crossing her arms high over her chest. "Where are we going anyway?"

I shook my head, doing a quick check of my mirrors for anything suspicious. "Some place safe."

"Do you have to blindfold me or put a bag over my head or something?"

Letting out a sharp breath through my nose, I squirmed in my seat, shooting a glare in her direction. "You want me too?"

She held up her hands. "Fuck no, man."

"Then don't give me any ideas," I advised, a threatening edge to my words.

Caleb cleared his throat pointedly in the back seat. Shaye and I shelved any further comments for a couple of blocks, retreating as it were to our respective corners. Internally, I chastised myself for letting Shaye goad me into ill-humor, even though I knew she wasn't really to blame. I needed to keep her on our side, at least for now, and being combative towards her wasn't helping. I took a deep breath, relaxing my grip on the steering wheel and leaning over to turn up the air conditioning.

"Listen," I said, doing my best to keep my tone neutral and even. "I'm taking you somewhere you'll be safe. It's a nice place, okay? You'll like it."

"I doubt that."

My hands strangled the steering wheel. Immediately regretting my choices wasn't an unusual sensation for me, especially when women were involved, but Shaye was proving to be a whole different level of pain in my ass. As she watched the city passing by outside the passenger side window, I examined her from the corner of my eye.

If she felt my gaze on her, she was careful not to show it. Her eyes were wide and round, light brown, the color of old photographs. Her hair was cut short, but to say it was hacked short was probably a better description, the dark blonde mop cut close to her scalp in some places and as long as her chin in others. Jagged and messy - those were good words to describe her entirely. She sat there, slumped down in my leather seat, drowning in her baggy mismatched secondhand clothes and practically begged not to be perceived; to be ignored.

I took a deep breath through my nose, but tried not to make it obvious, curious to catch her scent once more. Humans all smelled somewhat the same, but I had been surprised to find that Shaye did not reek of body odor and unwashed sweat. Instead, she smelled...clean. Soft, like fresh laundry drying under a clear, sunny sky.

I liked it.

Pulling me from these thoughts with a jolt, Shaye cleared her throat and straightened up in the passenger seat. "I need to pick up my things."

I wrinkled the bridge of my nose and did a double take at her. "Things, what things?"

Her look of confusion matched my own. She ticked items off on her fingertips. "You know – change of clothes, phone charger...just my stuff. Personal belongings. Don't were-wolves have those?"

I gestured to her with one hand, keeping my other on the wheel. "Don't you sort of... have all that on you?"

Her confused glare turned incredulous and angry. She twisted around in her seat to face me fully, straining at her seat belt as she did so. "Do I look like a bag lady to you?" she demanded, hands flying up and falling into her lap as she gesticulated her point. "Do you see me pushing a shopping cart down the boulevard? For fuck's sake, man..."

"Sorry, hey! It's no problem," I said quickly, shaking my head and lifting my hand in case she decided to do more than gesture at me. "You need to get your stuff, we'll go and get your stuff."

My acquiescence placated her for the moment, and she retreated back into her seat, glaring at me all the way. I was about to ask her where I should head for these mysterious 'things' when she spoke again.

"I'm going to have to let people know I'm not going to be working for a while too," she grumbled, her lips barely moving.

My mouth fell open, and I did another double take at her. "You have a job?"

Color rose in her tanned cheeks, and she snarled at me, "You really are an ignorant prick, Andy Vazquez, you know that?"

"Chica, tienes que calmarte, ¿vale?" I snapped. "I didn't mean anything by it, I'm just–"

"If you have a job, how come you're living on the streets?" asked Caleb from the back seat.

Shaye craned her head around to look Caleb in the face. "Do you know what a studio apartment goes for in this town?"

Caleb blinked at her and shrugged. "No," he answered honestly.

"More than I make doing odd jobs here and there, I can tell you that." She faced forward and sunk down in the passenger seat, folding her arms over her chest. "And you know how many leasing agents are anxious to rent to someone with no credit history for the last eight years? Or a bank account? Or who has a police record for vagrancy? The grand total is zero."

I licked my lips, shifting in my seat, adjusting my grip on the wheel. "There are agencies, aren't they? People who can help you?"

Shaye scoffed and shook her head. "Yeah, with waiting lists years long and more hoops to jump through than a three-ring circus." Squirming against the leather of the chair, she turned to stare out the window at the passing city, voice going quiet. "I can take care of myself. Been doing it for years."

"Hell of a way to live," observed Caleb from the back.

The muscles in Shaye's jaw tensed. She swallowed before speaking again. "I stand on my own two feet. That's more than a lot of people in this town can say." Leaning forward to peer out the windshield at an approaching street sign, she pointed to the right. "You're going to want to turn here."

I obeyed, cutting off a Honda in the process. "Where are we going?" I asked as I waved off the honking from the beat-up vehicle behind me.

"The Ketchum Y." Sinking in her seat, she explained, "They have lockers there you can rent out by the month. It's a good place to keep your stuff – safer than a train station, plus, if you get a membership, you can go in and use the showers whenever you want."

"That's..." I pulled my lips down in an exaggerated frown as I nodded. "That's pretty smart, actually."

A snort was her response. "Yeah, well, you can't be dumb and survive out here."

"I hear that," I muttered under my breath, shaking my head.

"Oh yeah," she drawled, putting her feet up on the dash and scowling. "With your Maserati and your thousand-dollar shirt – I'm sure you're just scraping by in the city of angels. I feel for you, vato."

I gave a mirthless laugh, blinking in shock at her vitriol. "You know, maybe you'd prefer to take your chances with this rogue wolf one on one, huh? I don't have to help you, Shaye Cassidy – I'm doing you a fucking favor."

"Am I not being grateful enough for the big bad werewolf's liking?" Shaye placed her hand flat against her chest, turning to look at me wide eyed. "Wow, thank you! Thank you for not eating me too!"

"La madre que te parió, I don't eat people!" I snapped, on the edge of losing my temper.

"So, what, you want a fucking medal?" shouted Shaye, straining against her seatbelt, her fingertips digging into the door handle.

"Hey!" Caleb barked from the backseat, his deep voice vibrating the air with a force that snapped my mouth shut before I could say something that I would regret. I looked back at him in the rearview mirror as he scooted up to rest his hands on both the front and passenger seat headrests. "How about we all stay quiet until we reach the YMCA, huh? How about that?"

"Great fucking idea," grunted Shaye, collapsing back into her seat.

I shot her a glare but didn't answer, throwing one hand up in the air in a gesture of acquiescence.

Parking was a nightmare, as it always was downtown, and by the time we managed to find someplace to leave the car it was nearing quarter to eight. Caleb and I followed behind Shaye as she hurried up the front steps that led to the main entrance of the Stuart Ketchum Downtown YMCA, an angular building of glass and steel. Silently, we passed by the sculptures that littered the front plaza like a yard sale of fine art. Los Angeles was like that – beautiful things everywhere you look, so much so that you stopped seeing the city for what it was.

Before we entered, I shot off a quick text to Lazlo, letting him know about our pit stop and to expect a slight delay in our return to the den house. I watched as my message went from sent to read and waited for a response, but none came. Frowning, I put my phone back in my pocket and followed the others inside.

The cavernous building had a distinctly deserted feel, strange for a place that was usually the hub of so much physical activity. A single YMCA staff member stood at the front desk, clearly ready to leave, a backpack half open on the counter beside him into which he was shoving various notebooks and pieces of technology.

He looked up as we approached, glazed expression shifting into confusion as he took us in. He nodded to Caleb and me before focusing on Shaye, brow furrowing.

"Hi Todd," said Shaye, shoulders hunched and eyes downcast.

"Hey Shaye," answered the bald man. Frowning, he fiddled with the Fitbit on his left wrist. "You know we close in fifteen?"

Shaye nodded, but didn't stop walking, gesturing towards the wide hallway to the right. "Yeah, I know. Just need to get some stuff real quick. That okay?"

Todd shrugged. "Sure, I guess. Just don't dawdle."

We walked quickly through the mostly empty gymnasium, past a huge indoor track and weight room, in which a few dedicated muscle heads still pumped iron. Continuing through the facility, Shaye pulled up short in front of the locker rooms, which sat across the hall from the closed pool.

Turning around to face me with a nod, Shaye held up a hand. "Okay, just wait for me here – I'll only be a minute."

"Oh no," I said, letting out a mirthless chuckle as I moved in front of her, shaking my head as I did so. "I don't think so. After all the trouble you put me through, tracking you down? I'm not letting you out of my sight."

Rolling her eyes, Shaye pointed over my shoulder. My brow furrowing, I looked behind me at the sign that read, in both English and Spanish, "WOMEN'S LOCKER ROOM".

Clearing my throat, I slid to one side, ushering her through the open door. "I'll wait for you here."

She flipped me off as she passed. "Right."

Muttering some curses under my breath, I shifted around so I could lean back against the wall, only to find Caleb staring at me, his arms crossed over his chest. Even from behind his sunglasses, I could feel his eyes boring into me – his frown was so sharp I could've cut glass with it.

I stared back at him. When I couldn't stand his disapproving silence any longer, I leaned forward at the waist, lifting my brows high over my eyes. "What?"

Caleb took off his sunglasses, revealing his comically wide green eyes. "Are you serious?" He shook his head. "Andy, after all the shit that happened last year–"

"How do you know about that?" I demanded.

"I keep my ear to the ground." He waved off my question, a lock of silver hair falling into his eyes. "That's not important. What are you doing? Telling a human about us? About werewolves?"

"We have to get her to trust us, don't we?" I said, more than a little defensive at his tone. I threw my hands in the air. "She's already seen a werewolf, it's not like we can keep her in the dark!"

He folded his arms over his chest, looking down his nose at me. "There is a big difference between keeping her in the dark and putting on a fucking dog and pony show for her," he insisted, glowering. "What's your plan here?"

Turning away from him, I stalked over to the glass wall that separated us from the pool. He was right and it rankled. I was dangerously close to making the same mistake twice. Leaning my forehead against the cool glass, I forced myself to take a deep breath. "Look: we take her in. We take her to Doña Sangre. Let her decide what to do with her."

"And you think Emilia is going to be happy that you were so loose with the big secret?" Caleb walked up and stood behind me. I watched him watching me in the reflection of the glass. "Again?"

I closed my eyes and swallowed hard. "I...didn't have a lot of options."

"This time or last time?"

I stood up with a start, forcing him back as I twisted around. "Either," I said. I cast a glance at my watch and growled in the back of my throat, rolling my eyes. "Madre de Dios, what is taking this woman so damn–?"

A series of loud metallic crashes shattered the quiet, followed by a muddle of shouting voices, and then the unmistakable crack of a gunshot. Before I had a chance to move, Shaye came barreling out of the locker room, a rucksack clutched to her chest, blood from an abrasion on her forehead dripping into her eyes, her mouth open in a shout.

"Andy!"

Caleb went for his gun. I went for Shaye, running forward to grab her, thinking I would shove her behind me, out of harm's way. But both Caleb and I were too slow for the two werewolves who rushed out at us from the locker room, their mouths crowded with fangs and claws unsheathed in their half-transformed state, a consequence of the absent full moon. I had just managed to lay hands on Shaye when the first wolf, a feral looking man with flaming red hair, charged into me. He sent us both flying backward, cracking into the glass window that separated the pool from the hallway in which we stood. I felt the pane give beneath my body, the air leaving my lungs at the impact as I tried to take the brunt of it for Shaye's sake, holding her tight to my side.

Caleb didn't fare much better, his gun knocked to the ground by a swipe from the larger of the two assailants. Disarmed, Caleb put his shoulder down and rammed the large wolf, pushing him back into the wall while the man's claws fought for purchase in Caleb's back.

The redhead in front of me drew back his hand and swiped at Shaye's face. Jerking her clear of his claws, I kicked at his groin, my heel making contact not with his genitals as I'd hoped but instead the fleshy part of his inner thigh. Howling in pain, the man instinctively grabbed my leg, and I wasn't quick enough to pull the appendage away from him.

With his hands wrapped around my calf, the man threw me back into the glass again, this time with enough lift and momentum to send both Shaye and I straight through the window and onto the unforgiving concrete which surrounded the enormous pool on the other side. I landed hard on my back and Shaye skidded across the ground a few feet away from me, her bag flying out from her hands.

Vision doubled, I did my best to stagger to my feet, not wanting to be caught on the floor if the bastard came for me again. But I needn't have worried. The redhead only had eyes for Shaye. He made a beeline to the barely conscious woman, dragging her up onto her feet with one hand even as he glared daggers into me.

"Stay down, motherfucker!" the man shouted, pulling a gun from the waistband of his trousers.

I had two options at that point. Freeze and let this maniac do whatever he came to do to Shaye. Or take my chances that he wasn't packing silver.

I chose the latter.

Keeping low, I threw myself towards him with a roar, aiming for his hips. I heard the gun fire, but by that point I was already colliding with him, hugging him tight around the waist and bringing all my weight to bear on him. Flung out of his grip, Shaye spun and tumbled into the pool with a weak, strangled cry that was cut off when she disappeared below the chlorinated water.

The next few seconds passed in a flurry of fists, my own, as I pummeled the redhead's face and head until I was sure he was unconscious. Blood dripping from my knuckles, I rolled off him and stumbled towards the edge of the pool, shouting Shaye's name.

There was no sign of her. I dove headfirst in the water, forcing my eyes to remain open but still seeing nothing: no body, no piece of clothing, just foamy, bubbling water on all sides. I came up for air, flailing this way and that in a panic. The relief that flooded through me when she surfaced on the other side of the pool, gasping for air, I put down solely to not having to explain another dead human to the authorities and having to start my investigations all over again.

Once she caught her breath, she caught sight of me. Coughing, she pushed her wet hair out of her eyes and splashed her way over to me, mouth gaping in horror. "Oh my God, are you okay?"

Spitting chlorinated water out of my mouth, I stared at her, my eyes wide. "Am I okay?"

Lifting an arm out of the water, she pointed towards my torso. "You–you've been shot!"

I looked down at myself as I treaded water in the deep end of the pool and was surprised to see a steady plume of red coloring the water around me. "Fuck!" I probed at my shoulder until I found the bullet hole and hissed in pain when my fingers dug into it. "That stupid piece of shit...I really liked this shirt too..."

Shaye shook her head violently, sending droplets of water into my face. "Are you fucking crazy?" she shouted, panic clear in her voice.

"No, I'm pissed off!" I shouted back at her, pain and anger for once getting the better of me.

She jerked back from me, her brown eyes wild with fear. Fear of me. The sight sobered me and, gritting my teeth, I pulled the wolf inside me back from the surface, shaking my head as I reached out towards her, mouth open to speak. But I was interrupted by Caleb rushing through the shattered window, shouting my name as his head swiveled from side to side, searching for me.

"Here!" I answered him, swimming over to the edge of the pool and waving one arm in the air. "I'm here. Did you get the other one?"

He jogged over to us, holstering his weapon as he did so. "No, I didn't – he ran, I chased, but I broke off to come back and make sure you were still breathing,"

I heaved myself up onto the concrete lip, shaking a little at the effort. "Carajo!"

Shaye paddled over towards us, gesturing to me. "Caleb, he's been shot."

Caleb jerked towards me, but I stepped back from him, shaking my head and waving off his sudden look of concern. "It's not silver, I'll be fine."

"Holy shit, that's true?" exclaimed Shaye from the pool.

Still crumpled in a heap at the edge of the pool, the shooter groaned quietly, shifting slightly as he tried and failed to return fully to consciousness. Watching him to make sure he wasn't going to pop back up and rush me again, I leaned down and grabbed at Shaye's arm.

"Come on," I said, pulling her up over the lip of the pool. "We've got to get out of here. I've had enough of the LAPD for one day and somebody would've called them after all that."

Struggling onto her feet, Shaye for once didn't disagree with me, nodding as she hugged herself tight, blood still streaming from the cut on her head. I put her agreeableness down to shock, sure it would wear off soon and she'd be back to her argumentative self in no time.

"What about him?" said Caleb, jerking his chin towards the still unconscious redhead by the corner of the pool.

I stared at the bloodied figure and, tightening my jaw, crossed to him, stooping down to manhandle him up into my arms.

"What the hell are you doing?" demanded Shaye.

"I'm going to get some answers," I replied grimly, slinging the man over my shoulders in a fireman's carry. "Now, let's go."

~ 6 ~

CHAPTER 6

Shaye

I'd never ridden in a car with a body in the trunk before. The fact that it wasn't a dead body did little to comfort me. In fact, it kind of made it worse.

"What if we get pulled over?" I insisted for the fourth time from the backseat as we crawled through late night traffic, sliding against the leather in my still damp clothes as I pulled myself forward between the two front seats.

"For the last time," groaned Andy from behind the wheel, throwing his hand up in my face. "Relajate, chica – we're not going to get pulled over!"

My face aching and head ringing, his casual address grated on me more than it should have, and I felt my short fingernails dig into the leather shoulder of his chair. "Don't call me chica, pendejo!"

That got his attention. Slamming on the brakes as we came to a dead stop behind a line of cars at a traffic light, Andy twisted round in his seat, his eyes wide as he repeated in a shout, "Pendejo?" He lifted a shaking hand, his pointer finger extended. "Escúchame–!"

From the passenger seat, Caleb reached out and slapped Andy's hand down with a growl. "For Christ's sake, could you two cut it out, please?"

"But she–!"

"This is not the time," said Caleb, his volume rising. "At the rate you're both going, he's going to wake up, and that I'd rather not deal with! Alright?" He looked from Andy to me, brows raised and then added, "And put your seatbelt on if you're so worried about us getting pulled over, Shaye."

I released my grip on the front seats and slumped back against the plush leather, grumbling aloud as I fumbled with the seatbelt. When I was securely fastened, I risked another look at the back of Andy's head, glowering, and caught him shooting me an equally angry glance in the rearview mirror. I stuck my tongue out at him.

"Did you recognize either of those boneheads?" asked Caleb, addressing Andy without looking at him directly.

Andy shook his head, readjusting himself in the seat to glance out the rearview mirror past me. "No. They must be from out of town."

Caleb hummed contemplatively, lifting his hand to rub some sweat off the back of his neck. "Well. Seems like there are a lot of us floating around all of a sudden."

Andy gave a noncommittal grunt in response, reaching down to switch on the radio as he continued to weave us through the Los Angeles evening traffic.

Brooding in the back, I watched the city go by and was surprised when I realized we were heading deep into the heart of the Fashion District. A hundred block section of downtown, the Fashion District was the hub of the West Coast apparel industry and was the best place to buy or sell just about anything in town – especially if a person wanted to pay cash for it and they didn't want the cops getting too interested in their business. It had been worse in the eighties and nineties, but there were still parts of the district a person wouldn't want to wander into unawares.

Even I avoided the place most of the time. Especially at night.

"What are we doing here?" I said, turning my attention from the dark store fronts, warehouses, and garment factories passing by outside to the two men in the car with me.

Neither of them answered me. Andy turned his precious Maserati into an empty parking lot at the end of a row of warehouses, the asphalt and concrete cracked and jutting up at such odd angles that getting from the road to a parking space was a tooth rattling experience. The warehouse was not the largest of the ones we had passed. It looked like it was storage space for some kind of mid-tier clothing manufacturer, or that it had been at one time. The paint peeled from the metal exterior walls, and trash littered the lot, enforcing the feeling of abandonment the property radiated.

Andy stopped the car, setting the parking brake with a jerk. He sighed and looked over at Caleb. "You want to carry him or...?"

"I got it," said Caleb, stepping out of the passenger side of the car. "No problem."

"What–?"

But the word was barely out of my mouth before Andy was also out of the car, the door shut firmly behind him.

My eyes followed his progress around the car to the back. Staring through the back window, my view was fully obscured when Andy unlocked and lifted the trunk. I heard some thumping, a grunt and then the shuffling of feet. Following the sound, I looked out the right-hand window and soon, Caleb walked into view, the redheaded youth who had attacked us slung over his shoulder, his head bouncing listlessly against the large man's back.

I scrambled across the seats and popped open the back right door. Swinging the car door shut behind me as I stepped out into the parking lot, I narrowed my eyes against the harsh glare of light coming from the tall streetlamps which dotted the warehouse's front. "I said, what are we doing here?"

Andy closed the trunk with a slam, pointing to me as he started to follow Caleb towards the warehouse's front door. "Stay in the car."

"Fuck you," I shot back, almost without thinking, my bruised jaw aching as I immediately ignored his command and began to walk after him.

Stopping abruptly, Andy let loose a growl of frustration, his hands curling into fists in front of him. "Mierda! Why do you have to make everything a fight?"

"I'm disagreeable – it's part of my charm." Moving through the darkness to stand in front of him, I shoved my hands into the pockets of my cargo pants, scowling. "Look: you said you'd keep me alive. So, I'm sticking with you."

He opened his mouth, and I closed my eyes, bracing myself for another round of shouting and cursing.

But it never came.

I eased my eyes open hesitantly to find him staring at me, a strange expression on his face. His jaw was tight, his brow furrowed. Andy looked me up and down, examining me with an intensity I hadn't experienced in some time.

He let out a sharp breath that might have been a word, but it was too quiet for me to hear. Without warning, without any kind of preamble, he took a step towards me, closing the distance between us to mere inches. He lifted his hand and brushed his fingertips against the side of my forehead, his palm touching my cheek.

I flinched away from his touch, not because he had caused me any pain, but for the simple fact that it had been a long, long time since anyone had touched me in such a gentle way. The sensation was shocking, like jumping into a freezing pool on a hot night, and I felt myself trembling as I stared at him with wide, accusatory eyes.

He sighed, lowering his hand and shaking his head. But his gaze did not release me, and it unsettled me even more than his touch had.

"We need to deal with that," he said quietly.

It took me a solid few seconds to realize what he had meant by both the gesture and what he had said. I lifted my own hand to my head and my fingers came back sticky and red – my head was still bleeding.

"Oh." I pressed my hand harder against my temple and felt the blood trickle down my wrist. "Yeah, shit."

"Come on." He jerked his head back towards the warehouse and started in the direction of the front door without waiting to see if I would follow him.

I looked behind me towards the deserted street. The city glittered, but where we stood was a black spot, a valley of void in the sparkling fabric of Los Angeles at night. I didn't feel any immediate fear. These were the places in which I had come to live over the past ten years, in between places that other people had forgotten about, whether by accident or on purpose. These were my streets.

A clatter of glass from somewhere across the street sounded high and clear. I jumped and my eyes sought out the source of the noise, all the hairs on my arms standing upright.

At least, they had been my streets.

Backing up slowly at first and then at a run to catch up, I followed Andy and Caleb inside the warehouse.

We strode quickly and silently through a large, dark room filled with display mannequins, most of them headless, which made the sharp angles of their plastic, still bodies even more unsettling as we moved in and around them. We eventually emerged from the forest of faceless plastic and headed into a hallway. Andy stopped at the entrance to the corridor to turn on a light switch, and a series of bare bulbs struggled to life along the length of the hall.

"Anywhere in particular you want this asshole?" asked Caleb, readjusting the still unconscious man over his shoulder.

"Fourth room on the right should have everything you need to keep him out of trouble," answered Andy. "I'm going to take a look at Shaye's head."

"Right." Caleb trudged down the corridor and disappeared into the room Andy had indicated.

I stared after him, curious despite myself what Caleb was going to do with my attacker.

"Shaye?"

I turned to see Andy waiting for me in the doorway of the first room on the left. He waved his hand inside. "Let's go."

I stayed where I was. "What's going to happen to that man?"

Andy looked at me for a long moment, his hand falling to his side. He leaned back against the door frame. "Do you actually care? He tried to kill you."

I closed my hands into fists. Lifting my chin, I repeated, "What's going to happen to him?"

Rolling his eyes, Andy straightened, pushing himself off the door jamb with a huff. "Nothing, okay? Nothing's going to happen to him. We just need to ask him some questions when he wakes up. Now, are you going to let me look at your head or what?"

Looking him up and down, I tried and failed to take the measure of Andy Vazquez. The longer I looked the more confused I felt rather than enlightened. Giving in with an annoyed shrug, I shuffled past him into the room.

The room was gutted, empty except for some old clothing racks shoved in one corner and a random collection of mismatched chairs, less than ten lining the far-left wall. There was also a counter, complete with sink and cabinets, which had clearly been built into the room more recently, which jutted out from the right-hand wall closest to the door.

Not seeming to care how much noise he made, Andy dragged one of the chairs, an old public-school style four-legged affair away from the wall and into the center of the room, pulling a burst cushioned black doctor stool along with his right foot as he did so. The stool he stopped first, unhooking his foot from around the wheels before adjusting the placement of the plastic chair just in front of it. He looked back at me and gestured to the plastic chair with both hands.

"Sit," he commanded, crossing the room towards the shop sink and counter.

I did as I was bid, holding up one sleeve of my still damp shirt to my forehead as I settled into the uncomfortable plastic seat. "You have a rag or a piece of cloth or something I can tie this up with?"

"We can do better than that." Andy flicked open one of the overhead cabinets to reveal clean towels of assorted sizes and, most impressive of all, a sizable first aid kit. He slung a hand towel over his shoulder before bringing the kit down and leaving it on the counter, still closed up tight. Crouching down, Andy dug around under the sink and produced a medium sized mixing bowl which he proceeded to fill with what I hoped was not freezing water.

I lowered my sleeve from my forehead as he approached, waiting as he perched himself on top of the ripped black stool. He placed the bowl of water on the floor beside him, leaning down to soak the towel in the water. Wringing most of the wet out of it, he sat up and examined my head from a distance, lips twisting into an empathetic grimace.

"This is going to sting," he said, bending forward with the towel stretched out before him.

Lukewarm water dribbled down into my eye as he pressed the cloth to the side of my forehead, and I hissed in pain. I shut my eyes and did my best not to pull away from him, grunting out, "Is it bad?"

"You'll be fine," he said. The cloth left my face, and I opened my eyes to see him bending down to run the bloody bunch of fabric through the water to clean it. "Head wounds bleed like a bitch, but the cut's actually not so bad. Just shy of needing stitches, I think." He looked up at me, still folded at the waist. "How'd it happen anyway?"

I took a deep breath through my nose, running over the somewhat hazy sequence of events in my mind. "Well, those guys jumped me in the locker room. Tried to muscle me out the emergency door, but I managed to get loose. One of them tried to cut me off from the door, punched me in the face and I fell and hit my head on an open locker door."

I was surprised to see Andy's face darken with anger. He straightened, shaking his head and swallowing hard as he placed the wet cloth once more on my face. "La madre que te parió," he cursed through gritted teeth, pressing the towel firmly against my cheek.

The worn, warm fabric felt good against my skin. Lost in the sensation for a moment, I came back to myself staring blankly at Andy's chest, his previously pristine white shirt now turning crusty brown with dried blood. Jerking forward, I gasped aloud. "Oh shit, what about you?"

Andy drew back from me, arms in front of himself, his brow furrowed. "What about me?"

Clicking my tongue off the top of my mouth, I fixed him with a disbelieving glare. "How do you keep on forgetting that you got fucking shot? Does that sort of thing happen to you a lot or something?"

This earned me a small, tense smile, and he shook his head. With his free hand he undid the first few buttons of his dress shirt as he spoke. "Like I said, it wasn't silver. And it was a through and through. So–" He pulled the ruined shirt towards his wound. "See? It's already healing."

The flesh immediately around the wound was still angry, red and raw, but it was no longer bleeding, and, just as he said, the bullet hole was clearly in the process of knitting itself shut. My stomach heaved a little, but I couldn't quite look away, the unnatural sight utterly enthralling.

"That's fucking wild," I said in a hushed whisper, gaze flickering between the half-raw wound and Andy's face.

He returned to cleaning me up with a shrug. "Being a werewolf has its perks."

"When did it happen?" I asked gingerly, unsure if it was a rude question and not wanting to get any more on his bad side than I already was. "Like, were you hiking in the hills, and you got bit or...?"

He gave a snort and ceased his dabbing, drawing back from me once again. "What? No. No, I've..." Andy gestured to himself, blinking rapidly. "I've always been like this."

"Holy shit," I exclaimed, my mouth dropping open as the meaning behind his words got through to me. "You mean you were *born* a werewolf?"

Frowning, his tongue came out to wet his lips. Andy rolled his head around his shoulders and gave a pained groan. "I, uh, I don't think I should really talk about it."

"Oh." I quickly directed my attention to the floor, suddenly embarrassed by the ease of our conversation up until that point. "Right. Yeah, okay."

We weren't friends. We were never going to be friends. Someone like him, a thing like him, had killed Jason. Was hunting me. I couldn't let my guard down around him more than I could let my guard down around anyone else. I couldn't tell him the whole truth about how I had come to be in that parking garage – about the visions – about any of it.

But Andy had saved my life.

I glanced back at the bullet wound, peeking out from his open shirt whenever he moved. I'd never thought I'd ever meet anyone who'd take a bullet for me. Literal or metaphorical. He needed me, I reminded myself, he needed what I knew, that was the only reason he was keeping me alive.

His fingers slid under my chin. "Look up for me," he murmured.

I complied without a thought, lifting my head. He drew the damp cloth down around my face and under my jaw in a firm, gentle stroke. I swallowed hard.

I understood why he was keeping me alive. What I didn't understand was why he was being so kind.

"What is this place?" I asked at last, the silence growing too awkward, even for me.

"It's one of our safe houses," he said, dropping the damp cloth into the bowl and standing. "We have a handful of properties like this around the city. Most of them are nicer than this though."

I swallowed again, glancing at him from the corner of my eye as he moved back towards the counter and sink. "Do I want to know what it is you guys do here?"

There was a pause. I turned to look at him fully. He was carefully picking through the first aid kit, setting out butterfly bandages one at a time, his back to me. Eventually, he shook his head. "No. You don't really want to know."

Andy pulled all the butterfly bandages together in a pile and walked back to me. I looked at the plethora of bandages in his hand and frowned. "I thought you said it wasn't bad?"

"And it's not," he answered. He peeled open the first butterfly closure and leaned towards me. "Come on, don't be a child."

Wincing a little as he pulled my wound shut, I allowed him to place the first few bandages without further comment, thinking about what he had said about the warehouse in which we were hiding. Finally, my brows drawing to a point and hindering his work, I pulled away to look up at him and ask, "Who is 'we'?"

Andy let out a sharp breath through his nose, clenching his jaw. "I've already told you a hell of a lot more than I should."

A snort was my response. I crossed my arms over my belly, slouching down in the rickety plastic chair. "Really? 'Cause I feel like I know jack shit."

"It's better that way," he insisted, hand following the level of my head as he attempted to complete the work on my injury.

"Better for who, for you?" My frown deepened and I started to shake my head but was stopped when Andy reached up and grabbed my chin in his hand. I huffed out a frustrated breath and said, "Why'd you tell me anything at all, then, if–?"

With a small jerk, he brought my face up and I found myself staring into his hickory brown eyes. His face was blank, but his tone was anything but when he demanded, "Do you have to answer everything I say with a question?"

Those eyes. Those damn eyes. A person could drown in eyes like that, dragged down inside them just as sharp and mercilessly as an inexperienced swimmer can get caught in a riptide. I hated him for having eyes like that.

It felt like he could see me. And no one had seen me in a long, long time.

I felt the muscles of my jaw move under his strong fingertips as I probed the inside of my cheek with my tongue. "No," I answered at last, petulantly as I could.

The corner of his mouth twitched upward, but the smile was smothered as soon as it appeared. Which was a shame really. He looked nicer when he smiled. Some of the sharp edges of him fell away and I could imagine that he might actually be a good man.

I thought of the man in the room down the hall, his face beaten to a bloody pulp and swallowed hard. Good men didn't do things like that – at least not in my world.

But I wasn't in my world anymore.

Final butterfly bandage placed, pulling the gash closed, Andy ripped open a package containing a tan colored dressing that would cover the wound in its entirety. The sticky edges of the plaster pulled against my skin as he stuck it to my forehead. I looked up at him when I heard him click his tongue against the back of his teeth. A look of consternation clouded his face, and he narrowed his eyes as he concentrated on lining up the bandage with my hurt. "Look: I told you what I told you because..." He finished placing the dressing and sat down heavily on the chair, his gaze falling to the floor. "...because after what you saw, you deserve to know the truth." He sat back, looking askance at me. "I'm sorry, by the way."

I started to lift my hand to the bandage but stopped midway, staring at him in confusion. "Sorry?"

"About your friend." He looked away again quickly, as if meeting my eyes pained him. Rubbing his knee with his fingertips, he shook his head. "It's... it's not supposed to happen. And I'm sorry you saw that. I'm sorry you got dragged into this."

My mouth dry, I stared at him, for once at a loss for what to say. His sincerity was as plain as it was surprising, and I didn't know how to react. My first instinct was to reject his apology, to lash out with an expletive and an insult, but that felt like hitting below the belt. In the end, I just nodded and said, "Thank you."

If I was surprised by his apology, Andy looked positively stunned by my gratitude. Adam's apple bobbing in his throat, he leaned forward, reaching towards me as if he were going to place his hand on my knee.

"Andy?" called Caleb, rounding the doorframe and stepping into the room from the hallway.

Andy started, pulling away like he was a dog that had got caught nosing around the kitchen trash can. Clearing his throat, he stood, shooting a quick 'yes' in Caleb's direction, but not turning to look at him standing in the doorway.

Caleb looked at me and lifted a brow. I shook my head and shrugged. Blinking, Caleb took in a deep breath, jerking his thumb out into the hall. "Uh, the asshole's awake."

~ 7 ~

CHAPTER 7

Andy

I walked out into the hallway with Caleb, all too aware of Shaye trailing after me, my blood thrumming in my ears. What the hell was I doing? Melanie's face briefly flashed in the front of my mind, and I shook it away.

I was not going to let history repeat itself.

No matter how Shaye made me feel.

I was not going to get another woman killed because I had a soft heart.

Caleb stopped halfway down the corridor and turned. I searched his face to see if he had noticed anything untoward, but if he had he wasn't giving anything away. He simply took a deep breath and tossed his head back towards the room in which he'd secured our unwilling guest.

"How do you want to run this?" asked Caleb, his tone light and conversational, as if we weren't about to face off with a man who'd tried to kill us all.

I gave the question a moment's consideration. A memory from our shared past popped to the forefront of my mind. I tilted my head to one side. "How about we do what we did on Angel Island, in '42?"

Caleb smiled broadly, hands sliding out of his pockets and onto his hips as he nodded. "Nice. Alright, okay – are the walls in here thin enough for that?"

"You should come through nice and clear," I assured him, waving him towards the door ten feet further down the hallway. "Give me five minutes and then start putting on a good show – but don't oversell it, okay?"

"You got it," said Caleb, firing off a lazy salute as he walked off.

I puffed out my cheeks as I released a heavy breath, running my hands back through my hair. Focus. I needed to focus. It was time to work. I thought briefly of texting Lazlo again, of updating him, but I shook the thought away. I could handle this myself. I had to prove to him, to everyone, that I could handle this myself.

Squaring my shoulders, I strode down the hall to the fourth door on the right, holding myself tall, working a stern expression onto my face. It wasn't until my hand began to twist the doorknob open that I heard the shuffle of feet behind me. I turned to see Shaye standing there, frowning deeply.

I looked between the door and her, my hand frozen on the knob. "What are you doing?"

Shaye crossed her arms over her chest and glared at me. "I'm coming with you."

I released the door, stepping back towards her as I shook my head. "Look, I really don't need an audience for–"

"I don't care what he did," she interrupted me, her fingertips gripping her arms so hard I could see the knuckles turn red and then white. "I'm not going to stand here while you beat the shit out of somebody for information."

I stared at her. "While I...?"

Words failed me as my mind went blank with disgust. Is that what she thought of me? That I was the kind of man who would torture someone? Did she think I was a monster?

Why did that bother me so much?

Tongue probing the inside of my cheek, I scoffed, looking away from her at last. I shook my head again and returned my hand to the doorknob, turning it. "You know what?" I opened the door wide and looked back at her, smiling without my teeth. "Come on in."

Shaye's veneer of self-righteous anger cracked a little at that. She looked from my face to the doorway and back again, her arms falling to her sides.

I swung my free hand through the door invitingly, lifting my brows high over my eyes. "Really. Matter of fact, I'd appreciate it."

She took a hesitant step towards the door. When I made no move to stop her, she sniffed and lifted her chin, turning away from me and striding past me inside. I followed after her without a word, closing the door softly behind us.

The room had, at one point, been some kind of maintenance storage space, though few vestiges remained aside from some dilapidated metal shelving lining the space on which were scattered handfuls of miscellaneous supplies. I assumed it was from this grab bag of materials that Caleb had found what he needed to restrain our attacker.

The redhead sat on a rolling chair that was missing two wheels in the center of the room, his arms duct taped to the back of the chair and his feet likewise duct taped to the wobbly base. A filthy rag protruded from his mouth, and I grimaced at the thought of what that was doing to his sense of taste and smell, knowing them to be as keen as my own.

I had done a number on the man's face, and even though our healing was accelerated, it wasn't instantaneous. His left eye was still swollen shut, purplish green in color, and his lips were split in multiple places. He looked up when we entered and began struggling against the duct tape, growling around the rag like some kind of wild animal.

Shaye stood frozen just inside of the room, her eyes wide, hands clenched into fists at her sides. I watched her for a moment, and almost offered again that she didn't have to be here, but stepped on my own words before I could speak.

With a quick shake of my head, I walked further into the room, the single bulb which hung from a wire in the middle of the ceiling casting long shadows around me as I went. The man stilled a little at my approach, enough at least for me to reach up and yank the rag out of his mouth, tossing it to one side.

"Hey there, carrot top," I said, peering down into the swollen face of our assailant. "How are you feeling?"

He spat, the glob of bloody expectorant landing somewhere to the left of my shoe.

I heaved a disappointed sigh, running my tongue along the front of my teeth as I considered him. "It doesn't have to be like that."

"Fuck you, dickbag," he snarled, not even looking up at me.

Rolling my stiff shoulders back, I tilted my head to one side, scanning the edges of the room for a quick moment as I considered how I wanted to proceed. Seeing what I was looking for, I moved past him, noting how, despite his big talk, he flinched away when I brushed by. I pulled a second battered office chair out from the back corner of the small room, putting it directly in front of him. I sat, and regarded him once more, my brow lifting. "You have a chance here, friend. One chance to walk out of here. I suggest you take it."

"What are you talking about?" said the redhead, his one good eye glaring at me in open distrust.

I reached forward and the redheaded man immediately jerked away, but there was nowhere for him to go, tied as he was to the immobile chair. I dropped my hand onto his shoulder, and it fell like a lead weight. Knitting my brow, I adopted an expression of sincere concern. "You do *want* to walk out of here, don't you?"

Looking from my hand to my face, the young man gave a hesitant nod. I drew back. Taking a deep breath, I shrugged off my jacket and twisted around to place it over the back of the chair. "Good. That's good. I can help you if you help me." I slumped down in the chair, unbuttoning the cuffs of my shirt sleeves as I stared at him. "So, tell me – why'd you come after the human?"

The young wolf huffed out what might have been a laugh, but it was a weak and poor attempt. "I'm... I'm not telling you shit."

I looked over my shoulder at Shaye and shot her an exaggerated frown. I shrugged. "He's not going to tell us shit."

Shifting her weight from foot to foot, glancing between me and the man tied to the chair, she nodded, letting loose a derisive snort. "Yeah, so I heard."

"Well...okay." I slapped my hands hard against my thighs and stood, pushing the rolling chair out from under me as I did so. "A real cool customer. I can respect that."

I picked up my jacket and slung it over one arm and headed towards the door. I felt Shaye's confused stare, but forced myself to ignore her as I moved through the space. Then, as if I had just remembered, I turned, one hand in the air, the other occupied with rolling my sleeve up towards my bicep. "Oh, by the way, your friend – is he as good under pressure as you are?"

The redhead went stock still in the seat. He turned his face towards me, his good eye wide with panic. "Nicky?"

Right on schedule, a series of violent crashes and thuds sounded from the room next to us. Shaye jumped at the sound of Caleb's muffled shouting, her eyes widening to the size of hubcaps as the large man let loose a high-pitched, pained wail that rattled the shelves around us.

"Is that his name?" I waited for the muffled cry to die away, sliding my hands into my trouser pockets. "My associate is talking to him right now. My associate isn't as...hands off as I am. And the first one who tells us what we want to know gets to walk out of here." More banging and another scream, this one more blood curdling than the last. I lifted my brows high over my eyes and winced theatrically. "Oh. Wow. Well, like I said, my partner has anger issues."

The walls shook as Caleb put on the good show he promised. I hoped he wasn't doing too much damage to the place – it sounded like he was throwing something thick and heavy against the floor, punctuating every strike with a scream in a voice not quite his own. I kept my gaze trained on the wolf in front of me. He whipped his head from side to side, jerking at the sound of every hit, beginning to whimper in time with the screams until finally he exploded with a loud shout of his own.

"Jesus Christ!" The redhead pulled against his restraints, panic written clear across his face. Another series of thuds and a garbled cry ripped through the air, and he shook himself from side to side violently. "Fuck, okay, stop! Just stop!" He looked around the room, tears welling in his eyes. "I'll tell you whatever, man, just, what do you want to know?"

Shaye harrumphed from the corner, and I turned to look at her as I walked back towards our captive. Her arms crossed high over her chest, she was struggling to hide a smirk. I answered her smile with a small one of my own, careful to keep it hidden from the wolf in the room.

Slowly and deliberately, I resumed my seat in front of him, my face blank. Then, leaning forward so that my elbows were resting on my knees, I jerked my head back towards Shaye. "Why did you come after her?"

"It was just a job, man," he answered miserably. He leaned forward as far as the duct tape would allow, his head hanging low between his shoulders. "This old fucker brought us down from Santa Barbara this morning. Told us he'd give us ten grand to track down a human and put her in the ground."

I nodded. "How'd you track her?"

The young wolf licked his lips and looked up at Shaye, nodding. "He had a–a jacket. With her scent on it."

The jacket. She had lost a jacket in the parking garage, hadn't she? We hadn't found it there, but I assumed some cop had logged it away as evidence before we arrived. Guess I was wrong about that one. "I was wondering where that went," I said to myself, before I refocused, straightening in my seat. "This old fucker have a name?"

The redhead glanced from me to Shaye, shrugging, his voice taking on a whine of desperation. "I don't know, we weren't like, hanging out, dude – we didn't exchange socials and shit!"

I thought hard for a long, quiet moment. Rubbing at the back of my neck, I looked at the redheaded man askance, asking, "How was this guy supposed to pay you? How were you supposed to let him know you'd done the job?"

The young wolf shook his head. "He said…" An unmistakable look of embarrassment crossed his face. "Look, he said when it was done, he'd know. Said to head back to Santa Barbara and he'd find us and pay us."

"And you believed that?" I rolled my eyes so hard my whole head moved in a circle. Shooting up from my seat, I brought one hand up to squeeze at my temple while I began to pace the room, muttering under my breath, "Just how stupid are you? Useless fucking…"

"I got his picture!"

I stopped at the far side of the room and turned to look at him, my hand falling to my side.

The restrained wolf nodded with enthusiasm, flashing me blood-stained teeth as he grinned. "Yeah, I snapped a pic of him when he wasn't looking just in case he tried to screw us over. Nicky doesn't even know I did it."

"Show me." I demanded, closing the distance between us with a long stride.

The redhead shifted in the chair, nodding down to his thigh. "It's on my phone, in my pocket."

A bit rougher than was perhaps called for, I dug the phone out of his pocket. It was a cheap, pay-as-you-go type phone, with a large crack across the screen. I brought it to life with a shake and turned the locked screen towards the captive wolf.

"Four, Six, Nine, Five," he spat out as quickly as possible.

I keyed in the code and the phone flickered fully awake. Flicking through the phone's storage, I searched for a recent photo that fit the bill, grimacing as I passed several unflattering shirtless selfies of the young man in question.

At last, a photo flashed onto the screen. My finger froze over the plastic. The figure in the photo was walking away from the person holding the phone, looking over their shoulder as if to say one final word. White-blond hair pulled back in a tight, high ponytail, brown eyes in a tanned face – a face I knew well. A face I had seen that very morning.

Lazlo.

I felt the blood drain from my face. My lips parted, but for a long moment no sound came out.

Shaye stepped closer to me. "Andy?"

"Puta madre," I cursed under my breath, my grip tightening on the cell phone, my knuckles going white around the plastic.

"What?"

I licked my lips, shoving the phone towards Shaye's face. "Is this the man you saw?"

"It was dark..." Shaye took the cell phone from me and moved into better light. "And he was...you know...not a man then..." She closed her eyes for a moment, swallowing hard. Opening them again, she looked at the slightly blurry cell-phone photo, doubtless trying to reconcile it with the flashes of terror-soaked memory.

At last, she nodded. She handed the phone back to me, taking a shaky breath. "Yeah, I think that's him. It's the eyes. The eyes didn't change."

My mind rebelled at the information that was being shoved into it.

Lazlo. Lazlo was the rogue wolf. He had been hunting openly in the city for months, bringing attention to the den, risking our exposure, risking our lives... for what?

It didn't make any sense.

Second only to Doña Sangre herself, Lazlo knew the rules better than anyone. How many times in the past year had he reminded me of how lucky I was not to be excommunicated for my own transgressions? He knew the cost of flagrantly flouting this law, a law not just of our den but for all were-wolves everywhere. This would cost him his life. Why – why would he do this?

And why would he let Emilia put me on this case?

Had he expected me to fail?

Or had he done something to insure it?

Caleb. He'd hired Caleb to help me...

Whipping around, my body shaking, I strode for the door. "Caleb!" I barked, throwing the cheap plywood portal open so hard that the knob cracked into the cheap plaster, embedding itself in the wall.

As I stepped out into the hall, I caught sight of Caleb, stepping out into the corridor, obviously concerned by the tenor of my voice as I shouted his name. When he saw me barreling towards him, he stopped and waited, his face clouding.

"Did you fucking know about this?" I shouted, closing the distance between us with a few long strides.

"What?" said Caleb, staring down at me with a confused quirk to his brow.

I slammed my open hand into Caleb's chest, forcing the larger man to stumble back down the hall. "Don't fucking lie to me – did you know about this?"

"Hey!" He shouted back at me, easily regaining his balance. "You need to calm down, Andy! Did I know about what, for fuck's sake?"

Without another word, I practically threw the redhead's phone at Caleb's chest. He caught it and turned it right side up, staring at the screen with a furrowed brow and narrowed eyes. There was a beat of silence. He looked up from the phone. His face was blank. "What is this?"

"This–" I shouted, pointing a shaking finger to the back of the phone in his hand, "–is our rogue wolf!"

A flurry of emotions fluttered across Caleb's visage, but he settled, after a moment, on a sickly mix of anger and confusion. "That... that can't be right."

"You didn't know?" I demanded, my chest heaving as I swiped the phone back from him and shoved it into my trouser pocket.

"Of course, I didn't know!" It was his turn to shout now. He turned away from me and walked down the hall, rubbing his hand against the back of his head. "This doesn't make any sense..."

Shaye looked between us, shaking her head. "Who? Who is that? Why is this bad?"

"Lazlo." I spat the name onto the floor like it was a sunflower seed that had been stuck in my teeth. Pacing the hallway, my hands on my hips, my eyes were fixed on the floor as I continued to talk to myself. "La concha de tu madre, what is he doing? Why would he do this?"

"Who is Lazlo?" Shaye pressed, trying to step in front of me and get me to look at her.

Staring at the top of her shoes, I struggled to compose myself. I didn't have time for this, for this panic, for this consternation. We needed to move.

I stepped around her and headed back towards the maintenance room where our captive was still sitting. Crouching down onto the balls of my feet, I ripped at the duct tape with too-sharp nails and growled, "You – get out of here."

When he failed to move, I lifted him up by the front of his bloodstained shirt and put him on his feet, adding, "If I see you again, I'll rip your throat out myself – entiendes?"

The young wolf wasted no time. As soon as my hands were no longer on him, he sprinted from the room, his heavy footfalls echoing down the hall towards the emergency exit in the opposite direction from where we had entered.

"Andy..." Caleb's voice was soft and clear behind me.

I turned as if in a dream, taking in the sight of Caleb and Shaye watching me expectantly.

His hands on his hips, Caleb shook his head, his eyes fixed on my face. "What the hell are we going to do?"

My mind raced through our potential options, none of them particularly appealing, until it landed back on the original plan, or at least a version of it. "We–we have to tell Emilia." I dragged my hand down my jaw and shook my head. "Now, tonight – this can't wait."

The silver-haired wolf threw his hand out towards Shaye, shrugging. "What are we going to do with her? We can't take her back to the den house."

"No," I agreed, darting my eyes from side to side as I tried to think. "There's another place that's near there, though – a safe house in Laurel Canyon. Come on."

Without waiting for agreement from my companions, I grabbed hold of Shaye's arm and dragged her out of the room and down the hallway. Consumed with thoughts of Lazlo, of Doña Sangre, or what I might say when I reached the den house, of what might happen to Shaye when all was revealed, I was only vaguely aware of Shaye attempting to pull away from me as we moved, protesting all the way through the warehouse.

It wasn't until we were back out in the parking lot, heading for my car, that Shaye, asphalt under her feet, had the leverage she needed to untangle herself from me.

"Hey! Stop!" she shouted for what must have been the tenth time. Shaking herself free of my grip, her sepia eyes darted between Caleb and myself in open alarm. "What the fuck is going on?"

One glance at her and I could see the fear hiding under the layers of performative anger and bluster. It plucked at my heart, and I opened my mouth to speak, when Caleb stepped between us, cutting me off.

"Andy!" Caleb faced me, his hands raised up in front of him as he stared at me from under set brows. "You can't."

I snapped my mouth shut, swallowing down the explanation that had been on the tip of my tongue. He was right. Of course, he was right. Den politics were nothing in which a human should get involved. Even if it looked like she was already in it up to her eyeballs without her knowing.

Turning around to face Shaye, Caleb shook his head. "He can't. You know all you need to know."

"No. That's bullshit." She pointed to the phone in my pocket, her face flushed. "Who the hell is that guy? You both are acting like I just told you that the dog catcher is on his way."

Eyes narrowing, Caleb and I shared a glance. He shook his head and I looked away, gritting my teeth.

Shaye let loose a frustrated grunt. "Come on! What is the big deal here? Why can't I know?"

"You're human," said Caleb, scoffing a little. "An unaffiliated human. You can't – you can't know about us!"

"But I do." Shaye rubbed at her forehead with her fingertips, screwing her eyes shut. "Jesus, I already know the big secret, right? Werewolves are real. Now, can you tell me exactly how many people would believe me if I were to go blabbing about it? Because I can." She looked from Caleb to me and back again, leaning forward. "Everyone would think I was just another crazy homeless woman."

The sleeping city hummed around us as we all considered the truth of her words. I crossed my arms over my chest. "She has a point," I said, shrugging.

Rolling his eyes, Caleb threw his hands up in the air and turned away. He started for the car, growling, "We don't have time for this..."

I nodded, wrapping my hand around Shaye's bicep once more. "He also has a point. A particularly good point. We have to go."

She immediately began to pull against me, sputtering. "I said I'm not going anywhere–"

I spun around to face her but did not release her. "Listen: get in the car and I'll tell you everything." Staring into her eyes, I asked for what I knew I was a fool for wanting. "Please trust me."

~ 8 ~

CHAPTER 8

Shaye

A ndy drove. As he drove, he talked. He talked and I listened. I listened as he moved us out of the Fashion District and through the city, heading up into Laurel Canyon, the city suddenly and abruptly giving way to bungalows and suburban-lite neighborhoods.

There was an entire world underneath the one I knew. Which was crazy because I already thought I lived in a world that existed under the one most people knew. I did my best to follow Andy's story, to wrap my head around the idea that all across the country, all across the world there were gangs, families, of werewolves who didn't live on the fringes, but had weaved themselves in the warp and woof of modern life in ways I couldn't even begin to fully appreciate. Andy was a member of a family – he called it a 'den' – called Sangre Sagrada, that had existed in Los Angeles for hundreds of years. This den had leadership, had rules, and these rules had been broken, the leadership defied, and now...

Now we were all in deep shit.

Me especially.

We coasted to a stop at a light and Andy glanced over at me after a long pause, lifting his brows over his eyes. "Hey, you okay?" he asked. "You look a little dazed."

"Yeah." I rubbed my forehead with my fingertips, frowning. "This is just... a lot to absorb." I straightened in the passenger seat, bringing my feet down off the dashboard where they had been resting. "So, this guy that killed Jason–"

"Lazlo Cabral," supplied Caleb from the darkness of the backseat. I looked at him in the rearview mirror to find him staring out the window in a deep, petulant brood.

"Cabral, he's like the right-hand man to your Queen or whatever, right?" I continued, squirming in my seat so my back rested against the passenger side door.

Andy shook his head, nose wrinkling. "Doña Sangre, she's not a queen, she..." The light turned green, and his foot slid off the brake and onto the gas pedal. He rolled his eyes. "No se como explicarlo, she is like el presidente, okay?"

I leaned forward, the seat belt biting into my collarbone. "But her dad was the leader before her?"

"Yes, and Lazlo was his right-hand man too," Andy said, propping his elbow against the open window frame and leaning his forehead against the fingertips of his left hand.

I gave a loud harrumph, lifting my brow and rolling my eyes. "Sure as shit sounds like a monarchy to me..."

"¿Tienes una pregunta?" Andy snapped through frustration and clenched teeth.

I blinked rapidly, bringing my mind back to the thread of thoughts I had been attempting to follow. "Yeah, right, sorry. Anyway, so, Cabral, if he's in so tight with this Doña Sangre of yours, and your Doña Sangre doesn't want hunting in the city–"

"Nobody does," said Caleb. He leaned forward, his hands hanging between his knees. "Sangre Sagrada, Nameless, doesn't matter what den you're a part of – flashy kills like that are a big no no. They're way too public – attract too much attention."

"Then why the hell is he doing it?" I looked between Caleb and Andy, my arms open wide. "Why kill Jason and all those other people?"

"I don't know," Andy admitted. "I just... I don't know. I don't understand. It doesn't make any sense."

I swallowed down a protest, a demand that he must know, that he must have some idea why Jason had been killed, why I had a target on my back now, and instead I turned to roll down the passenger side window, letting in a warm blast of smoggy LA nighttime air.

I could see it written all over his face – Andy honestly didn't know. When it came to the whys of all this, he was just as in the dark as I was.

Which was a terrifying thought.

The silence felt awkward and oppressive. Fingers fiddling with my lower lip, I let my head drop to one side. "What do you think your Doña Sangre is going to do when you tell her? About Cabral?"

Andy exchanged a glance with Caleb in the rearview mirror. Rolling his shoulders back against the plush leather seat, he ticked his head to one side. I got the feeling he was choosing his words carefully as he answered, "She... she won't be happy."

I tried to imagine an unhappy werewolf president – how would she choose to air her displeasure?

Would she kill this Cabral guy?

"I want to be there," I announced, setting my jaw.

Andy jerked up straight in his seat. "No, no way," he exclaimed, his eyes widening. "Lazlo lives at the den house. Taking you there would be like handing you to him on a silver platter. I am not letting anything happen to you, remember? That's our deal."

I pushed my hand through my hair, grumbling. "I don't like this. Being stashed away like I'm some kind of dirty secret."

"That's exactly what you are right now, Shaye," answered Andy.

"It's bullshit."

I was surprised to hear him chuckle at my displeasure and felt a twinge of embarrassment at my behavior flare in my belly. He looked over at me, rubbing his chin. "You know, you may not like it, but it's going to keep you alive."

I didn't have an answer for that. I had trusted Andy Vazquez this far with my wellbeing, it seemed petulant and unwise to suddenly balk at his counsel and insist on a course of action that even I had to concede was reckless at best.

As I sat in the dark cab of the luxury car, I tried to get my bearings. The car wound up the residential back streets, headlights illuminating sleeping households in brief flashes of electric light. We turned down a street, Chandelle Place. The paved road was tight, barely allowing more than one car at a time down the middle, the houses huddled close to the edge. The residences were strictly middle to lower class, small two-story bungalows with green lawns and dirty, weather damaged walls.

Without warning Andy pulled the car into a steeply sloping driveway, parking the car in front of a white, dirt caked garage. To the left a series of steps led up to large wooden double doors that were partially hidden from the street behind yuccas and bushes.

"Here we are," announced Andy, unbuckling his seatbelt as he unlocked the car's doors, getting out without waiting for the rest of us.

I stepped out of the car and looked at the sleeping bungalow, noting the single light that burned in the upstairs window. Without warning, the garage door rumbled up and open. Starting, I moved my gaze down to take in the sight of two people exiting the blindingly lit storage space. I could tell little at first except that one person was male presenting, the other female. But as my eyes adjusted to the light cast by the handful of bare bulbs suspended from rafters in the garage and the pair stepped further out into the night, I could make out a little more. The woman had long black hair bouncing around her shoulders in tight tiny coils. She stared at me with piercing green eyes. The man was slightly older, his head shaved close to the scalp, and he walked with a limp.

"Who are those people?" I asked, keeping my hands loose at my sides, my stance wide, in case a fight was to suddenly break out.

"They're ours, don't worry about it," Andy said in a hushed voice, even though I noticed that his eyes did a quick scan of the two approaching wolves. Moving forward, he adopted an air of tired nonchalance, lifting one hand in a wave as he shouted, "Claudia! Nico! ¿Qué tal están?"

The male werewolf stepped ahead of his female counterpart, his hand outstretched and gesturing directly at me. The expression on his face was less than welcoming as he demanded, "¿Qué diablos está haciendo esa cosa aquí?"

Andy gave an exaggerated look behind himself before returning his attention to the one called Nico, his brow furrowed. "¿Qué? ¿La humana?"

The female werewolf, Claudia I was guessing, came to stop beside her partner, crossing her arms over her chest, looking at Andy down her nose, scowling. "Si, la humana, Andy." She and Nico shared a glance and then she smiled cruelly. "No la has vuelto a joder, ¿verdad?"

"No, no esta vez." Andy stopped a few feet in front of the other two werewolves, resting one hand on his hip. "We need to keep this woman here for a few hours. Maybe a day, but probably no more than that."

The smirk was wiped clean of Claudia's face. Her arms dropped to her sides as she shook her head. "¿Estás loco?"

"Andy–" started Nico, frowning hard.

"Come on, Nico." He stepped between the two wolves, wrapping an arm around Nico's shoulders as he moved forward. He drew him away from his partner to stand closer to the garage, lowering his voice, but not so much that I couldn't make out what he was saying. "This is on the up and up, te prometo."

I stepped forward, straining my ears to catch the words of the two male werewolves' conversation. Claudia, seeing me move, snarled at me in a half-hearted way, flashing teeth that didn't belong in a human mouth. I stilled, grimacing at her, unable to look away. Heart in my throat, I lifted a shaky hand and flipped her off.

Her snarl widened into a grin. She licked her lips.

I forced my attention back to Nico and Andy, lowering my hand as I looked away. Seeing that Nico remained unconvinced, Andy rolled his eyes, forcing a small smile onto his face as he patted the other werewolf's chest with his open hand. "La Doña quería un bocadillo especial...¿entendides?"

As my brain took an extra second to translate what had been said, my blood, which had been pounding in my ears, stilled and went cold.

So...they *did* eat humans.

I looked at Andy and swallowed hard, his joking smile making my stomach churn. Maybe they had to, maybe it was part of the curse of being a werewolf, maybe...

Oh God, was he a monster?

"A ella le gusta jugar con su comida," quipped Nico in reply, grinning from ear to ear.

I turned and stepped out from behind the car door, heading for the lawn and the bushes with a jerk, my stomach betraying me with a lurch. But I wasn't sick. Instead, I stood there, head spinning, breathing shallow, and tried not to remember the sound of snapping bones as Jason had been devoured.

"Shaye," Caleb's voice rumbled out behind me. "You okay?"

I nodded, lifting up my hand and waving in case he had any misguided thoughts about coming over and checking on me. The last thing I wanted was one of them near me right now. The sound of footsteps made me turn, a snarl on my face, but it disappeared when I saw Andy walking back towards Caleb and the car.

"Caleb." Andy put his hand on the open passenger door and shook his head. "I want you to stay here with Shaye."

Caleb looked hurt. He swallowed, lifting his chin. "You don't want me backing you up? I told you, Andy, I didn't know anything about–"

Andy gave him a far more genuine smile than the one he had used on Nico. Clapping him on the shoulder, Andy shook him lightly. "I know. I believe you, okay? It's just that I'd rather have you here – anything happens to Shaye and all I've got is a shitty cell phone picture of Lazlo and a wild story."

Lest I forget: I was just a means to an end to these people. I stared at the front door of the bungalow, lost in thought. What would happen to me once they got what they wanted? Would I become someone's next meal? I swallowed hard and blinked slowly. I couldn't think like that. I couldn't think that far ahead. I was safe for now and I needed to take this time to recuperate, to gather myself and my strength. Especially if my visions had come back.

Besides, I had no intention of going down without a fight.

Next to me, Andy cleared his throat and I jumped, my gaze snapping to him as if he had shouted my name.

"Sorry," Andy said quickly, lifting his hands in supplication. "I just... I'm going to go. You'll be alright here. Caleb is going to stay and keep an eye on you."

I looked from him to Caleb, who had moved up into the garage and was talking with Nico and Claudia. I waved my hand through the air, shrugging. "Okay. Whatever. I still think I should go with you."

Scowling, Andy shook his head. "I told you I'd keep you safe," he said. "Will you stop being difficult and let me hold up my end of our deal?"

I shrugged sharply, rolling my eyes like a teenager being told to finish their homework before going out with their friends. "Fine." I threw my arms across my chest and then, as if it were an afterthought, spat out a half-hearted, "Dickhead."

The expletive garnered a snort of laughter from him for which I think neither of us could account. He looked at me for a long moment, as if trying to memorize exactly how I looked standing there. I pulled at the hem of my still some-how damp shirt and avoided his gaze, discomforted by the unfamiliar sensation of being perceived so totally.

His head falling to one side, Andy took a tentative step towards me, his hand outstretched in my direction. "What is it?"

"You're staring," I mumbled, gritting my teeth as I stared at the top of his expensive shoes.

He stopped moving and I glanced up at his face. Creased with confusion, he swallowed hard, his Adam's apple bob-bing. "Oh. Uh, sorry." He waved his outstretched hand up and down, indicating all of me in a broad sweep. "You just...you just seem like something's wrong."

"How would you know?" I snapped. I rubbed at the back of my neck, irritated without really knowing why, tired of the tension I carried there between my shoulders. "Besides, what about all this shit is supposed to be right?"

"Right. Well...try and get some rest," he said finally, his arms hanging awkwardly at his sides. "I'll... I'll be back in a few hours."

He turned and a sense of dread overtook me, sudden and strong, like the pressure of a summer thunderstorm when it crests over the mountains.

I couldn't make myself believe he was a monster. It didn't matter why he was helping me, the fact was he had saved my life. And something that had been dormant for many long years stirred inside me and sent a shiver up my spine: this man was not a danger – he was *in* danger.

Shaking my head, I moved towards him, my mouth open and forming his name before I could stop myself.

"Andy!"

Before he could turn to answer me, I reached forward and grabbed his hand. I didn't know why I did it, but once I had clasped onto him, it felt like a magnet was holding me to him and I knew the last thing I wanted was to let go.

Andy gave a small jerk when our hands touched. He came to a dead, sudden stop, and twisted round sharply, staring at me with wide eyes.

I squeezed his hand tighter. "I don't like this. This isn't going to go right."

Something in the back of my mind stirred and I closed my eyes tight. There it was again. Ten years of nothing and now, twice in the space of forty-eight hours, that familiar, hazy tug at the base of my skull. I forced my eyes open and stared at Andy, fear closing up my throat. Would I have a vision right here? Right now?

I couldn't let that happen.

Andy closed the distance between us with a hesitant step. I didn't recoil from him, or release his hand, but stayed staring at him, searching his face for some sign that he understood. That he could tell me why it suddenly mattered so much to me what happened to him. Why a part of me that had been asleep for many long years was waking up to make sure he was going to be okay.

He had to know. He had to be able to tell me, to see…

But instead, he let out a sharp, short breath and reached up, pinching my chin between his thumb and pointer finger, shaking my head playfully from side to side. "What, you psychic, chica?"

The jibe hit me like an open hand across the face. I dropped his hand with a jerk and stepped back from him, eyes darting around the driveway, as if by keeping them moving I could stay the tears I felt welling in them.

"I just..." I swallowed hard and hugged myself. "I have a bad feeling about it, okay?"

I glanced back up at him, blinking in shock at the hurt in his gaze. But it was only there for a moment, overtaken by a practiced disgruntled air as he cleared his throat and leaned away from me.

"I'll be back in a few hours," repeated Andy, shaking his head in an attempt to dispel the last of the disappointed expression off of his face. Waving up to the house, he stepped backwards towards the car. "Change your clothes, take a shower, sleep. Just relájate, ¿está bien?"

Nodding, I let loose a heavy sigh as I watched him climb behind the wheel of the Maserati. I heard Caleb call my name from the garage and, with a final, hesitant glance through the dark windshield, I turned around and headed up the drive.

~ 9 ~

CHAPTER 9

Andy

I t was a thirty-minute drive from Laurel Canyon to Bel Air. Alone in my car for the first time since this morning, I switched on the radio, grimacing a little at the bombastic dance track Recuerdo had opted to put on at this time of night. I turned it down low, but kept it on, feeling the need for noise, not wanting to be left one-on-one with my thoughts.

I took a breath and caught Shaye's scent on the recycled air in the cab of the car. The pit of my stomach contracted. Shifting uncomfortably in my seat, I rolled down the windows, desperate to dispel her presence.

This couldn't be happening. Not again.

Smog-soaked air buffeting my face, I let myself think, for the first time in a year, of Melanie. Her long red hair, her soft, shy smile. Sweet and airy, like cotton candy, she had worked at one of the Sangre Sagrada production companies as an intern, completely unaware of what or for whom she was really working. She had just been excited to be in Hollywood, to be "in the business", to get her foot in the door and start a career in entertainment.

Her enthusiasm, her optimism, was infectious. When I was with Melanie, I honestly believed that no problem was insurmountable, that life was precious, a gift – that I had been put on this planet to enjoy myself. To love her forever.

What did I know about love? What did I know about forever?

Everything changed the day I told her the truth about what I was. I wanted to be honest with her, to give myself to her completely. It never occurred to me that she wouldn't want all of me.

The fear in her eyes. The disgust. She ran from me, avoided me for days, weeks, until... Until Sangre Sagrada found her. And made her disappear.

Melanie was right to run. I was a monster. I had loved her, and because of that she was dead. I couldn't, I wouldn't let that happen again. My hands flexed around the steering wheel. Not that I was falling in love with Shaye. I glanced at my reflection in the rearview mirror and rolled my eyes.

Sure. Sure, I wasn't.

My car climbed up into the hills that surrounded the city. I thought of the last things I'd said to Shaye and shook my head. I'd as good as lied to her. Back in a few hours? The truth was I didn't know what was going to happen next. After I told Emilia everything, what happened next to Shaye was not up to me. Most likely she'd be hidden away, moved out of the city, or somehow otherwise placed under watch to make sure she didn't expose our secret. Given my own recent history, it'd be doubtful I'd be allowed to keep in any kind of contact with her. In fact, the likelihood was high that I would never see Shaye again.

If I wasn't falling in love with her, then why did that thought pain me so?

No. No, it was good that I wouldn't see Shaye again. For the best. Whatever I was feeling for her, whatever it was, lust, love, it would lead to nothing good. Better for her to stay away from me, to stay alive.

The Bel Air retreat was silent and dark as I approached the front door. Ringing the doorbell, I wondered briefly how long it might take for someone to answer when, to my surprise, the door swung open almost immediately. A young wolf, shirtless and clad only in silk pajama pants, stood in the doorway, his chestnut brown hair mussed, a pair of over the ear headphones slung around his neck. He looked at me expectantly, his brows raised.

"I need to speak to Doña Sangre," I said by way of hello as I sidled through the doorway, forcing the wolf at the door to step back or be stepped on.

"Oh, uh, alright," he said, scratching at the back of his head. "I think she usually has an open audience session around noon on Monday–"

"Now."

He stopped scratching and stared at me from under his brow. "Uh...it's the middle of the night."

I pointed my finger up, indicating the second floor of the spacious mansion above us. "Is she still up?"

Blinking slowly, he didn't immediately answer, pausing instead to shut the door. Turning on his heel, he crossed his arms over his chest. "Yeah. Yes, she is."

I waved him away and started to walk farther into the house. "Then I won't be disturbing her."

His hand gripped my shoulder and I stopped, twisting around to look at him. He shook his head, rolling his eyes, and moved past me. "Just...wait here, vato."

Shoving my hands in my trouser pockets, I watched as he disappeared into the Retreat. As soon as I was alone, I let loose a heavy sigh, tilting my head back and staring at the high ceiling. What was Emilia going to do when I told her what was going on? She'd be devastated to learn that Cabral had betrayed us like this, and I couldn't provide her with a ready explanation as to why. Only Lazlo Cabral could do that, and I had no doubt that when Emilia was done with him, he'd be more than happy to talk.

Still, this would change the way the den operated at a fundamental level. Emilia was already making substantial changes, implementing rules that severely limited members' ability to engage in the Sacrament. But this? This would shake people's faith in leadership, open us up to unpleasant questions from others. This was the last thing we needed with the Nameless practically on our doorstep. But Emilia had given me a task. And I had to see it through to the end.

I heard someone call to me and I looked down, shaking myself a little from my thoughts as I refocused on the unpleasant task before me.

The young wolf's bare feet padded against the hardwood floor as he walked towards me, and he jerked his head back the way he had come. "You know the way."

Nodding to him, I moved through the house until I reached the sweeping white oak staircase, climbing up to the second floor of the Retreat and taking the steps two at a time. Stopped at the top of the stairs by two guard wolves, I waited impatiently as they patted me down. When they found no weapons on me, they stepped back to let me through, and I hurried to the rooms I knew Emilia to occupy.

When I entered, I stopped short, my eyes widening at the scene in front of me. Emilia, dressed in a nightgown and robe, had her back to me, her attention rapt on an open portfolio of papers in none other than Lazlo Cabral's outstretched hand.

Of course. Why wouldn't he be here? My luck had to be that bad.

"Doña Sangre," I said, hurrying into the room towards her, a half-formed idea in my mind of pulling her away from Lazlo's side. "Thank you for seeing me."

"Andoni–" Her eyes went wide as she turned to look at me. She gasped aloud.

Her shock stopped me in my tracks. I followed her line of sight and covered the bloodstained hole in my shirt with a start, having quite forgotten that I'd been shot an hour or so ago.

"Mi querido," she exclaimed, moving towards me in a rush. "You've been hurt!"

"Andy, were you shot?" demanded Lazlo, snapping the folio in his hand shut, his brow furrowing.

I glared at the old wolf but cut it short to address the woman now standing in front of me, her hands reaching for my chest. "Doña Sangre–" Letting out a huff of frustration, I captured her hands before they could touch me, holding them gently in my own. "Emilia, please. I need to speak with you."

Nodding, she allowed me to put her hands at her sides, though her gaze took on a quality of confused curiosity. "Speak, Andoni, speak."

Releasing her, I looked over her shoulder at Lazlo, my gaze hardening. "Alone."

The mood in the room shifted palpably, tension thickening the air like flour thickens gravy. Lazlo met my gaze and I saw something flicker in the depths of his eyes. He lowered the portfolio to his side, gripping it tightly.

He knew that I knew.

Scoffing, Emilia waved at the older man still standing by the open patio doors. "Oh, I have no secrets from Lazlo, Andoni – any more than I have secrets from you."

"But he can't say the same," I said, shaking my head and stepping forward, putting myself between my den leader and the traitor. "Can you, Lazlo?"

Lazlo's head fell to one side. He blinked at me in disbelief, putting on a good show of innocence. "Andy, I don't...what the hell are you talking about?"

His manufactured bewilderment grated, and I turned my back on him, pulling myself up tall. "Doña Sangre, Lazlo Cabral is the rogue wolf we've been looking for."

The room went as silent as a mausoleum. Emilia stared at me in frank amazement, her mouth slightly open. As I watched, her eyes flicked over my shoulder and settled on Lazlo. I heard a step behind me and the hairs on the back of my neck bristled. It took all my self-control not to turn and see what, see who she was looking at. Instead, I kept my gaze straight ahead, my jaw set, my hands fists at my sides.

With slow, measured steps, Emilia walked behind her desk and settled into her chair, crossing one leg over the other as she examined me. "That..." She shook her head and cleared her throat. "That is a very serious accusation, Andoni."

I strode forward to stand in front of her desk, reaching into my trouser pocket for the redhead hireling's cell phone. "I can prove it, Emilia."

She gave a curt nod, resting one hand on top of the papers scattered over the desktop. "Do so. At once."

Pulling up the photo as quickly as I could, I presented the phone to Emilia. She leaned forward but made no move to take the device from me, so I placed the cell on the desk in front of her. Staring down at the picture, her brow furrowed, her lips contorting in a grimace. She shook her head, withdrawing back into her seat. "No entiendo, Andoni. What am I looking at?"

"Lazlo." I leaned down, resting my hands against the desktop. "There was an eyewitness to the last attack. A human woman. I managed to track her down and–"

"A human?" Emilia's hands clenched into fists, crumpling the paper that lay beneath them. She surged to her feet, forcing me back as well, her eyes wide with panic. "Mierda! This is exactly what I was afraid of. We can't risk exposure at a time like this!"

"You said you tracked her down?" interrupted Lazlo, stepping towards us with one hand outstretched, face drawn with concern.

I scowled at him, crossing my arms over my chest. "Yes, I did. And she–"

Emilia moved out from behind her desk to stand by Lazlo, nodding with enthusiasm and smiling at me for the first time since I entered the room. "Good! Good, that's good. She's taken care of then?"

Her meaning could not have been more clear. Internally, my self-righteousness faltered for a moment as I began to realize that perhaps my friend's priorities and my own were not aligned. I shifted my weight onto my back foot as I grimaced. "She's..." I shook my head and gritted my teeth. "No, not exactly, Emilia. You see–"

"Not exactly?" Emilia's low-heeled slippers clicked across the hardwood floor as she strode towards me, her arms flung wide. "Andoni, the Nameless will be here tomorrow. Do you know what they will do to us if they find out about any of this? I know how you feel about killing humans – I feel the same, but in this case it's entirely necessary!"

Swallowing hard, I lifted a defensive hand, my eyes flickering shut. "I understand, Emilia, but Shaye–"

A sharp, stinging pain – my eyes shot open. Emilia gripped me by the face, her fingernails digging half-moon crescents into my cheeks. With a jerk, she forced me to meet her eyes. "Shaye?" she repeated the name I had used so carelessly, whispering it back to me with a shudder of barely concealed rage.

I was well aware of the way Emilia felt about me. I would've been a fool to be ignorant of her desire, of her affection for me that went deeper than the love one feels for a friend. It had been strange, flattering in a way, to know that she saw me in such a favorable light. But what I didn't realize until that moment, until she looked deep into my eyes with Shaye's name in the air between us, was that I would never feel the same way about her.

Ever.

I looked away from her, gaze focused on the floor. There was nothing else I could do.

"Oh, Andoni..." The corners of her mouth fell into a deep frown, her eyes shining with, what for the briefest moment, looked like tears. "What did you do?"

"Andy," chided Lazlo. "Not again."

"Wait, Emilia, you – you don't understand," I exclaimed desperately, yanking my head free of my den leader's hand. "Shaye – she saw the wolf who killed that man. She can identify him! And she did! She saw Lazlo Cabral–"

The back of Emilia's hand cracked hard across my face and for a moment the world went white. My teeth cut jagged holes in the inside of my cheek and blood coated my tongue as I stumbled back, blinking in shock.

Emilia stared back at me, her expression closed off and cold. Breathing quickly in and out of her nose, she rolled her shoulders back and, with earnest effort, turned so she was only half facing me, her attention instead focused on the view out of her bedroom windows.

"Kneel," she commanded.

Keeping my eyes on her, I slowly lowered myself onto my knees, my arms limp at my sides.

Cradling one hand in the other, Emilia did not look at me when she spoke, staring instead over the glittering city that lay below the hills. "What did you tell this woman about us?"

I shook my head, swallowing down the blood in my mouth before answering quietly, "Nothing she didn't already know, Doña Sangre."

She slapped me with her open palm, sending my head jerking in the opposite direction from her first strike. I swayed to one side, stopping myself from falling over with a quick movement of my outstretched hand, bracing myself against the floor. The side of my face was warm where she had hit me, but I resisted the urge to reach up and touch my hurt, straightening instead and returning to my pose of supplication.

"Why?" Her voice was low and quiet, filled with pain. She shook her head once, but still did not look at me. "Why are you making me do this, Andoni?"

I took a deep, steadying breath, but still I heard a waver in my words when I said, "Emilia, por favor, listen to me–"

The back of her hand struck me again, harder this time, and I felt a tooth in the back of my mouth loosen at the impact. Desperation started to creep into my heart, and I struggled to remain upright as I almost shouted, "Emilia, Lazlo is slaughtering humans openly in the city! He's going to expose everything, expose us–!"

Finally, she looked at me, her head whipping round to stare down at me. The muscles in her clenched jaw rippled and her eyes burned into me. "Like you have exposed us?"

My protestations died on my lips. I looked back at Lazlo and realized in a flash how badly I had miscalculated this encounter.

I was dead. And I had taken Shaye down with me.

Emilia took a deep breath, intentionally lifting and dropping her shoulders. Reaching down, she pulled up the hem of her long nightdress and brought up the skirt to clean my blood off her hand. "Where is this human now?"

I stared at the floor and did not answer.

Grabbing the front of my shirt, Emilia lifted me off of my knees, shaking me like a snow globe as she demanded, "The human, Andoni, where is she?"

My hands clenched instinctively over hers. "One...one of our safe houses."

"You brought her–!" Emilia's breathing became labored with anger, her eyes widening. "How could you—! Bastardo!"

With a roar, Emilia flung me to the floor, my head cracking against the hardwood. Through blurry eyes, I looked up at her, watching helplessly as her claws unsheathed, her hair growing wild as she shifted partly into her wolf form. She drew her hand back, aiming for my face.

And then stopped.

I was ready to die. I wasn't ready for the cold look that crept across her enraged face. For the deep, deep breath she sucked into her lungs and the slow drawing away from me.

"I... I won't kill you, Andoni." Emilia flexed her fingers, and I watched her claws recede. "I won't. What you have done – killing you would be kindness."

A sudden rush of panic, hot and sticky, like molten metal, flooded my mind, running down my spine and settling in the pit of my stomach. Struggling onto my feet, blood dripping from the corner of my mouth, I sputtered, "Emilia, please, you have to listen to me–"

"As of this moment, you are excommunicated from the Sangre Sagrada." She swallowed hard, lifting her chin a little as she spoke, her eyes fixed on the city – her city. "You are denless. You are alone, Andoni. You have turned your back on your family. And so, your family will turn their back on you."

My tongue felt dry and heavy in my mouth, thick and useless, like a piece of worn-out leather. I needed to say something. Something to make Emilia change her mind. She couldn't do this. She couldn't... Not when everything I'd done had been to protect her, protect the den, to try and make up for my past mistakes...

But it was already done.

As I watched, struck dumb by her pronouncement, Emilia brought her hand up to her forehead, her voice breaking a little as she quietly asked, "Lazlo, por favor–"

The older wolf placed a fatherly hand on the small of her back. "Consider it done, Emilia."

Turning from her, he walked quickly through the room, not sparing me so much as a glance as he went. Lazlo's head disappeared out the bedroom door as he called quietly, "¿Guardias? ¿Por favor?"

Stepping quickly and quietly from their station outside, the two guard wolves entered the room. There was a brief, hushed conference with Lazlo and then they both nodded and strode towards me. Grabbing me by the arms and lifting me off the ground, the two wolves began pulling me back towards the bedroom door. The part of me that was still aware of such things heard someone shouting, cursing, and after a few seconds of the words reverberating off the soaring ceilings of the mansion and coming back to ring in my ears, I realized with a start that it was me who was protesting so violently.

Literally kicking and screaming, the guards dragged me backward down the stairs and through the front part of the house. The wolf who had opened the door for me poked his head out of the living room, eyes wide, but said and did nothing as I was forced out onto the front porch.

Once outside, the guards changed tactics. No longer content with simply restraining me, the sallow faced wolf kicked the back of my knees, forcing my legs out from under me, before landing a punch under my eye. The larger of the two wolves picked me up under my arms, bashed me against the side of the house, and then threw me bodily out into the driveway.

I landed just inside the radius of the porch lights' glow, my body skidding against the stones and gravel that made up the walkway leading to the front door. Head spinning, partly from physical trauma and partly from emotional, I tried to push myself up off the ground, heedless to the guards who walked towards me.

"Danos un minuto, por favor," said Lazlo from behind them, stepping forward off the porch as he motioned the guards to back away. They obeyed without a word, moving back into the doorway.

I had just about managed to sit up when Lazlo's foot landed on my shoulder. He pushed down on me with his full weight as he leaned towards me, my bloodied face rubbed into the stones.

"I should've known better than to hire outside of the family," said Lazlo, his voice a low murmur in my ear, his rueful chuckle grating against my eardrum as he ground his shoe into my shoulder. "But when Emilia told me she was going to put you on the case, I got a little desperate, I'll admit. Sloppy. Should've known you wouldn't be able to resist shooting yourself in the foot, though, mi hijo. You do have a talent for that."

Kicking me onto my back, Lazlo stepped away, smiling down at me for a long moment before turning to head back into the house. I watched him go, disbelief, rage, confusion, and a whole toxic cocktail of emotions churning inside me. As it often did, though, rage got the upper hand and I scrambled up onto my feet, the edges of my vision narrowing as I focused all my attention on the retreating Lazlo.

"Hijo de puta, te voy a matar!" I roared, rushing towards him, my claws out.

The guards were on me before I had gone more than a foot. Flanking me, the muscular wolves grappled me into stillness handily, heedless to my kicking and straining. Lazlo, for his part, turned neatly on his heel and came striding back to me, leaning down so his face was level with mine.

"Estoy seguro de que te gustaría," he hissed in my face, spittle hitting my cheek, before he buried his fist in my stomach.

It was a good shot. Practiced. The breath in my lungs was forced out in a painful cough and I found myself temporarily unable to draw in fresh air, left gasping around his fist like a fish on the end of a hook. My feet twisted under me, and it was only the strong arms of the guards holding onto me that kept me standing.

Stepping back, Lazlo nodded to the guards restraining me. "Let him go," he said, shaking out his fist. "He won't be any more trouble."

The guards dropped me, and I crumpled to the ground, the stones of the front walkway digging into my knees. I managed to stay upright, but only just, leaning forward onto my hands as I sucked in air. Lifting my shaking head, I glowered at Lazlo, who grinned back at me with all his teeth.

"By the way," he said, lifting his pointer finger into the air. "I really should thank you for bringing that human to my doorstep. I hate loose ends." Waving over his shoulder, he walked back into the house, calling out, "You might want to keep that in mind when you decide where to run."

~ 10 ~

CHAPTER 10

Shaye

S tanding in the kitchen, my hands resting on the lip of the sink, I stared out into the dark street. Nothing moved, not even a stray cat or a dead leaf. Everything was still and quiet out there.

So why did I feel so on edge?

Was it because Andy wasn't there?

I gritted my teeth a little at the thought. I had gotten by just fine before I met Andy Vazquez, for fuck's sake. I could get along for a few hours without him. No, that couldn't be it. What was it? I rolled my head around my shoulders, and the truth dawned on me with sudden, bitter clarity.

I couldn't remember the last time I'd been inside a house.

"Everything okay?" asked Caleb from behind me.

"No," I responded petulantly.

There was silence for a moment, and then Caleb stepped closer to me. "It's alright," he said, hesitantly placing what I was sure was meant to be a reassuring hand on my shoulder. "It's going to be alright. This place is secure. Only people in Sangre Sagrada know about it."

Nodding, I stepped out from under his hand, moving back into the kitchen. Caleb followed me, clearly as uncomfortable in the role of keeper as I was in the role of being kept. He gestured to the cabinets around us.

"Are you hungry? Or thirsty, maybe?"

I shook my head but made no other answer as I paced around the edges of the square space like a tiger in an enclosure.

He shrugged, sliding his hands onto his hips. "Well, help yourself if you like."

Rolling my eyes, I was about to apologize for my reticence when Nico turned the corner from the living room. He shot me a distrustful glare before nodding to Caleb. "Hey – you got a moment?"

"Yeah, sure," responded Caleb.

Nico waved his hand, and the large werewolf followed him out of the kitchen and into the living room, leaving me alone. I waited for a few moments, my shoulders tense, but when no one came to collect me, or called my name, I relaxed a little at last.

I was fine with being ignored. In fact, I preferred it. A person living out on the streets soon found out that being ignored was a kind of superpower. It lets a person go places and do things that the average citizen would never dream of getting away with.

Secure in my anonymity once more, I wandered away from the kitchen, passing the group in the living room to go deeper into the house itself. Generic art hung on the walls, landscapes with lighthouses and watercolors of sea creatures, and the overall vibe of the interior of the place was more like a sample unit rather than a space where real people lived.

Moving down a hallway that branched off from the main living quarters, I pushed open the first door I came across, searching for and finding the light switch easily on the wall just inside the door. Entering the modest bedroom suite, I made an immediate beeline for the attached bathroom, giving a low hum of approval as I entered and turned on the light. The bathroom was spacious, with a large gleaming white hot tub style tub that was big enough to lay in, a vanity style two sink counter, and a separate shower stall on the other side of the toilet.

Exiting the bathroom, I gave the room it was attached to a closer inspection. Once again, the room was pristine, almost untouched. The bed was pushed against the back wall in the center of the room, carefully made in soft blue sheets with a dark blue comforter and dark blue pillows that looked like they'd never felt the weight of a head.

With great care, I perched myself on the end of the bed, testing the firmness of the mattress with tentative care. I realized I was half-expecting someone to jump out of the walk-in closet on the other side of the room and demand that I get up and get out. Snorting a little at the ridiculousness of the thought, I bounced once or twice, enjoying the give of the springs under my backside.

How long had it been since I'd slept in a bed?

Laying back, the toes of my shoes still resting against the carpet, I took in a deep lungful of machine cooled air. It was strange to lie prone without the sounds of the city buffeting me. I strained my ears but could hear nothing but the low hum of the soccer game on the television in the living room down the hall. Spreading my arms over the comforter, my hands traced the stitching patterns of flowers in the fabric beneath me. Jordan and I had a bedspread like this. Lifetimes ago, I slept every night in a bed just like this, in a house just like this. Slept... and dreamed...

"Shaye?"

I jumped up from the bed, bouncing off the balls of my feet like a wound spring that had just been released. My eyes wide open now, I saw Caleb watching me from the doorway, jerking back a bit at my oversized reaction.

He shot me an apologetic look, his hand still on the doorknob as he leaned inside. "Jeez, you startle easy, don't you?"

I let out my held breath and shook out my hair with my hand, attempting a smile but coming up short. "I'm not used to people..." Searching for the right words, I realized that anything I ended that sentence with was going to sound more pathetic than playful. I shrugged instead, my not-quite-a-smile dissipating like mist in the sun. "Well, I guess I'm just not used to people. What's up?"

The older man released his grip on the door and took a step inside, lowering the volume of his voice a little. "I haven't heard anything from Andy yet, but he should've made it to the den house by now. I'm thinking that no news is good news." He jerked his thumb back towards the hallway. "I was going to wait out in the living room with Nico and Claudia – unless you need anything?"

I pulled my lips down into an exaggerated frown and shook my head. "No, no – that all sounds good." I turned to look into the room behind me. "I think I'll actually take Andy's advice – this place has a really nice bathroom and I'm all sticky from the pool."

Caleb nodded. "Well, if you want some fresh clothes after, there should be some in the closet and the dresser."

I eyed the massive walk-in closet and ornate dresser across from me with deep suspicion. "I can just...take them?"

"Yeah." Caleb glanced around the room. "This house is sort of a place for wolves to go after a change – get cleaned up, patched up if they need it, you know. So, there's all kinds of supplies in here. Clothes being the least of it. There should be something around that'll fit you. Just... take whatever you'd like."

I gave an oversized nod, rocking backward and forward from my heels to the balls of my feet. "Cool. Thanks."

Caleb waved and started back out the doorway, pausing for a moment on the threshold to grab at the doorknob and repeat, "I'll be right out here if you need anything."

I flashed him a thumbs up. "Right."

Shrugging, he closed the door behind him. At the sound of the door clicking shut, my whole body relaxed. I hadn't been lying when I'd said I wasn't used to people. I couldn't remember the last time I had spent such an extended period of time with others, and I was unsurprised to find that the togetherness was beginning to grate on me.

I had gotten used to being alone.

A twinge of guilt assailed me as I took a moment to revel in my solitude. Caleb and Andy had saved my life after all. They were risking a lot by continuing to protect me against this rogue wolf, this Lazlo Cabral character. Even if ultimately, it was all for the good of their den, their family, they were also keeping me safe, and I should be grateful.

I remembered a time when I would've done anything to protect my family. But that was a long, long time ago. A lifetime. I had been a different person then.

"What, you psychic, chica?"

Andy's words ringing in my head, I hurried into the bathroom, shedding my clothes as I went. It had just been a stupid thing for him to say. A joke. He didn't know. He couldn't know. My secret was still safe.

So why was I so scared?

Scowling, I crouched down and pulled open the cabinets under the sink. I let out a happy snort when I found not one bottle of bubble bath, but a whole slew of bath salts, beads, and other goodies hidden there. Grabbing the first bottle I could reach, I stood and walked to the bathtub. I turned on the hot water, making sure it was scalding before pulling the stopper on the tub shut and letting the basin begin to fill. I poured in a steady stream of the blue goo and the scent of hyacinth and lavender filled the air, the water bubbling up beautifully.

Of course, I was scared, I reasoned with myself. I was being hunted. By fucking horror movie monsters. I'd seen a man, my friend, die, for Christ's sake. Anyone would be scared. If it hadn't been for Andy...

I twisted off the water, making sure to leave just enough room for myself in the enormous tub. I stared at the bubble topped basin without really seeing it.

Andy. He saw me. He looked at me, not through me. He saw me and he didn't look away.

And good Lord, he was handsome.

I blinked slowly, my mind miles away from my body as I stepped one foot, then the other into the stinging water. I sat down carefully in the tub, hissing as the water lapped at my skin, staring out into nothingness, my mind fixated on its current train of thoughts.

His eyes were so deep...and his voice...like putting on a cool silk robe on a warm night...and his hands...when he touched you just a little, his hands promised he could do so much more...

I groaned, letting my head fall back against the lip of the tub. What the hell was I doing? He was one of them. He wasn't even human. He was...was I really falling...?

Taking a deep breath, I pushed myself under the surface. Water filled my ears and covered my head. Curling into a fetal position in the tub, I focused for a few seconds on the beating of my own heart in my chest. *What the hell*, I thought. *When was the last time anything in my life happened the way I thought it should?*

I didn't soak in the tub for as long as I would've liked, hopeful that when I got out Caleb would reappear with word from or at least about Andy. Toweling myself dry, I listened for the sound of approaching footsteps. But they never came.

Wrapped in a towel, I sat down once again on the edge of the bed, sighing heavily. How long had it been since I'd slept? At all? Over twenty-four hours at least. I was exhausted. And Andy had told me to relax...

I lay back onto the bed, my bare legs dangling off the end of the mattress. I wasn't even sure if this was a room I was supposed to sleep in. Maybe there was another place they wanted me to stay. Maybe I should get dressed and ask Caleb...

As I lay there, my limbs grew heavy, my breathing deep. I felt sleep coming for me and, not having the strength to fend it off, succumbed to it, nuzzling the side of my face into the comforter and breathing in deep the scent of domesticity, of safety.

Opening my eyes, I found myself standing in a large, luxurious bedroom, far more ornate than the one I had fallen asleep in. A figure moved by me. Andy. Looking past me, his mouth moved, but I couldn't hear him, could only follow his gaze to a beautiful woman with long black hair. Next to her, a concerned grimace on his face, an older man, with white-blond hair pulled back in a ponytail.

The rogue wolf. The one who'd eaten Jason.

Anger, thick and metallic, coated the vision like forest fire smoke. My throat closed up, and I felt like I was choking, my heart beginning to race as fear flooded through me.

The vision went white. Sharp pain radiated across my face, stinging like antiseptic, and when the blinding white cleared, I saw Andy falling to the floor. The beautiful woman in the nightgown turned her back to me and the blond man moved forward towards Andy on the ground, smiling a cruel, fang filled smile, his hands outstretched, his fingers curling into claws. I tried to run to him, to get between Andy and the blond man, but my feet were stuck to the floor. No, they were stuck in the floor. I was sinking. Being consumed, subsumed, I sank faster and faster until the floor closed up over my head and I was in suffocating darkness. I couldn't breathe. I couldn't breathe. I couldn't-

I woke up, gasping for air, my hands at my throat as I jerked up from the mattress. Taking in giant, rasping breaths of air, I began to cough, leaning forward so my head was between my knees.

Not now. Not again. Two in a row, after all this fucking time?

My shoulders shaking, I looked towards the alarm clock on the bedside table. I'd been asleep for ten minutes. Was that all? The vision must have been waiting for me, crouching on the other side of consciousness, ready to pounce into the light like a rat poised to escape from a closed dumpster.

Rocketing up onto my unsteady feet, I careened across the room towards the dresser and closet, haphazardly tearing through clothes until I found items that fit. Caleb. I needed to tell Caleb. Andy was in trouble, but Caleb would know what to do.

I unthinkingly put on an outfit that cost more money than I'd seen in five years, all my attention focused on my vision and its potential consequences. There had to be some way to help him, though I wasn't even really sure what kind of danger Andy was in. That man, the blond, was dangerous. I knew that like I knew the feel of my own skin. He would hurt Andy if he could.

I couldn't let that happen.

Hurrying back towards the living room, I stopped short when I saw Nico standing at the end of the hallway, talking quietly on his cellphone. He glanced up at me and stepped to one side, allowing me room to pass even as he turned his back to me.

I skirted around him as quickly as I could. When I entered the living room proper, I found Claudia sitting close to the television on one end of a large multi sectional couch, staring intently at the soccer game in progress, and Caleb on the opposite end of the couch, watching the screen with glazed disinterest.

"Caleb?" I called to him, hearing the waver in my voice and hating myself for it.

"Yeah?" he said, turning away from the television to look at me.

I don't know what he saw when his eyes met my face, but it must have been bad. He rose to his feet, his own brow furrowing as he hurried toward me, green eyes wide. "What, Shaye, what is it?"

"I think..." Looking down at my feet, I forced the words out, ignoring the tightness in my chest. "I think something might be wrong with Andy."

"With Andy?" Caleb's eyes darted around the room, his lips twisting up into a grimace. "Why?"

Running my tongue along my teeth, I tapped my foot against the floor. "Listen, I just–"

"Look out!"

Caleb reached forward and grabbed me hard by the shoulders, shoving me down and to the right. As I fell to the floor, my shoulder clipping the corner of the hallway, I saw him lunge forward, his hands outstretched.

A gunshot rang out and I knew in that instant that Andy wasn't the only one in serious trouble.

~ 11 ~

CHAPTER 11

Andy

Lazlo's parting words pressed down on my chest like cement blocks. With a last glance at the guards that were still eyeing me warily from the porch, I scrambled to my feet and rushed to my car.

He knew. He knew Shaye was at one of the Sangre Sagrada safe houses. How long would it take him to reach out to all of the safe house stewards? Hell, he probably had everyone on a text chain – he could alert them all in the length of time it took to type and send a message. And I knew just what that message would say – what the order would be.

Shaye was dead. I had killed her.

I threw myself into the driver's seat, slamming my finger on the ignition button and tossing the gear shift into reverse. Peeling out of the driveway, I shouted at the car's computer to call Caleb's cell phone.

There was no answer.

Battering the steering wheel with my fist, I gave a wordless shout of frustration that reverberated off the car's interior and back to me. I slammed my foot onto the gas pedal, careening down from the hills and into the city as fast as I could.

This was my fault. All my fault. It was good that Emilia had excommunicated me. I deserved it. I didn't deserve a family, a home, I didn't deserve any of it. I couldn't even do one thing right, couldn't save my den when it mattered.... couldn't save one person who mattered...

I called Caleb's phone again. Still no answer. I took a corner hard and popped the curb, but didn't slow down or stop, just continued flying down the road. I couldn't accept that I was too late. I couldn't accept the totality of my failure. My mind wouldn't allow it.

Like a broken record, I ordered the computer to call Caleb's phone again. The phone rang, and rang, and rang and then–

"Yeah?" said Caleb, the word slightly muffled through my car's speakers.

"Caleb!" I shouted his name, leaning forward in the driver's seat as my hands strangled the steering wheel. "Caleb, you need to get out of there, both you and Shaye, you need–!"

"Andy, Andy, Andy!" responded Caleb, volume growing with every repetition of my name until I fell silent. "Relax! We're okay. It's okay. The house is secure."

I shook my head, my foot pressing down harder on the gas pedal as I flew through a yellow light. "It's not! Lazlo–"

"Found out where we are?" Caleb gave a loud harumph. "No kidding."

"You..." I looked down at the speakers from which Caleb's too-calm voice was emanating, narrowing my wide eyes. "Wait, you know?"

There was a long, beleaguered sigh. "Trust me, Andy – the house is secure. Get back here and we'll figure out our next move."

Swallowing down the lump in my throat, I gave my assent to him and signed off. My heart continued to pound in my chest, however, for the remaining quarter of an hour it took to reach the house in Laurel Canyon. I couldn't shake the feeling that something awful had happened – that the worst was yet to come.

Turning into the driveway, I shifted the car into park and had my door open in the next instant, running up the front walkway to the door. I tried the knob, and finding the door unlocked, burst inside. I rushed past the kitchen and into the living room, where I could still hear a television on at a low hum. I heard no movement of people and the sinking, sucking feeling in my chest returned. Maybe something had changed in the time it took me to get here. Maybe Nico and Claudia had overpowered Caleb, killed Shaye, and left...

Reaching the living room, I skidded to halt, my eyes widening. The room was wrecked. The TV sat askew on the wall, still on but fritzing badly. The broken remains of a coffee table were scattered in the center of the room, where it looked like someone had landed on top of it, crushing it to bits. One half of the large sectional couch was tipped onto its back, the exposed springs underneath dusty and grit covered. Caleb sat on the still upright portion of the sofa, his elbows resting on his knees as he pressed a damp dishtowel to his bleeding lip. He had a bruise on his neck that looked like someone had tried to strangle him, and another that disappeared under his hair on the side of his head.

I stood there, frozen on the edge of the living room with my chest heaving, staring at Caleb with wild eyes.

Caleb shifted his weight on the couch. He blinked and looked up at me. "Things didn't go well with Sangre Sagrada, I take it?" he asked, his tone deadpan.

"I'm out." The two words took a second to say, maybe less. But hearing them out loud, hearing the truth in my own voice, hearing me admit to another wolf what had happened to me...

The silence that echoed back at me seemed to stretch on forever.

Caleb dropped the hand holding the towel to his split lip into his lap. His eyes widened. "You're...*out*?" Looking away from me, he shook his head, getting slowly to his feet. "Oh, shit, Andy. Shit!"

Swallowing hard, I closed my eyes, forcing myself to focus on what was most important and not the roiling of my stomach. "Is–is Shaye okay?"

At that moment, the door to the walk-in pantry in the kitchen swung open. I looked up to see Shaye sliding out between the door and the frame, pushing back on the unconscious body of Claudia, who appeared to be bound and gagged. I looked down at her feet and saw what I could only assume to be Nico's crumpled form stuffed in the pantry as well.

"Caleb, I don't think this stuff from the garage will hold them if they wake up," she said, struggling to extricate herself from the tangle of bodies. "Could you try calling Andy again? We need to–" Looking up, her eyes widened and then softened when they took in the sight of me. "Oh, thank Christ, you're here. You okay?"

"Do you, uh, need help?" I said, taking a step towards her.

"No, I got it." She stepped out of the pantry and leaned against the door until it finally clicked shut, grunting a little at the effort. "I thought you said these assholes were with your den?"

"They are," I answered, part of me wanting to laugh without really knowing why. "That's, uh, that's the problem, actually."

"What?" Shaye locked eyes with me, even as she moved into the kitchen to grab a wooden chair from underneath the table. She moved back to the pantry door and shoved the back of the chair under the doorknob, wedging it closed. "Hold on, what are you talking about?"

"I'm out," I repeated, the words sticking a little in my throat this time. I blinked hard. "I'm excommunicated. Denless." Struggling to catch my breath, the sucking sensation in my chest returned and my sense of balance left me for a moment as I muttered aloud, "Fuck."

Caleb stepped towards me, his arms outstretched. I felt one of his hands slide between my shoulders and the other wrap gently around my arm. "You don't look so good, Andy. Maybe you should sit down."

It wasn't until Caleb touched me that I realized I was shaking, shivering like I'd spent all night out on the beach without a jacket. With wobbly legs, I let him lead me to the corner of the sofa, where I collapsed ungracefully onto the cushion, folding in on myself like a falling souffle.

"I'm okay," I protested, "I'm..." My lies trailed off into silence and I drew my hands down my forehead. Leaning forward, dropping my head so low my chin was almost even with my stomach, I tried to focus on breathing.

Over one hundred years of living and I had never been alone. I'd always known I'd belonged somewhere, that people would back me up, that there was a safe place to run to and now, when I needed it most – I was alone. My family was in danger and instead of listening to me they had cast me out for trying to protect them in the only way I knew how.

I heard Shaye walk into the living room. "I don't understand – you're just kicked out of the family? For good?"

I nodded. It was all I could do. I couldn't even bring myself to look at her, too ashamed of myself to meet her eyes. I was lost. Worthless. Unwanted.

Shaye crouched down in front of me, her hands folding one on top of the other over my knee. She looked up into my face, forcing my eyes to meet her soft sepia orbs. Wetting her lips with the tip of her tongue, she squeezed me gently. "It's going to be okay."

I stared at her, my chest heaving. How could she know that? How could she say that after I'd lost everything?

And why did I believe her?

I put my hand over hers. She was warm and soft, and I took a deep breath in, her scent filling my lungs. I held my breath as long as I could and let her out again.

It was going to be okay.

Shaye was here.

"Why would she do this?" asked Shaye, gaze flitting up to Caleb before returning to me. "Why would you be-?"

"She... she didn't believe me," I said weakly, a tear rolling down my cheek. I wiped it away with the side of my hand. "And when I told her about..." My gaze flickered to Shaye's face and then away. I forced the truth back down my throat and choked on it a little as it went down, coughing out. "She-she just didn't believe me."

Shaye pulled her hands back from me, her face losing some of its color. "This... this is my fault, isn't it? Because you told me- shit, this is my fault-"

"No," I insisted, lunging after her hands and holding them tight in mine as I shook my head. "No, no, no, por favor, Shaye, this is not your fault, this is my fault. I-" I rubbed the back of her hands with my thumbs, staring at the floor. "- I broke the rules. That's it. I broke the rules."

But the damage was done. I saw the guilt in her eyes, and it killed me to know she was blaming herself. I wanted to say something, anything to convince her that she was innocent in all of this, but Caleb interrupted the silence with a gruff clearing of his throat. "Look, we can sit around here, and trade blame all day, but that doesn't change the fact that we've got a big problem. Did you get a verdict on Shaye? What does the den want to do with her?"

I looked up at Caleb, my face drawn, misery oozing from me.

Caleb turned away, shaking his head as he drew his hand down his face. "Fuck."

"What?" demanded Shaye. "What, do they want to-?"

I felt her hands begin to shake in mine as the realization of what the den had decided dawned on Shaye. She sunk fully onto her knees, her brows drawing up to a point. "Wait. They want to...kill me?"

I released her hands from my grip, nodding. "Yeah."

"We've got to get her out of town," said Caleb, pacing the living room furiously. "Right? Andy? That's the smart play here, right?"

I opened my eyes and my gaze fell, as if drawn by a magnet, onto Shaye. Sitting at my side, she stared at the floor, lost in thought, her face pale and haggard.

She had already been through so much. This needed to stop.

"No." On weak, shaky legs, I stood, one hand falling to my hip. "If we don't fix this here, now, there's no telling what's going to happen." Looking down at the top of Shaye's head, I made up my mind. "No. We don't run."

Caleb pivoted mid-stride, his hands in the air as he moved back towards me. "Jesus, Andy! Have you lost your goddamn mind?" Caleb waved a hand between all of us. "The three of us are not going to be able to take on Sangre Sagrada by ourselves! They'll run us to ground and then they will kill Shaye and there won't be a damn thing we can do about it."

"Maybe we don't have to," I said, probing the inside of my cheek with my tongue as my exhausted brain tried to piece together a plan. "Do you still know people in the Nameless?"

"Who are the Nameless?" asked Shaye, struggling to her feet.

"Another den," answered Caleb, blinking at me in confusion. "And, yeah, actually. Kassandra Arnaud and I go way back. Why?"

I nodded. "They should be in town by now for the big meeting with Sangre Sagrada. Reach out to them. Tell them we have information about Sangre Sagrada they're going to want to hear. Tell them it's theirs in exchange for protection."

"Hold on a second," protested Caleb, his hand slicing through the air, his gaze boring into me. "Think about what you're saying for a second. You know what they'll do. When they hear that one of the ranking members of Sangre Sagrada is killing for sport, it'll be just the excuse they need to take over the territory."

"I know," I said, standing akimbo, staring at the floor.

The older wolf let a deep breath out slowly. "And you're okay with that?"

"If you have another play for us here, Caleb, I'd love to hear it," I snapped at him, glaring.

"What if they don't go for it?" he said at length, pushing his hand back over his hair, his head falling to one side.

"Then we get Shaye out of town."

"To where?" Shaye, looking on the verge of tears herself, rubbed her arms. "Where would be safe?"

"There are places–" I started, but the sight of tears welling in her eyes was too much for me at that moment. I looked away from her, forcing myself to focus on the plan I hoped would save her life – would save us both. "This is a good plan, though. It'll work." I pointed to Caleb, nodding. "The Nameless should be in LA by now for the meeting tomorrow. Work your magic, old man."

"Right." Caleb clapped me on the shoulder and lifted a brow. "Okay. That's the plan. But for now, let's get you both somewhere out of sight."

I leaned back from him, but he didn't release me. "Both?"

"You think Lazlo is going to want you walking around knowing what you know? He's not stupid. He'll take you both down if he can." Pulling me along with him, Caleb headed towards the front door. "Come on, we can all lie low at my place."

~ 12 ~

CHAPTER 12

Shaye

Caleb insisted on driving Andy's car, arguing that the other wolf was too distracted. Andy put up no resistance, a fact which clearly concerned Caleb, but since it met his own desires, he didn't press. I crawled into the back of the car and tried my best to be invisible, a skill I had perfected over the last decade.

As we drove, I watched Andy. The change in him could not be more pronounced. Slumped against the passenger side window, bruises on his cheeks that I could see even in the dim, intermittent glow of streetlights, his beautiful dark brown eyes were hollow; haunted. He didn't speak during the hour-long drive to Caleb's place, didn't look out the window, just stared unseeing at the floor of his own car, seemingly focused on keeping his breathing steady.

I wished I could pretend I didn't know what he was feeling at this moment. Andy was alone for what seemed like the first time in his life. He'd been kicked out by his family, a family made of blood ties and bonds that went beyond what I could possibly comprehend.

I knew a little about how that felt.

But this time it was my fault that it had happened to someone else.

Maybe that's what the dream had been trying to warn me about. Maybe that's why I had them. Because I was a danger to every person I got close to. Toxic, I was a poison in the life of people I even began to care for. First my parents...then Jason...now Andy...

How many people were going to get hurt because of me?

I closed my eyes and leaned my head back against the seat, willing the bile in my throat back down into my stomach. The answer was no one. No one was ever going to get hurt because of me again.

When Caleb had said we were going back to his place, I had envisioned some crappy apartment somewhere downtown. Ending up in El Segundo, in the heart of suburbia, was hardly what I had in mind.

A modest, two-story affair, the house was on a postage stamp lot, surrounded by other houses that looked almost identical to it except for differences in paint and outdoor decoration. Caleb punched in a code on the number pad lock and opened the front door, ushering us inside with a sweep of his arm.

"I'm going to do a sweep," said Andy, his face stony as he hurried into the entryway.

Caleb shrugged. "Hey, whatever makes you happy, man." He stepped in after him, shouting after the already out of sight Andy. "But you're not going to find anything, the house is clean!"

There was a muffled call in response, something dismissive in Spanish. Caleb shook his head and turned back to me, his brow lifting as he once more waved me through the doorway. "You want something to drink, Shaye? Or something to eat? Let me show you where the kitchen's at."

I stepped through the door cautiously, following Caleb through the house with my hands shoved in my back pockets. We immediately passed by a small office space at the front of the house, moving through an archway that led to an open plan style living space, where living room, kitchen, and dining space all flowed together without much of anything separating one from the other.

Andy was prowling the edges of the rooms, examining every nook and cranny for God knows what. I turned my back on him, just the sight of his frantic searching making me feel paranoid, and instead walked into the living room area, stopping in front of a large television that was mounted to the back wall, looking at it curiously.

"Shaye?"

I looked over my shoulder to see Caleb in the kitchen, a glass full of water held out in his hand. I shook my head. "I'm good, thanks." Shuffling my feet, I gestured awkwardly to the house around us, feeling as out of place here as I had in the safe house bungalow. "So, what is this place?"

Downing the glass of water in several gulps, Caleb shook his head. "Just a house I rent when I'm in town. I know the owners, we go way back."

Andy rocketed out of the living room, heading for the staircase which led to the upper level of the house. "Does Lazlo know–?"

"He has no idea," responded Caleb, coming around the kitchen island to follow Andy for a few steps, but stopping at the edge of the living room and shouting up the stairs after him. "You know Lazlo, he doesn't much care about how his hirelings live, just that they get the job done." Lifting his brows, he turned back into the room, walking slowly past me as he fumbled his phone out of his trouser pocket. "Speaking of which..."

Caleb began typing something on his phone, his brow furrowing with concentration as he wrote what seemed like a fairly long missive of some sort. I walked over to him, dropping my arms to my sides. "What, what are you doing?"

"Just submitting my resignation from Sangre Sagrada's employment." He hit a final button with a flourish, waited a moment and then nodded in satisfaction to himself. "I do like to be formal about these kinds of things. I have a reputation to uphold, you know."

"Wait a minute," I said, nose wrinkling. "Employment?"

Caleb looked at me and shook his head in confusion. I scoffed. "I thought...so you're not a member of the den or whatever? You're not part of Sangre Sagrada?"

Now it was Caleb's turn to wrinkle his nose, not in confusion but in disgust. He took his jacket from over his arm and draped it over the back of the nearby couch. "God, no. They just needed a hand and I happened to be available."

"So, what den do you belong to?" I pressed, perching my bottom on the arm of the lazy boy which sat behind me.

"I'm not a part of any den. Never have been."

I narrowed my eyes. "Huh. Really?"

He nodded. I ran my tongue along my teeth, my head falling to one side. "Sorry, that...that's confusing. The way you and Andy talked about it, it sounded like every werewolf belonged to a den like...automatically."

Caleb gave a grunt, shifting his weight onto his back foot and sliding his hands into his pockets. "The dens haven't existed forever. Only the last five or six hundred years. I was turned before that."

Nearly losing my balance on the arm of the chair, I pitched forward, landing on my feet with a thud. "Excuse me, what?"

Caleb watched me, the ghost of a smile turning up the corner of his lips. Pushing a hand back through my hair, I looked at him askance, dropping my head low between my shoulders. "Wait, are you– you're telling me you're over six hundred years old?"

"Give or take a half-century," he said, wobbling his head from side to side. "Yeah. I am."

I tried to imagine it – living for centuries. For lifetimes. Watching human history in all its complexity and all its drama from the sidelines, knowing you could never truly take part in any of it, because you were going to outlast it all.

And I thought I knew about loneliness.

"Damn." Sensing that this was not sufficient, I snapped my gaping mouth shut and gestured at him. "Uh, you look...good."

He crossed his arms over his chest. "Thanks." Shrugging, he tossed his head back. "I try to stay fit, you know. Active. Like to think it helps."

I was about to make a joke about dog-years when a thought occurred to me. I felt some of the blood drain from my face, the corners of my mouth falling into a contemplative frown. On the second floor, I could hear Andy pacing from room to room.

"Um. So... how old is...?" I pointed a finger up to the ceiling, indicating the werewolf who was careening around the place above us.

Caleb smiled and shook his head. "Oh, he's a baby. Barely a hundred."

My stomach flip flopped as I tried to grapple with the fact that I had been having impure thoughts about a centenarian. "Fuck."

Tearing down the stairs and back into the living room, Andy came to an abrupt halt between Caleb and myself, looking around the space as if he had lost something. After a moment he nodded once, and then again.

"Okay," said Andy, letting out a huff of breath. He stood, one hand on his hip while he clawed through his hair with the other. "Okay, yeah. Yeah, this place should work. It looks clean."

Caleb frowned. "I told you it was."

"Yeah, but you know." Andy rubbed at his bloodshot eyes, wincing. "Can never be too careful."

Running his tongue along his teeth, Caleb stepped towards Andy, reaching his hand out and gripping the younger wolf hard on the shoulder. "Andy, listen – you need to get some rest." He turned his gaze to me, lifting his brows. "Frankly, you both do."

Grimacing, Andy attempted to shake off Caleb's grip, eyes darting to and away from me as he protested, "What? No, I'm fi–"

"You are not fine," said Caleb sternly. "When was the last time you slept?" He didn't even wait for Andy to answer, rolling his eyes and continuing with, "If it was over twenty-four hours ago, that's too long. Even for us."

Andy threw his hands up into the air before resting them on his hips. "How the hell am I supposed to sleep?"

"You go upstairs, lay down on a bed, close your eyes, and go unconscious for a while." Caleb smirked, but there was real affection in it, and I found myself wondering, not for the first time, how long Caleb and Andy had been friends. "You're not good to anybody half-out of your head with exhaustion. You know I'm right."

Hanging his head low between his shoulders, Andy sighed loudly. "Okay, okay – I'll try." He started to back out of the room before stopping, turning to me on the sofa and gesturing towards the upstairs with one hand. "Shaye, do you–?"

"I'm good right here." I moved to the couch, sitting down first before settling back into the worn pillows, letting the cool leather caress the back of my neck. "This couch feels amazing."

"Are you sure?" said Caleb. "There's two bedrooms upstairs."

Closing my eyes, I sighed in only partly fake contentment as I toed my shoes off my feet. "I can't remember the last time I fell asleep on a couch." I lifted a clenched hand, pleading jokingly, "Let me have this."

I heard Andy give a snort of laughter and the sound lifted my spirits. "Suit yourself."

Caleb's heavy tread sent vibrations into the couch as he walked away towards the office at the front of the house. "I'll reach out to the Nameless while you both rest. Andy, I'll wake you if I hear anything back."

Waiting until I was sure I was alone, I eased my eyes open and looked around, letting out a deep breath through my nose. I knew I should try and get some sleep, but I dreaded what might come to me in my dreams.

The floor above me creaked. Andy, hopefully settling in for some rest of his own. Unbidden, my imagination conjured up the image of him lying in bed – of waking up next to him.

Scowling, I turned over to face the back of the couch, embarrassed at my own desires. The man – werewolf – the guy had just been through something traumatic and here I was, drooling over him, wanting him in a way he would never want me.

I needed to get a grip. Or else things were just going to go from bad to worse. If that were even possible at this point.

Burying my face in the pillow, I focused on my breathing, losing myself in the steady, slowly elongating rhythm of push and pull. Before I knew it, I had fallen asleep.

The next thing I was aware of, the old pendulum style clock on the wall was clanging out the hour, several long bongs that in my half-awake, half-asleep state I couldn't be bothered to count. I groaned as I rolled over onto my back, pushing my bangs out of my eyes gingerly. Diffused afternoon sunlight warmed the whole living room to a pleasant, cozy temperature. I relaxed back against the sofa cushions, letting my body go limp again.

No visions this time.

Thank God for that.

A creaking, wooden sound from the other side of the high couch back caught my attention. Furrowing my brow, I gripped onto the couch with one hand and pulled myself upright just enough to see Andy sitting at one of the stools that surrounded the tall breakfast nook table. He had a book open in his hand, some kind of reprint of an old pulp mystery, but it clearly wasn't holding his interest. As soon as my head crested the edge of the couch, his dark brown eyes met mine.

I didn't know what was weirder – the fact that he'd been watching me sleep or the fact that it made me feel kind of good.

"Hey…" The word felt thick in my mouth, and I smacked my lips, swallowing in an attempt to get some sleep out of my throat. I looked at the clock hanging on the wall. I'd been asleep for about eight hours. A sudden flash of self-consciousness and I wiped the back of my hand across my mouth. I hoped he hadn't been watching me for that long. I had it on good authority I was an ugly sleeper.

"Feel better?" Andy asked, putting down the book he hadn't been reading and standing up from the stool.

I rubbed my eyes, blinking and wincing in the glow of the lights over the table where he was sitting. "Weren't you supposed to be sleeping too?"

"I did," Andy said, moving over to stand behind the back of the couch, his hands sliding into his trouser pockets. "But Caleb woke me up about a half hour ago. The Nameless got back to him. He's gone to meet them."

Nodding, I stifled a yawn as I asked, "Just him?"

He shrugged, trying and failing to hide a dissatisfied grimace. "He's the one who knows Arnaud, the head of the den. She wanted to meet with him one on one before deciding if she wanted to take the chance on bringing us all in."

"It's not what you were hoping for," I said, sitting up fully.

Rolling his shoulders back, Andy looked up at the ceiling, tapping his foot as he conceded. "It's not a bad idea. I'd probably have done the same thing in her position. But no, it's not what I was hoping for. Just means more time that Lazlo has to look for us. More time we're out in the open and exposed."

"So," I brought my knees up to my chin, hugging my legs to my chest. "What do we do in the meantime?"

"Sit tight." Andy looked away from me, pulling his phone out of his pocket and turning it on with the press of a button. "Caleb will call with an update when he has one. But he said it could be a while."

I lifted my brows. "Oh. Great. I *love* waiting."

~ 13 ~

CHAPTER 13

Andy

The hours passed by slowly. I tried to lose myself in a book but couldn't find one that was capable of holding my interest for more than a few moments. Shaye seemed likewise unable to settle, although television was her distraction of choice. She would flip through the hundreds of channels for what felt like five or ten minutes, finally decide on a show, watch it until a commercial break and then start the entire process over again.

We ate separately, foraging from out of the fridge and the cabinets in the well-stocked kitchen. I couldn't muster much of an appetite, managing to make it through half a sandwich before I gave up and threw the rest in the trash. Shaye, on the other hand, did not make herself a meal but rather grazed intermittently for about an hour, eating her fill of grapes, clementines, tortilla chips, cheese, and other various sundry snacks.

Eventually I found myself standing at the back sliding glass door, eyes glazed over as I gazed out into the fenced backyard. I couldn't stop thinking about what Caleb might be up to, hoping against hope that this plan of mine would work.

I didn't want to send Shaye away.

I closed my eyes, resting my head against the doorframe. I was pathetic. Here I was, excommunicated, denless, and I was worrying about trying to protect a human. A woman I'd just met – who probably hated my guts as much as any other werewolf out there.

The feel of her hands in my hands came back to me in a flash. The sincerity in her eyes when she told me everything was going to be alright. The sorrow in her voice when she tried to take the blame for what had happened to me.

God, she was so much more than just some human woman. And I let myself start to hope that maybe she saw me as more than just a convenience, a means of survival. Would she ever... could she ever...?

"I can't sit here any longer," Shaye said, throwing the remote onto the couch she rocketed to her feet. "You're driving me fucking crazy!"

Jumping at her sudden outburst, I looked at her over my shoulder, scowling. "Me? What am I doing?"

Shaye gestured in my direction, hands flailing. "Just look at you – look at the way you're standing!"

I looked down at myself quizzically, pushing away from the frame of the door as I did so. I shrugged. "What?"

"Oh please," said Shaye, walking through the living room to stand a few feet behind me. "You've been standing at that door, staring out into the backyard for almost an hour, like you're just waiting for a squirrel to run by so you can chase it."

She had a point. She had a point and that got on my nerves. I leaned back against the door frame, crossing my arms with a huff. "I've... I've got a lot on my mind right now, okay?"

Rolling her eyes, Shaye dropped her hands to her sides, her palms slapping against the tops of her thighs. "And I don't?" She took a step closer to me, brow furrowing in concern. "Look – you told me to relájate, ¿sí?"

"Sí, pero–"

"No!" she exclaimed, reaching out and pushing my shoulder with the heel of her hand. "No 'but's! Take your own advice. Fuck. You're so goddamn tense." Crossing her arms over her stomach, she looked up at me with narrowed eyes. "Don't you ever just relax, Andy?"

I didn't know how to answer her question. I didn't know how to explain to her that the last time I relaxed, the last time I let my guard down with a human, with a woman, that person had ended up dead.

I didn't know how to tell her how terrified I was of history repeating itself.

"That shouldn't be a brain stumper, Andy," said Shaye, grimacing.

"Of course, I relax," I answered at last, trying to be as flippant as possible, turning away from her to look back out into the backyard. "But have you ever tried to relax with you around? Imposible. I never know what trouble you'll get into next."

"Oh, fuck you," she said, but there was teasing in her tone that I did not anticipate, and I looked down to see her smirking up at me. "You love getting me out of trouble."

That smile. That *damn* smile. It was the kind of smile that reached right into a person's chest and squeezed the air from their lungs, leaving them as breathless as a drowning swimmer. I hated her for having a smile like that.

"I'm getting used to it," I admitted, my voice quieter than I had intended.

If she noticed what she was doing to me she didn't show it. Instead, she lifted a brow, throwing her arms behind her back and peering up at me through narrowed eyes. "So?"

I narrowed my eyes back at her and shook my head. "So what?"

"What do you do to relax?" she insisted, more gently this time, genuine interest in her gaze that disarmed me completely.

I was fighting a losing battle, trying to resist her. I uncrossed my arms and turned to face her. "You really want to know?"

"Wouldn't ask otherwise," she quipped back.

"Fine. I'll show you," I said, reaching down and taking her hand in mine.

As I led her out of the living room, towards the foot of the staircase in the entryway, Shaye's annoyed facade cracked for a moment and a worried look crossed her face. "Hold on, what if Caleb–?"

"Come on, if anything comes up, he'll call." Still, she hesitated, pulling back on my hand a little but not letting go. I stopped, my foot on the first step, and I looked over my shoulder at her, grinning. "Come on. I promise I won't bite."

As we headed up the stairs, I kept my grip on her hand loose enough that she could easily slip her hand out of mine should she wish. When she chose not to, keeping her fingers wrapped around my own as we climbed, my throat tightened, and my pulse quickened. The effect was only slightly dampened by the all too sincere suspicion in her voice when she asked, "You're not about to do some kind of weird werewolf thing and make me watch, are you?"

I shook my head, letting loose a small laugh. "Like what?"

"I don't know – find a pair of shoes and chew on them or–"

I interrupted her with a breathy, frustrated exclamation. "Por el amor de Dios, I'm not a dog, Shaye!" Glancing back, I shot her an admonishing look. "I don't dig holes in the backyard, and I don't hate cats and I don't chase cars."

Shaye tipped her head to one side. "Can you eat chocolate?"

I felt my eyes widen and I quickly turned back around. "...Sure...Most of the time..."

She hurried up the steps, appearing beside me instead of behind me, grinning wildly, her free hand held up in triumph. "Aha, but sometimes you can't!"

"I don't want to talk about it," I admitted sulkily.

We reached the second-floor landing, and I led us down the hall past the bedrooms to an open doorway at the far end of the house.

"Welcome to the rec room," I said, gesturing into the room and relinquishing her hand at last. "After you."

Looking at me with curiosity, Shaye complied. I followed after her, my hands sliding into my trouser pockets.

"Woah..." breathed Shaye, taking in the room with wide eyes as she stood in the middle of the space, the waning sunlight creeping in and casting long shadows.

The room was beautiful and looked barely used. I wondered if it was a newer addition to the house, something the owners had put in to make the property more attractive to potential renters and vacationers looking to fill their down time with entertaining pursuits. It certainly entranced Shaye, who wandered first to the small bar, sliding her hand across the silky-smooth wood, and then to the large sectional couch that filled the far-left corner of the space, facing an enormous flat screen television.

"Wow," she exclaimed again, walking towards the wall to ceiling windows at the back of the room, her eyes bright and wide. "This looks like something out of a movie."

She turned as the light above the billiards table flicked to life, catching sight of me standing by the switch. Her head fell to one side. "What are you doing?"

"This–" I said, moving away from the switch and towards the rack of pool cues on the far-right side wall. "–is how I relax." Picking a cue out from the rest with one hand, I undid the top button of my shirt with the other. "You ever play before?"

She walked towards the polished table, shaking her head as she ran her fingertips along the wooden lip. "Some. A long, long time ago."

"But you remember how it works," I pressed.

Shaye shrugged. "In theory, sure."

"Well then?" I lifted a second cue free from the rack and tossed it to her. "It's no fun to play alone."

Shaye scowled at me as she stumbled backward, catching the pool cue awkwardly in both hands. I smiled and made myself useful by setting up the table, racking the fifteen billiard balls in a tight triangle, with the eight ball in the center.

"Where's the chalk?" Shaye asked, still frowning as she moved by me in her search.

Removing the wooden rack with a flourish, I used it to gesture behind me towards the cue rack. "Should be over there somewhere. What do you say we make this a little more interesting?"

There was silence from behind me. I picked up my own cue and turned to see Shaye observing me silently, rubbing the end of her pool cue with a small cube of blue chalk. She met my eyes and shrugged languidly. "Alright, I'm game," responded Shaye.

"How about this: for every ball I pocket–" I pressed my hand flat against my chest. "–you have to tell me one thing about your life from before you started living on the street."

Her jaw dropped open, her eyes going flat and wide, like I had just dumped a bucket of ice water on her head. "Wha–wh–" She sputtered, the hand holding the cue turning red and white as she strangled it in her grip. "Why the fuck do you want to know about that?"

"Because I don't get you." I closed the distance between us, keeping my gaze fixed on her. "You're not stupid. You're not crazy. And you're not an addict. So, what are you doing on your own like this?"

Tip of her tongue flicking out to wet her lips, Shaye turned away to put the cube of chalk back on the rack. "There's all kinds of reasons someone ends up homeless," she said after a moment, twisting back towards me, but keeping her face towards the floor. "None of them are good."

I took another step towards her and took a breath, her scent filling my lungs, unaccountably familiar and utterly intoxicating. "I know."

She swallowed hard and looked at me from the corner of her eye, her sepia orbs burning into me like a heated brand. "Do you?"

I had to look away from her face then, not trusting my next words if I were staring into her eyes. "I'd know if you'd tell me."

Silence. I risked a glance in her direction. She was staring at my chest, the muscles in her jaws flexing beneath the skin. I took a step back, spinning the cue in front of me with one hand. "I am willing to earn it, Shaye. What do you say?"

Shaye let out a long breath through her nose and closed her eyes. "Fine," the word forced itself out from between her gritted teeth. I watched as she forced her body to relax almost muscle by muscle, rolling her shoulders back and rubbing her neck. "Fine. Okay." Then, with a suddenness that should have alarmed me, her eyes snapped open, a light sparking in the depth. She grinned. "But for every shot I make," she announced, lifting her cue into the air like a baton, "you have to take off a piece of clothing."

A bark of laughter escaped me before I could control myself.

Shaye lifted an eyebrow in response, her smile undimmed.

The skin on the back of my neck began to tingle. "Shit, are you serious?"

"Absolutely."

I felt my face begin to flush but I did my best to adopt an air of nonchalance, leaning my weight against my cue as I smirked. "Uh, I'm a werewolf, remember? Being naked in front of people doesn't bother me."

"Then you should have nothing to worry about." Shaye proffered her hand to me, meeting my gaze. "Do we have a deal?"

My brow furrowing, I looked her up and down. But her body language, usually so transparent, revealed no insights into her end goal with this particular move. Clicking my tongue off the top of my mouth, I reached forward and took her hand, giving it a single shake. "Deal. Let's flip for the break."

"Fine by me," she answered, following me over to the walnut bar, on the end of which some drunk had left a stack of red Solo-cups and a handful of quarters. Measuring the weight with my hand, I balanced the coin on the edge of my fist and, when I was sure Shaye was ready, I flicked it high into the air.

"Call it," I said.

She watched it spin and for a split second I thought she hadn't heard me. But as it started to fall down towards my open hand she called out, "Heads."

I caught it and flipped it onto the back of my opposite hand, revealing the coin with a flourish.

"Tails," I said, grinning. "I get the first shot."

Frowning, Shaye said nothing but gave a sharp shrug, stalking away towards the table in a snit. Tossing the quarter on the bar, I smothered my smile and followed her, looking over the table with a practiced eye and letting muscle memory mostly take over. Heading for the far end of the table, I picked up the cue ball, letting the heavy resin orb cool my skin as I chose the best place on the head string to place it.

In the end I settled on an angled break. The pool cue slid through my fingers, and I closed my eyes at the sharp crack of the wood as it struck the ball, finding the sound and vibration enormously relaxing. The off-white ball bounced off the left rail before crashing into my carefully constructed triangle of billiards and the orbs scattered like marbles falling to the floor. I watched with satisfaction as the striped ten ball bounced off the right rail and rolled placidly into the left corner pocket.

At the other end of the table, Shaye tossed her head back, gritting her teeth. "Well, fuck."

"Deals a deal, right?" I said, straightening up over the table, lifting a brow at her in challenge.

Rolling her eyes, Shaye waved a hand towards me. "Fine. Come on, what do you want to know?"

"Anything. What you did, who you did it with, just...what was your life like before all this?" She gave me a blank stare and I shook my head, letting out a sharp breath through my nose. "Okay, like – high school. What were you? In every school play? Or head of the chess club?"

"Neither." She passed her cue from hand to hand, watching me with an intensity that was almost unsettling. At last, she looked away, scratching her chin. "I was on the cheerleading squad, actually."

My mouth fell open. "Christ. You're kidding."

She rolled her eyes. "I wish I was."

I nodded, clearing my throat as I attempted to curb my reaction. But the image of Shaye, the Shaye I had come to know, taciturn, foul-mouthed, and grumpy, suddenly in a skimpy cheerleading uniform, enthusiastically chanting out mind numbingly dumb rhymes in front of a crowd – it was too much. Unable to control myself any longer, my carefully neutral facade cracked, and I began to sputter out laughter, folding in on myself as I cackled.

"Hey, don't laugh, asshole!" Shaye chided, but there was a lightness to her voice and when I composed myself enough to look over at her she was grinning, the slightest blush coloring her cheeks. "I was damn good at it too! I could turn a hell of a somersault, you bastard."

I held up my hands, backing away from the table with a smile. "Alright, alright. Fair's fair, go ahead and take your best shot."

Bemused, I watched as Shaye surveyed the table. I hadn't left her with any easy shots to take. I actually felt a little guilty that I wasn't giving her much of a chance to get her own back and was about to move towards her, ready to offer some advice, when she bent at the waist, leaned across the table and sent the cue ball flying down the felt. It ricocheted off the top right corner rails where I was standing, clattered into and bounced off the striped thirteen ball and then rolled to a gentle stop just behind the solid five ball, which it nudged ever so tenderly into the right-side pocket.

"Jacket," Shaye demanded, pulling back from the table with a satisfied air.

"¡Hostia!" I exclaimed, staring at the table in disbelief. When I looked back up at Shaye she looked as pleased with herself as a cat who had discovered a year's worth of nip. I narrowed my eyes. "I think you hustled me, tía..."

"Jacket!" she repeated, shaking her head from side to side.

Sighing gruffly, I complied, still glaring at her as I pulled my arms free of the sleeves. I crossed back to the bar to drape the expensive jacket over the back of a stool, keenly aware of Shaye's sepia eyes following me as I went. I looked over my shoulder at her, my head crooked to one side in question, but she only smiled and kept on staring at me, fingers tapping against her pool cue.

Rolling my shoulders, I forced my mind back to the game, attention shifting from Shaye to the table beside her. "So," I said, walking back and lining up my next shot somewhat carelessly, not even watching the striped twelve ball as it bounced into the left side pocket. "What did you want to do after high school?"

"I..." Shaye swallowed hard and some of the color left her face. But her smile remained, dim though it was, like a light bulb that was on the verge of going out. "I did it. I did what I wanted to do after high school."

I waited a beat for her to continue, but when she didn't, I prompted her with a soft, "And? What was that?"

"I married Jordan," she said, gaze focused on the table. "He was my high school sweetheart. And I got busy being the perfect all-American housewife."

I blinked hard and deliberately. I don't know what I was expecting to hear, but that had certainly not been it. "Married?" I managed, my brows high over my wide eyes. I stared at her openly. "You?"

"Yeah." She sighed heavily. "Me."

"Shit," I managed at last, pulling my eyes off of her with difficulty as I struggled to come to terms with what I had just learned. "Wow. Are, uh, are – are you still married? Did you break up?"

"Uh uh," she chided, leaning down to take her shot. "My turn."

She made quick work of this one, neatly pocketing the one ball in the top left corner. Shaye straightened up, fixing me with a none too friendly stare of her own before commanding, "Shirt. Off."

Keeping my attention on the floor, I unbuttoned my shirt mechanically, mind still reeling with what Shaye had said. Married. Someone's wife. Was she still – did she belong to someone else? I tugged the bottom of my shirt free of my trousers, shaking my head a little bit as I did so, internally chiding myself. What did it matter? So, she was married, or had been married, or whatever.

She was here with me now.

I looked up as I pulled the dress shirt down off my shoulders, somehow still surprised to find her once again watching me. When our eyes met, I expected her to look sharply away, as she almost always did, but this time she let her gaze linger over me, falling down across my body like a billowing sheet, soft and cool.

My skin prickled and I worked hard to keep my breathing steady. I crumpled the shirt in one hand and threw it to the floor, the muscles in my jaw tensing as I forced myself to turn away from her and move back towards the billiard table.

Steadying my hands, I managed somehow to sink the striped thirteen into the left side pocket, though it rattled off the edges of the railing more than it should have. I swallowed and straightened, slipping one hand into my trouser pocket.

"What was this Jordan guy like?" I asked, wanting and not wanting to know the answer at the same time.

"He was...sweet." Shaye rolled the word around in her mouth like it was something that she was trying to decide if she liked. She swallowed hard and shook her head, smiling a small, tight smile with trembling lips. "Jordan was simple. It was easy being with him. You always knew where you were with Jordan; there were no surprises. When he said he loved you, you knew he meant it. And it was easy to say it back."

Envy clenched at my heart. My throat went tight and dry. To have a love like that – I'd never known that sensation. Ever. Not in over a hundred years.

I looked into Shaye's face. Pain, clear and hot like blown glass, shimmered in her eyes – maybe there was a cost to such a love that I was lucky I'd never had to pay.

Shaye cleared her throat and cracked her neck, closing her eyes as she stepped towards the table. "My shot, right?"

I nodded. It was all I was capable of doing.

I heard rather than saw the ball land in a pocket. I honestly didn't care at that moment. All I could think about was the pain in Shaye's eyes. Should I go to her? Comfort her? Maybe we should stop. But I needed to know...

"Dealer's choice," said Shaye, turning away from the table, not even looking at me now as she was clearly lost in her own memories.

I nodded and looked down at myself, taking stock for a moment before wriggling my right foot out of my shoe. I hadn't even started on the second shoe before a loud guffaw ripped through the air.

"Oh, come on, that's not fair!" whined Shaye, throwing her free hand up over her head as she turned to watch me.

"They're a piece of clothing, it counts!" I insisted, smiling weakly as I worked the remaining shoe off my left foot with my toes.

"The socks have got to go too, then, same time," she insisted, starting forward as if she were going to pull them off my feet herself if I didn't comply.

I rolled my eyes before bending down to acquiesce to her demand. "Fine."

Tucking my socks into my shoes, I nudged them under the pool table where'd they be out of the way. I surveyed the spread of billiards atop the green felt, assessing my options, making calculations and trying hard not to think about the next question I was going to ask her, the question that begged to be asked.

With a soft, satisfying clatter, the striped eleven disappeared into the bottom left corner.

"Any kids?" I said, careful to keep my voice neutral and calm, as if I was asking if she'd ever had any pets or was allergic to shrimp.

"No." Shaye swallowed hard, but didn't turn away from me, lifting her chin a little as she spoke. "We... we never got around to that."

Nodding slowly, I read the regret on her face like it was a billboard for the latest Hollywood blockbuster. "But...you wanted some."

She smacked her lips together, ticking her head to one side. "Yeah. Yeah, I did."

We stared at each other, the light from the setting California sunshine giving the room a warm glow that contradicted the chill in the air.

Without warning, Shaye started towards me, her brow set and determined. I backed up automatically, my hands lifting in front of myself, half-convinced she intended to strike me. Instead, she slid in front of me and made an unnecessarily complicated shot, bouncing the cue ball off the head and foot rails before it collided with the solid three ball at a sharp angle – the orb went careening into the top side of the left handrail, rolling almost languidly into the top right corner pocket.

She stood up straight and turned around, face expressionless. "Pants," she demanded coldly.

Another flush threatened to crawl its way up my neck and into my face, but I forced it back with a deep breath, prodding the inside of my cheek with the tip of my tongue as I propped my pool cue against the table and begrudgingly fumbled with the buckle of my belt.

I had meant what I said earlier – normally being naked in front of others didn't bother me. It happened more often than a human might think when someone was a werewolf, and after a while the shock of seeing another naked body in front of you, or being the naked body in front of someone else... Well, it sort of wore off.

But as I unbuttoned and unzipped my trousers, as I hesitated for just a moment before hurriedly shoving them down my legs and stepping out of them, my senses were as sharp and keen as they were before a change. The air felt fuzzy, almost electric. I kicked the expensive trousers away from myself and under the table.

I glanced up at Shaye and my breath stilled in my lungs. I found her examining me with something less than cool detachment, something more akin to eager anticipation and I swallowed hard.

She looked at me. I looked at her, working hard to squash the unfamiliar urge to cover myself. I was usually so comfortable in my own skin, but with her...*looking* at me like *that*...

"Yes?" I said with an upward inflection, my eyebrows lifting over my widening eyes.

She tugged at her bottom lip, her head falling to one side as she observed, "Boxer briefs man I see."

I crossed my arms over my chest. "You sound surprised."

"Would've thought you went commando."

I gave a snort of laughter, cracking a smile. "Hey, I like wearing clothes. I don't get to sometimes, so it makes a nice change." Reaching for my cue, I nodded at the pool table behind her. "My go?"

Shaye stepped to the left, her arms wide. "Please."

Humming a light, poppy tune to herself, Shaye meandered around the table. I did my best to ignore her as she made a circuit, bending over to line up my shot as she headed back towards me. Eventually she moved behind me. I waited for her to appear on the other side of me and when she did not, when I realized she had stopped behind me, when it occurred to me that she was behind me, silent, *staring* at me bent and stretched out across the table, I felt my face finally flush bright red and hated myself for it.

"Ah...can I help you?" I asked, not trusting myself to look over my shoulder at her.

"Oh, you are helping plenty," she drawled appreciatively.

Part of her was enjoying this. She was enjoying me. Did she actually...?

Could it be that she wanted me the same way I wanted her?

Shaye hummed again, this time a low, appreciative purr that sent a fizzle of pleasure up my back from the base of my spine to the back of my skull. I couldn't help but close my eyes and imagine, just for a moment, that sound echoing in my ear, her lips close, her body under mine.

The thought was all consuming and entirely antithetical to concentration. I knew my shot was off as soon as the end of the cue cracked against the ball, hitting it at an awkward angle and sending it spinning uselessly down the felt. As I watched the cue ball roll past all the playable billiards on the table and landed softly at the far end of the table.

"¡Carajo!" I growled, straightening up and clenching my hand into a fist.

"Ooo, so close!" Shaye moved up beside me, slapping me hard on the shoulder.

"You don't have to rub it in," I said, glaring without malice as she walked to the far end of the table.

"Rubbing it in? Me?" She held her hand flat against her chest and shook her head, her eyes wide with mock innocence. "I'm just trying to give you some words of encouragement. I don't want you to feel bad – this game can take a lifetime to master."

With the ease and grace of a professional, Shaye leaned over and made her shot, sending the cue ball careening past the few playable balls that remained and striking the solid six billiard, knocking it cleanly into the left side pocket.

"Or you can just be really, really fucking good at it, like me," she crowed in triumph. Stepping back from the table, she pointed to my chest with the butt of the cue. "That'll cost you your undershirt."

I looked at her from under my brow, wanting to say something smart, to respond with some quip, some nonchalant barb, but ultimately finding myself utterly bereft of any clever repartee that would cover the nakedness of my feelings in that moment. "Okay," I said after a moment, eyes never leaving hers. "If that's what you want."

Shaye's smile faltered, losing its sardonic edge and softening into something altogether hungrier. "I think I've earned it," she responded, lifting her chin and looking down her nose at me. "Fair's fair."

Without another word, I lifted the thin black t-shirt I wore up over my head. I dropped it onto the floor.

In the silence, I heard Shaye let out a huff of air. I looked back at her. Her eyes trailed up and down my body like I was a map she was desperate to decode.

"Enjoying yourself?" I asked point blank, just as desperate to hear her confirm what I hoped was true.

I had hoped for a blush, an embarrassed smile, or for her to look away shyly. What I got was her eyes snapping to my face and a mirthless laugh. "Hey, you want to ask a question, you better take a shot."

Her coolness grated on my raw nerves. Tip of my tongue held between my teeth, I looked back at the table. I mapped out my shot in my mind and bent down to execute it. The pool cue slid through my fingers with a shushing sound, the tip cracking against the cue ball like a firework. I straightened and turned away from the table, leaning my cue against the edge, not bothering to watch as the striped fifteen found its way home in the bottom right pocket.

All my attention was for Shaye.

"Okay, then: last question," I said, closing the distance between us with a few slow steps. "Were you happy?" The look of confusion that clouded her beautiful face almost broke my heart. I looked away from her for a moment, shaking my head. "You know, in your old life. Were you happy?"

A silence stretched between us. Then, Shaye spoke.

"Was... Was I happy?"

The tremor in her voice was unmistakable. I whipped my head back up to look at her, to see tears rolling freely down her stunned, pale face.

I had gone too far.

Shaye shook her head, blinking rapidly as if that would force the tears back behind her eyes. "I... I was twenty-one. Living out in Chino Hills, California. Married to my high school sweetheart, who was a partner in his family's ridiculously profitable real estate business. I was a stay at home, soon-to-be mom with a husband who adored me, a house with a pool, and not a care in the world." A hollow laugh tore itself from her chest. "Of... of course I was fucking happy."

She threw her cue onto the table. It landed with a clatter that seemed to shock her, making her jump as she turned away from me, clearly desperate to try and regain some semblance of control.

"Shit," she whispered to herself, hands pawing at her cheeks as she struggled in vain to stop herself from crying.

"Shaye," I reached for her, my hand sliding against her shoulder. "I'm sorry."

She rolled her shoulder back, brushing my hand away from her even as she forced a shaky, insincere grin onto her quivering lips. "You're sorry? Ha, I'm not the one standing here in my underwear." Gesturing over me, her eyes looked me up and down. "You look..."

Even with tears welling in them, I saw the hunger in her gaze. She took in and released a deep breath, eyes drinking me in like a man in the desert might drink a gallon of cold, clear water. "Fuck...Andy, you look–"

In the span of half a heartbeat, I pulled her into my arms, silencing her with a kiss.

~ 14 ~

CHAPTER 14

Shaye

"I'm sorry," said Andy, jolting back from me, stuttering a little as he blushed an even deeper shade of pink than he had when I'd gotten him to take off his pants. "I don't – I – I shouldn't–"

I wrapped my arms around him, my blunted nails digging into his bare shoulder blades as I yanked him forward. "Don't stop," I demanded, panting a little as I struggled to catch my breath. "Don't you dare fucking stop."

My lips collided with his and I dragged my nails down his shoulders to his lower back, gaining the most delicious moan from him as we kissed. His mouth opened and I slipped my tongue inside. He responded in kind, one arm around my waist, the other holding the back of my head, his fingers buried in my hair.

Breaking away from me, Andy leaned down even further to send a trail of kisses and nips down the underside of my jaw and neck, resting for a moment in the place where my neck met my shoulder, sucking hard. I gasped and held on to him tightly, my eyes fluttering shut as I shuddered in pleasure. He stopped after a few seconds, replacing his lips with his tongue, lathing the sore spot gently.

"I can make you happy," he spoke into the cradle of my neck, smattering kisses against my skin between every heavy breath, his eyes closed tight. "I can try. I can try if you'll let me...I'll make you happy..."

I raked my hands through his hair, leaning back in his arms as I lost myself to the sensation of being held close again by someone. "You really are a romantic, aren't you?"

"What can I say?" I felt him smirk against my skin before he straightened, his hands sliding across my back as he brought me forward to capture my mouth once more with his. "I like a challenge."

Bending at the knees, he wrapped his arms under my thighs and then straightened back up, lifting me off my feet and fully into his embrace. I wrapped my legs around his hips, hooking my feet at the ankles, moaning as every part of him pressed against every part of me.

And it still wasn't enough. I wanted to drown in him, feel him in my blood, see him behind my closed eyes. I wanted to crawl inside him and never come out.

It'd been so long. It'd been so fucking long since someone had kissed me, touched me, *wanted* me...

"You want me," I said aloud as soon as the thought crossed my mind, needing to hear him say those words.

Andy looked into my eyes and nodded without hesitation. "I want you." He shifted his grip on me, so his fingers dug into my ass. Grinding his hips into me, I felt the truth of his words, his cock rock hard and straining against his tight underwear. "Ay, Shaye, I want you so fucking bad, me voy a volver loco..."

I lunged forward, taking his shoulder into my mouth and biting hard, muffling my own groan at the sound and the feel of him. I felt a bump against my backside and Andy's hands were gone, replaced by something smooth and cool. I looked down and realized he had maneuvered us back towards the pool table, propping me up on the edge so his hands were free to wander elsewhere.

Smirking, I released his shoulder, bringing my mouth up to his ear and nibbling at the lobe before murmuring, "Now I see what you really like to do to relax..."

That earned me a low chuckle from him, and he brought his forehead to rest against mine as he chided, "Eres la diablo. It's not like I planned this, you're just...I can't resist..."

"Show me," I challenged, and he obliged, kissing me once more. He pulled my bottom lip between his teeth and flicked at the sensitive skin with the tip of his tongue, leaving me squirming.

As we kissed, I felt his hands glide over my thighs, alternately squeezing firmly and petting with featherlight touches of his fingertips. Taking his lead, with one arm still wrapped over his shoulder and my legs still hooked around him, I reached down between us and began to stroke his cock through his last remaining piece of clothing.

Andy's hips bucked and he jerked away from my mouth to let loose a lurid moan that sent my pulse pounding. His dark, deep eyes flickered shut and his fingers dug into the soft flesh of my thighs as he practically purred, "Oh, *yes...*"

Delighted by this reaction, I watched his face carefully as I released and reworked my grip around his shaft, not quite holding him fully because of the fabric in the way. "Oh, do you like that?"

"Mmhm," he answered, rolling his lips under his teeth, his head thrown back, eyes still closed.

"Andy..." I leaned forward, trailing my hand gently down the clothed length of him. "Look at me."

Blinking against the light, he craned his head down to meet my gaze. Desire and pleasure, already hot and roiling deep in my belly, gave a little jolt and I couldn't help but smirk at the sensation.

"What are you smiling at?" Andy questioned, attempting to sound put out as he stared at me, his lips parted.

"You," I admitted, my smile only growing wider. I scooted forward to the very edge of the table, pulling him as close as I could with my legs while still allowing enough room for my hand to work between us. "Fuck, Andy, you're so fucking hot. I wonder if I can make you come just like this?"

That earned me a grin. He wobbled his head from side to side. "Take your best shot, *princesa*."

The term of endearment turned my brain fuzzy. I bit the tip of my tongue to keep from laughing, lifting my hand out from between us only to snake around him and grab his ass tight. "Alright, vato," I shot back, lifting my brow as I lost myself in his eyes. "But I should warn you, I've been told I'm pretty good at this."

Slipping my hand underneath the band of his boxer briefs, his hard cock slid into my palm, heavy and warm. It took considerable control not to grab him tight and start pumping for all I was worth, the urge to drive him to distraction fast and hard was difficult to deny. But I bit my bottom lip as I slowly moved my hand down the length of him, my fingers fully exploring the shape and feel of him without taking hold of him just yet.

My toes curled behind his back as I moaned just from touching him.

The corners of his mouth twitched upward into a smile as he looked into my eyes, his lips parted. "You like?"

"I like," I answered, pushing my hand even farther down and cupping his balls. "Very, very much."

He hissed at the sensation, and I felt his cock jerk up and down as I massaged him. Leaning forward, I slowly scraped my teeth along his shoulder. Bringing my hand back up the length of him, I finally wrapped around him at the tip and pumped downward in a long, slow stroke.

Starting up this slow, steady rhythm, I held him close to me with my legs and my free hand. When I grew tired of tasting his shoulder, I licked across his collarbone and up his neck, stopping to suck and bite at the underside of his jaw, marking him as he'd marked me. Every few pumps of my fist I'd release him and trail just the tips of my fingers down the underside of his cock to his sensitive balls, cupping them in my hand and toying with them for a few seconds before returning to my work. Soon they were high and tight against his base, and as my fist worked over him, I felt slickness at his head.

"How does that feel?" I asked, not needing him to say it for me, but wanting to hear him own up to it for himself.

"G-good," he admitted without a fight, his forehead dropping against my shoulder, his breath hot against my collarbone.

"God, Andy, you're so big..." I whispered as I worked, the fingers of my free hand petting the back of his neck. I looked down at him in my hand and groaned a little at what I could see. "I can't wait to put this in my mouth."

Andy lifted his head, letting loose a weak laugh into the shell of my ear. "You think you can take it?"

"I think I'll manage," I said teasingly, moving my hand from the base of his shaft to his sensitive, swollen head. I flicked my thumb over the tip of him, back and forth, mimicking the movement of a tongue. "Would you like that? Like your cock inside me?"

His hands slid from my thighs and onto the raised lip of the pool table as he bucked against my hand once again, seemingly unable to control the motion as he cursed from between clenched teeth. "¡Mierda! You have a filthy mouth, don't you?"

"I don't have to ask if you like that," I said, gripping him tighter and pumping my fist painfully slowly up and down his length. "I can tell you do. I can feel you getting even harder in my hand."

Lifting his head off my shoulder, he breathed out words so softly they almost sounded like a prayer. "Dios mío, Shaye, you feel so *good...*" He peppered quick, hot kisses against my cheek. "Faster, you have to go faster, mi querida..."

I leaned back from him so that I could look into his eyes, my free hand coming up to cradle his jaw and force him to look back at me. "Is that how you want to fuck me? Fast? Hard?" Increasing my speed, but only by a heartbeat, still going far slower than I could tell he wanted, I licked my lips. "You want to be on top of me, inside me, making me come on your–"

He lunged forward, cutting me off mid-sentence with an open-mouthed kiss. The tip of his tongue teased the top of my mouth and I shivered, moaning into him. When he finally allowed us to come up for air, he shook his head, his eyes wide and serious. "If you talk like that, lo juro por Dios, I'm going to–"

"Don't make promises you can't keep," I cautioned with a grin, my grip on him tightening.

"Oh, Shaye..." My name came out from between his lips in a breathy groan. I felt his legs shudder under him as he gripped the edge of the pool table, fingers digging into the felt railings. "Don't fucking stop."

"Don't close your eyes," I asked in return, moving my hand ever so slightly faster over him. "Let me see."

Andy shivered and writhed in front of me, at times almost seeming to attempt to pull away from me, but always returning, allowing me to hold him in place with my legs and my hand. His eyes were wide, pupils blown and dark with pleasure, and he panted wantonly, guttural groans shuddering from deep in his chest. "Shaye," he begged at last, "Por favor, I-*fuck*-"

Removing my hand from him at the last possible moment, I quickly pulled his boxer briefs back up and over him. He made a strangled noise of protest, staring at me with wide, confused eyes, before his questioning cry was cut off by a loud shout of pleasure as he came uncontrollably inside his underwear.

I watched him as he rode the wave of his pleasure, transfixed by his loss of control and deeply aroused by it. I wrapped my hands around his shaking biceps, reveling in the feel of the muscles contracting under my fingertips, and waiting patiently for him to come down from his high.

His chest heaving, he slowly relaxed his grip on the pool table on either side of me, his breathing deepening as he lowered his head between his shoulders. The expression on his face slid from ecstatic bliss to confused annoyance with a rapidity that was frankly amusing.

"Shaye..." he started, glaring at me from under his brow as he shivered. "What the fu-?"

I shook my head, laughing as I leaned forward, capturing his ear lobe between my teeth and licking it. "Caleb would kill us if you ruined this pool table," I said by way of explanation, unhooking my legs from behind his back. "And I don't have a change of clothes."

Free from my grip, he stepped back and looked down at himself, still breathing heavily. "And I do?"

I shook out my hand, flexing it. "Well, I did say I'd like it if you went commando."

"I'm going to have to now, aren't I?" He shook his head and carefully pulled the soiled clothing away and off of him. Muttering words in Spanish that I couldn't quite catch, he began to wipe himself clean with the boxer briefs as best as he could, shaking his head the entire time.

"Now who's filthy?" I teased, watching him fumble in his attempts to clean himself off.

"Still you," he announced, grimacing with chagrin. He attempted to find a dry, clean square of fabric left on his boxer briefs and, finding one, continued dabbing at his skin half-heartedly as he sighed. "Ay, what a mess..."

I waited patiently while he fussed over himself, taking this opportunity to fully appreciate his naked form without him noticing. Lithe and lean, hard muscles moved beneath tan skin, every line of his body hinting at concealed power, at strength just below the surface. His arms, legs, and chest were dusted with dark brown hair.

"I'm going to make you pay for that," he said with a glare, crumpling up and tossing away his ruined boxer briefs with both hands.

I leaned back, resting my hands flat against the pool table, my feet swinging. Smiling wide, I shrugged. "Take your best shot, princesa."

He gave me an assessing glance, taking a deep breath through his nose. Shrugging sharply, he started towards me and said, "Okay."

Before I could read his intentions, Andy bent at the waist, wrapped his arms around my hips and heaved me up off of the table and over his shoulder, reminding me that he was somehow a great deal stronger than he looked.

"Hey!" I exclaimed, struggling to push myself away from his bare back as he strode towards the rec room's door. "What are you–?"

"Bed," he said by way of explanation, turning left out of the rec room and heading up the hallway where we had passed several bedrooms.

"Aw," I said, letting my arms hang limp so they bumped against his bare ass. "What's wrong with the pool table?"

He didn't immediately answer me, one arm still wrapped up around my waist, holding me securely in place on his shoulder as he strode naked through the house. He pushed open the door to one of the bedrooms with his foot and walked inside, heading straight for the large, king-sized bed that filled the center of the space.

"I can't do this–" he said at last, tossing me face up onto the mattress so hard I bounced a little. "–on the pool table."

The impact with the bed forced a huff of laughter out of my lungs. "You're right, that would've hurt on the pool table."

The light in the room was murky and dim. But even in this semi-darkness, I could make out Andy clearly: his small, sly smile, the sparkle of sweat on his chest, and the outline of his rapidly hardening cock.

His gaze raked hungrily down my still clothed body and his smile grew wicked. I backed up on the mattress, pushing myself away from him with my heels as I laughed again and held up a waving hand. "Hey, now, hold on–"

"Oh," he intoned, still smiling as he mounted the mattress on all fours, stalking up and over me. "Now you want me to hold on?"

Nervous excitement was making me dizzy, but I felt the need to put up some defense. Resting flush against the pillowtop, I protested, "Just remember that these are the only clothes I have, alright?"

Andy shook his head, smirking as he leaned over me, one hand outstretched. "You really should've thought of that before you got me so worked up, princesa," he chided.

I couldn't help it – I leaned into his touch as his hand cupped my cheek, my eyes flickering shut as he reverently moved his fingertips across my jaw, down the column of my throat and onto the plane of my chest. The warmth of him radiated across my exposed skin and I sighed contentedly as he leaned down and kissed me more gently than I had thought possible, his other hand coming to rest on my hip, the rest of his body still hovering above me.

Which made the shock all the more acute when his hand slid down under the collar of my shirt and pulled down hard on the row of buttons that fastened the blouse shut. The buttons popped off the shirt in a flurry and I yelped at the sensation of tearing fabric against my skin, the sound swallowed by Andy's lips against mine.

I wriggled beneath him, trying to push him away, my cursing protests muffled against his face. I felt him chuckle, felt his lips curl into a smile as he pressed against me, his hand sliding underneath the cup of my bra to fondle my breast.

"Now we're even," he mumbled into my mouth.

"Bastardo," I shot back, even as I wrapped my arms around his shoulders and held him close.

He responded by teasing and pinching my nipple, taking it from sensitive to rock hard in an instant. I ground my hips against him as I moaned, one hand sliding down his bare back while I buried the other in his thick hair.

Relinquishing my lips, he moved down to my neck, sucking and licking at the tender flesh. Fingers digging into his sides, I gasped and shuddered as he kissed me in one of my most sensitive spots, getting lost in sensation as his hands continued to explore my chest and torso.

"Fuck, Andy, please don't stop," I pleaded.

He hummed his assent, and I went dizzy for a moment as he lifted me upright, freeing me of my ruined blouse and undoing my bra with a flourish. I held onto him, breathing in the scent of him, my eyes fluttering shut as he replaced me on the mattress, moving from one side of my neck to the other.

As he kissed me, I felt him fumble one-handed with the belt and buttons that fastened my shorts shut. After a moment, he pushed himself away from me and stepped off the bed, yanking the expensive shorts down and off my legs as he went. Andy tossed them aside into the darkness while his gaze drunk in the sight of me. Lying there almost naked, I felt a thrill of pleasure go through me as he put one knee on the bed between my legs and reached out to trace the lines of the silk and lace underwear I had chosen for myself, his eyes unnaturally bright and completely fixed on what his hands were doing.

"Que linda..." he muttered, his fingertips feather-light against me, touching across my belly and hips, but not where I wanted to be touched most.

"¿Te gusta?" I queried, giving my hips a slight shimmy and propping myself up on my elbows.

His eyes flicked up to my face and he grinned. "Sí, me gusta."

Backing up off the mattress, he dragged me towards the edge of the bed by my hips. My breath caught in my throat as his left hand drifted from my hip, down my thigh, all the way down the length of my leg to my ankle. His eyes never leaving my face, he lifted my left leg into the air and turned to plant a kiss on my ankle. His lips were soft as silk and slid down my skin slowly. He kissed from my ankle to the side of my knee. Every so often his teeth would scrape against my skin – never enough to cause pain, but just enough to titillate.

His other hand was hardly idle, rubbing small circles on the inner thigh of my opposite leg as he worked his way back towards me. When he lowered himself to his knees, reverently bowing his head as he kissed my inner thighs, I felt myself shudder in anticipation.

A potent mixture of shock, pleasure, and rueful annoyance shot through me when he pressed his mouth against my still-covered pussy, a mouth that quickly and skillfully sucked at my clit through the cloth, forcing the rough fabric to rub against it. His tongue licked long, light strokes across me, the pressure alone driving me wild, the full experience I was being denied so close and yet so far away...

"Oh you–" The expletive that was on the tip of my tongue was swallowed down in a gasp as his lips moved across the fabric, pressing against the center of me as his fingers dug into my thighs, holding me open for him. I tried to grind down onto his tongue, but he held me still and I gave a grunt of frustration, tossing my head to one side as I shut my eyes tight. "I take it back. I take it back, you're not a romantic...you're a fucking tease..."

He nuzzled against me, and I felt the huff of a laugh against my warm skin. "And you're soaking wet," he observed. He moved one of his hands from my thigh down to my hip, slipping his fingers up under the elastic band of my underwear, but staying well away from where I needed his touch the most. "Making a real mess of this pretty little thing..."

"Then take it off!" I grunted, trying once again to press myself into his face, growing desperate for more intense sensation.

"Hmm..." Andy, quite opposite to my wishes, pulled away from me entirely, getting back to his feet. He stared down at me in mock thoughtfulness and then said, firmly, "No."

Before I had a chance to spit a string of expletives into his handsome face, he reached down and grabbed me by the hips with both hands, lifting me once more into the air.

"Andy!" I exclaimed in surprise, bouncing face down on the mattress as he flipped me onto my stomach without warning.

"You said I wanted to be on top of you," he said, lifting me up onto my knees by my hips, massaging my ass in his hands. "Inside you–" The mattress shifted under his weight as he got fully onto it on his knees behind me. "–making you come." With one hand still on my hips, he used the other to pull my underwear to one side, exposing my hot, wet, center to the open air. "Think you know everything, don't you?" I felt the head of his cock press against my entrance as he growled, "I don't want to be on top of you, princesa."

He sank every inch of himself inside me in a single, rough thrust. I cried out, some strange mix of a curse and a groan. I couldn't stop myself from pushing back against him, wordlessly demanding more of the same as I scrambled onto the palms of my hands, breath coming out quick and shallow.

As his hips set a firm, fast pace behind me, I was at first only vaguely aware of one of his hands sliding around my side and under me. When the pads of his fingertips began to play with my clit, his knuckles pushing against the underwear I was still wearing as he worked his hand inside them,

I gasped sharply, tossing my head back as my arms began to shake under my own weight.

"Andy!"

"Sí, me gusta," he grunted, and I could hear the grin in his words. His free hand moved over my ass and squeezed me hard as he fucked me. "I like you screaming my name." Leaning down over me, he kissed my back, breathing out, "Un sonido tan bonito de una boca tan sucia..."

It'd been so long since someone had touched me. So long since I'd been wanted and taken. And never like this.

I closed my eyes, overwhelmed by sensation, and still, I could feel him all around me, consuming me, making me a part of him. Jordan's lovemaking always had a sort of lazy quality to it, an inevitability, a feeling that this is what was supposed to happen between two people in our situation.

Being with Andy was nothing like that.

Being with Andy felt like stealing fire from the gods. A moment snatched from the hands of fate and enjoyed to the fullest. I pushed myself back against his body and he dragged his teeth across my skin and all I could think was *more, please, more...*

I was almost disappointed to feel my orgasm racing towards me. But I was as powerless to stop it as I was to stop a speeding train.

The best I could do was go along and enjoy the ride.

"Andy, Andy, Andy–!" I screamed his name in time with the snap of his hips, my shaking arms giving out from under me, my cheek buried in the comforter as I neared the brink of my control. Still, he kept touching me and soon I jerked upward, hands scrambling back to grab onto his side and hip as I came, shouting, "Oh God, *Andy!*"

Wave after wave of pleasure washed over me as I relinquished control of myself for a few moments to sweet sensation. As I returned to myself, my tense body beginning to relax, I waited for Andy to change his pace, to speed up towards completion himself, to move his hand away from my center and take what he needed. I waited for the pleasure to slowly recede and then stop.

But it didn't stop. *He* didn't stop.

"What... what are you doing?" I demanded breathlessly.

He didn't answer, but continued to move inside me, fucking me through the shuddering end of my orgasm, shifting us so he was sitting on the edge of the bed with me perched on top of him, my back flush with his front, my legs wide around his hips even as he held me upright with one arm. His other hand was still pressed against my wet pussy, sending almost painful jolts of pleasure deep into my core.

I shivered against him, every inch of me alive with sensation, alive in a way I hadn't been in years, if ever. Shaking my head, I struggled to speak, my hands sliding down his arms. "I...I came... Andy, I–"

"And you think you're done?" His teeth captured the top of my earlobe and he almost purred as he continued to pump into me, rubbing my clit in small, sharp circles. "Oh no, mi princesa. You're not done until I say you're done." Andy's mouth left the side of my face and landed on top of my shoulder. I felt the muscles of his core contract and relax as he fucked me. "You deserve so much more than that..."

His arm slid up from around my waist and across my chest, his hand kneading my breasts, fingers rubbing my nipples in rhythm with my clit. The sensation was too much, and I was tired of not being able to give as good as I was getting. I reached up and pulled at his hand, directing it across my shoulder and neck and up to my jaw, so his fingers were pressed against my lips. I opened my mouth and licked at his thumb, drawing it inside with my tongue until I could suck on it properly.

His hips stuttered and I felt the rumble of the moan deep in his chest. He threw his head back, muttering, "Oh, *fuck* yes, princesa, *yes...*"

I never knew praise could physically feel so fucking good.

I came again, even harder than before, and I think my shouts would've carried well past the walls of the house if Andy hadn't angled his head towards me and captured my mouth with his, his tongue dancing with mine as he continued to thrust in and out of my shaking body.

This time there was a moment of relief from the constant pleasuring of my clit as he moved to wrap his arms around my shoulders, cradling me as he twisted us around and down onto the mattress. My sweat-slicked back immediately stuck to the sheets and the comforter tangled under us. I closed my eyes and whimpered as he began to move inside me once again. I curled my arms around his neck and shoulders, holding on for dear life.

"¡Maldita sea! You're so fucking wet..." His words came out in a hushed groan, almost as if he were talking to himself. Forcing my eyes open, I found myself looking into his face, his soft brown eyes with pupils blown wide with pleasure. He leaned forward and kissed me hard, pulling away only to whisper, "Shaye, mi princesa, you feel incredible..."

"Touch me," I begged shamelessly.

"Where?" he asked, his lips sliding against the skin of my throat.

I tightened my grip on him, certain that I never wanted to let him go again. "Everywhere..."

As we moved together, his hands roamed over my body, touching, squeezing, rubbing, reminding me constantly of his presence. That he was here, that he was with me. That it was us, just the two of us together in this moment, that this was ours and ours alone.

I felt his cock pulse inside me, and he moaned, lifting his head up towards the ceiling as he called out my name. "Oh, Shaye..."

"Come inside me," I said, nodding as I pulled him tight against me, my legs wrapping around him, my hips lifting to match him thrust for thrust.

"Ay, Dios mío," he moaned, clearly on the edge of losing control. But still, he tried, his breath ragged as he rested his forehead against mine, looking deep into my eyes. "Are–are you–?"

"Fuck, Andy, *please*, I need–" My fingers scrabbled against his shoulder blades as I arched up into him, trembling beneath him, almost embarrassed to be cresting into orgasm *again*. "Ah, shit, I'm– Andy, goddamnit, please!"

"Yes, ah! ¡Jódeme!" he shouted in return, burying himself deep inside me with one last hard thrust, his arms shaking around me as he came.

The sensation of him losing control so completely, the sight of him unraveling on top of me, the sound of his ecstatic moans drifting into almost pained whimpers – it was all too much. I came around his cock, vision going white as I cried out.

For a few long, quiet moments, there was no other sound than our ragged breaths in the stillness of the dim room. When my eyes could focus again, it was to the sight of Andy still hovering over me, looking down at me with undisguised affection, even as his chest heaved, and his arms began to shake slightly.

I slid my hands down his sweat-slicked shoulders to rest just above his hips, unable to break away from his gaze. "Andy..."

"I could listen to you say my name forever."

The sincerity in his voice – it frightened me more than I cared to admit.

The shaking of his arms intensified as he withdrew from me, his eyes flickering shut. "Ah, princesa, you ruined me..."

He laid himself down carefully next to me, letting out a deep breath as he did so, his face pressed into the mattress, his arm snaking around my waist. I curled into him, almost as if on instinct, some part of me still wanting to feel his skin against mine, even as my tired mind wondered, as it drifted towards sleep, if I hadn't just made a huge mistake.

~ 15 ~

CHAPTER 15

Andy

I woke up face down in a plush pillow, soft cotton sheets draped loosely around my waist and legs. Looking around myself through bleary, half-lidded eyes for what had stirred me from unconsciousness, I slowly focused in on a handset phone sitting on the bedside table next to my head. As I watched it, the number pad lit up, flashing slowly. I realized the chiming I had heard in my dreams was not in fact, imaginary, but was actually the ringing of this phone.

Reaching up with one heavy arm, I knocked the handset off the cradle and fumbled it towards my head. Running my tongue along my lips, I pressed the phone to my ear.

"Hello?" I mumbled, still half-asleep.

"Why aren't you answering your goddamn cellphone?"

The sound of Caleb's ire, so cold and crisp coming down the line and into my ear was better than a bucket of ice wa-

Moaning, she slowly twisted away from me, pushing her face deeper into the pillow. Smiling, I got up fully on my knees, crawling across the bed towards her and putting two hands on her this time, one on her shoulder, the other on her elbow and giving a little shake. "Vamos, princesa–"

With a loud gasp, Shaye flailed into wakefulness with such force that she shot upright in bed, forcing me to tumble backwards. She cast about herself for a few frenzied moments, seemingly at a loss for where she was, her eyes wide, her face a mask of terror.

"Woah! Shaye!" I said, hands raised partially in defense, partially in supplication as I righted myself and leaned towards her. "Mi vida, it's okay! You're okay."

Her eyes found me, and she jerked forward squeezing my shoulders tightly in her hands. "Andy!"

I held her in return, frightened to feel her shaking under my touch. "What, Shaye, what is it?"

She opened her mouth, but no words came out. A change came over her face, the fear draining from her eyes. Color returned slowly to her cheeks as she shut her mouth with a snap. She relaxed under my hands. The shaking diminished and then ceased completely. As I watched, Shaye clenched her jaw, screwing her eyes shut as she shook her head.

"Damn it," she hissed out, sounding upset, but much more like herself than she had a moment ago.

"Are you okay?" I ventured after a moment, dropping my hands back down to the mattress.

"Yeah." Shaye pulled her hands down her face, stretching the skin around her eyes. She shook her head. "Yeah, I'm fine." She plastered on a thin smile and looked at me at last. "Sorry. Bad... dream."

I nodded, resisting the urge to wrap her up in my arms and collapse back beneath the sheets. "Uh, sorry to wake you, but Caleb called. There's a car from the Nameless coming to pick us up. We've got to hustle if we're going to be ready to meet it."

She took a deep breath. "Right. Okay, we better get going then." Pushing away the covers, she got out of the bed and began to gather her clothes. I got up as well and was headed for the door when she let loose a quiet "um". I turned around to see her holding up her torn blouse with a grimace.

"Just take something of Caleb's," I offered, nodding to the armoire in the corner. "I don't think he'll mind."

"Guess I'll have to," she said, dropping the ruined shirt back onto the floor.

I smirked in spite of myself, shaking my head as I padded down the hall towards the rec room.

Caleb was probably right to be upset – this wasn't a smart thing to have done. Things were complicated enough as they were without adding a sexual relationship into the mix.

Of course, this wasn't just strictly sexual.

The thought popped into my head before I could stop it. I grimaced at myself, mumbling with frustration as I bent down and collected my discarded clothes from the rec room floor. Why couldn't things ever be simple? Why did I have to be like this? Was I really going to let myself get romantically entangled with *another* human woman after what happened last time? I had promised myself that I was done with all that.

So much for promises.

I made a quick trip downstairs to pick up Shaye's shoes and socks for her, arguing with myself all the while. It didn't matter how I felt, or how I didn't. Shaye would certainly not be interested in me, not like that. So that was that. We were having fun if you could call it that. That would have to be enough.

My eyes focused on the floor, I reentered the bedroom, entirely engrossed with my own thoughts. I dumped my pile of clothes onto the end of the bed, likewise dropping the few things of Shaye's onto the mattress. I only looked up because I heard her heave a heavy sigh.

My heart leapt to my throat and despite my best intentions, I felt myself getting hard again. Standing in front of a floor length mirror in her underwear, her hair still a tousled mess, she had gotten herself into one of Caleb's black undershirts. It was, of course, enormous on her, so she had improvised by rolling up the excess fabric and tying it off in a knot at her hip.

I had never seen a sexier sight in my entire life.

Turning to face me, Shaye batted at the large knot at her side, shaking her head. "God, this looks stupid." Then, seeing the expression on my face, her brow furrowed, and she put her hands on her hips. "What?"

"It really doesn't look stupid," I assured her. I gave a cough of laughter, scratching at the back of my head and looking at her from under my brow. "It's just... I don't know how I feel about seeing you wear another man's shirt after everything we did."

Her face turned a perfectly adorable shade of pink and she looked away from me quickly, striding towards the mattress where I had dropped her shoes and socks.

"Well, you should've thought about that before you went all caveman on my top," she quipped as she passed, her bare feet padding against the floor.

"No tengo excusas," I said, following her back to the bed. "I did what I had to do."

We were silent for a few moments as we both busied ourselves with dressing, Shaye pulling on her shorts and sitting down on the mattress to fumble on her socks, while I put on my trousers and shook some of the wrinkles out my shirts.

"Do you want to talk about it?" I asked.

I saw her eyes widen and her blush return. I realized she had misconstrued my meaning. I couldn't hide a smile as I corrected her, pushing my arms through the sleeves of my undershirt as I said, "I meant your dream."

The pink in her face deepened to red. She bared her teeth in a pained grimace. "Oh. Uh, no, it's fine."

"Alright. If you say so." I swallowed hard but attempted to sound casual as I continued. "As for the other thing..."

Her eyes darted around the room before settling on my face. I lifted a brow at her and smiled. "¿Eso fue agradable, no?"

I was beyond relieved when she returned my grin with a shy smile of her own, rubbing at the back of her neck as she answered, "It was a little more than nice." The smile almost disappeared in the next moment, however, as she shook her head, standing up from the mattress to finish fastening her shorts. "But let's just focus on surviving whatever is coming next, alright? We can talk about anything else later."

"Fair," I admitted. I opened my mouth to speak but was interrupted by the cheery chiming of the doorbell. I hurriedly pulled on my shirt, starting for the bedroom door as I fumbled with the buttons. "Mierda. That must be them."

"I'll be right behind you," called Shaye, shoving her feet into her still laced up tennis shoes.

I hurried down the stairs, running my hands through my hair in an attempt to tame it into some semblance of kemptness. The doorbell rang again, and I put on a burst of speed, lunging for the handle and yanking the portal open.

A young, alert female wolf stood on the porch, her arms loose at her side. Her hair was pulled up on top of her head, an intricate pile of black braids, and her umber eyes shone with a playful air in a diamond shaped face. In the driveway behind her, a large black car idled. When the door opened, she straightened a little, leaning forward at the waist and looking up at me from under her brow.

"Andy Vazquez?"

I nodded, tucking my shirt into my pants as I did so. The woman eyed me questioningly, a wry smile playing around her lips. "I'm Naomi. Caleb Beck sent us. He did let you know we were coming, right?"

Heat rushed into my cheeks, and I avoided her appraising stare, hoping I didn't look as rumpled as I felt. "Yeah, he, uh, had a little trouble getting hold of me." There were a series of loud bumps from behind me and I turned to watch Shaye hurry around the corner from the direction of the stairs. I took one look at her, wearing an oversized men's undershirt, hair tousled beyond repair, and looked down at myself, still struggling into my clothes, and realized immediately how improper it all appeared.

I winced and turned back to face the young woman at the door. She was grinning now, her brows high over her eyes. I licked my lips and nodded. "Yeah, Caleb let me know. We're ready."

"Great." The woman turned on her heel, gesturing to the black Escalade idling in the driveway. "Let's get going then."

I shifted to one side in the doorway to let Shaye exit ahead of me, reaching around to lock the door before closing it behind me. We climbed into the backseat of the SUV while Naomi resumed her seat in the front passenger side, murmuring something to the petite Asian woman behind the wheel. The driver laughed, glanced back at us in the rearview mirror and, seeing that we were strapped in and ready, backed out of the driveway and into the street.

We drove in silence for a few miles before Shaye tapped me on the arm, leaning away from her window to whisper, "Anything I should know about these Nameless people?"

I cast a quick glance up at the two wolves in the front of the car before turning my head fully towards Shaye, keeping my voice at a low murmur. "They're a Seattle-based den. Been expanding their territory over the last year. Sangre Sagrada has some joint operations with them, so relations

are generally friendly. Well, as friendly as relationships between dens ever are." I looked up at the ceiling of the car,
struggling with how to phrase what to say next. "They're
also more... liberal-minded than Sangre Sagrada."

"Oh? In what way?"

I sat back, shrugging. "Lots of ways. Let's just say they're
more for co-existence with humans rather than...well..."

"Eating them?" she supplied with just a touch of venom.

Grimacing, I nodded. "Yeah."

She gave a loud harrumph, readjusting in her seat and
pulling at the safety belt. "Well, that's good for this human
to know."

It took us almost an hour to wind our way into West
Hollywood, and about halfway to our destination. I realized
where we must be headed. Where else would an important
dignitary visiting Los Angeles want to stay? Only the
Chateau Marmont would do.

First opened in 1929, the building housed the rich, famous, and reclusive. By the time it was converted to a hotel
in 1930, the ultra-elegant, the bawdy, the depraved, the op-
ulent, the perverted, and the gaudy – all the weird and
wonderful famous folk of Hollywood -- had crossed its
threshold. Like an aging starlet, the property would occasionally fall into disrepair, but some new beau would come
along, fix her up, and she'd find a second life with the next
generation, who were taken with her legacy.

Before parting ways with our escorts in the gothic lobby,
they directed us to one of the penthouse suites. The ride
up in the elevator was quick compared to the long drive

through Los Angeles. It felt like no time at all before I was knocking on a thick wooden door.

The door swung open, and we were greeted by a slim, petite werewolf, in an ankle-length yellow sundress and pink pearls. Her hair was a platinum blonde that would've given Monroe's a run for her money, and her green eyes and long lashes had probably gotten her in and out of trouble more times than I could've guessed. She looked like she would be just as home modeling in front of a camera as she would be behind an executive assistant's desk. Her face lit up when she saw us.

"Welcome," she said, her green eyes sparkling as she smiled. She stepped back from the door and gestured for us to come inside. "We've been expecting you!"

After exchanging a glance with Shaye, I stepped forward, trusting her to follow after me. The entryway was small, but the suite was spacious. As soon as we stepped inside, my eyes fell on Caleb, his head bowed in close conversation with a tall, muscular blonde woman with hair down her back in a thick Dutch braid. The petite movie-starlet-type tapped her way towards them, whispered something up at Caleb, and then stepped back. Caleb nodded, looking over his shoulder, his face grim.

"Kassandra." Caleb turned away from the tall blonde woman and gestured back to me, stepping away so she could have an unobstructed view. "This is the wolf I was telling you about, Andy Vazquez."

I moved forward to take the hand that Kassandra Arnaud extended towards me. I had heard that she had been tapped to take over the den when the next in line had abdicated her position. The former head of the Nameless' elite security force was a good candidate for leadership -- it was unlikely that she would suffer the same fate as her predecessor, Mama, who had died at the hands of a Hunter. At least that was the story circulating amongst the dens. Arnaud had brought a military tactician's eye to running the Nameless, focusing on strengthening their hold on the Pacific Northwest region and absorbing some of the neighboring, much-smaller dens. She had a reputation for ruthlessness, but her slight smile was warm, if a little unsure.

"Good to meet you," said Kassandra, her voice low, yet undeniably feminine, reminding me of an old-Hollywood movie star, like Garbo or Dietrich. Her grip was firm, her gaze steady. "Sorry to hear about what happened."

"Yeah," I said, doing my best to keep eye contact with the den leader and return the bone-crunching handshake. "Thanks for meeting with us."

Her calm facade cracked a little, her smile growing broader and more genuine. "Hey, when Caleb Beck calls in a favor and says he'll owe you? You let him write that check."

I nodded in understanding, and opened my mouth to respond, but closed it sharply when I realized that Kassandra's attention had fallen over my right shoulder. Taking in a steadying breath, I released her hand and stepped to one side, giving her full access to Shaye.

Kassandra waited a moment, assessing the woman standing in front of her before moving forward, her hand outstretched. "And you must be our human interloper: Shaye, right?"

Shaye took Kassandra's hand after a moment, but did not return the verbal greeting, instead asking: "Do all the dens have women in charge?"

Kassandra smiled again, but this time the expression was far more natural. She shook her head. "No, unfortunately. Just the best ones. So–"

A high-pitched giggle, like chandelier crystals stirred by the Santa Ana winds, interrupted the elder wolf's friendly interrogation.

Shaye's eyes slid over to the younger woman who had, until now, remained silent and unobtrusive at the side of the entryway. Kassandra followed Shaye's attention and brightened considerably, waving the female wolf forward with one hand.

"Oh, please," said Kassandra. "This is Sylvia Laurent – my right hand."

Stepping forward, Sylvia looked at each of us from under her lashes, grinning. "And her left hand. And most other things in between. Nice to meet you all. Shall we sit?"

~ 16 ~

CHAPTER 16

Andy

Shaye and I followed Kassandra, Caleb, and Sylvia further into the suite, where a large, well-appointed living room awaited us. Kassandra waved us into a pair of armchairs before taking a seat on a couch across from us. Sylvia stood behind her at a respectful distance, and Caleb followed suit, standing behind me. Shaye, looking more uncomfortable with each passing moment, slumped in her seat, her eyes roaming around the room as if she expected something to jump out at her at any moment. I was about to say something to her when Kassandra instead addressed me.

"So, Vazquez," said Kassandra, leaning back as she crossed her legs. "Tell me about your situation."

"Oh." I shifted onto the edge of the overly plush chair, my hands clasped between my knees. "Uh, I'm sorry, I assumed Caleb would've–"

"He did," she said, examining me with the same interest as a person considering an expensive bauble. "But I'd like to hear your version of things. Best to get things straight from the source, in my experience."

So, trying as best as I could to leave out nothing pertinent, I told the story of everything that had happened since Emilia had summoned me to the den house two days ago. I explained the situation with the rogue wolf and how we had come to track down Shaye, what she had seen and how the wolf had attempted to permanently silence her before she could identify him. Lazlo's hiring of the Santa Barbara outsiders was, as Kassandra observed, "a sloppy mistake" that ended up ultimately working in his favor. I had thought I had him – but he managed to turn the situation to his benefit and get me excommunicated and Shaye slated for execution, all while keeping Emilia blind to his true activities.

Kassandra listened quietly, asking a question or making an observation only on a few occasions. When I finished, she was silent, probing the inside of her cheek with her tongue, her gaze focused somewhere near my left shoe.

"Lazlo is dug in deep with your den," said Kassandra after a moment. She shook her head and scratched her chin. "It's not going to be easy to convince your la Doña that he's turned against her. Especially without knowing why he's doing it."

"That's what's confusing me as well," I confessed, straightening in my seat. "I don't see his logic – the why behind his actions. I mean, if he's caught, if Emilia does find

out that he's gone rogue, she'll kill him. And if he isn't...
well, what does he gain?"

Sylvia nodded, frowning. "I agree. What the hell does he
want?"

"Maybe he's just lost it," offered Caleb from behind me.
"It happens sometimes with the older wolves. All that living, it can take its toll on the mind."

"You speaking from experience, old man?" said Kassandra, smiling sourly. "No, Cabral doesn't sound crazy. This is
something else..."

"He wants a war."

We turned almost as one body to look at Shaye.

For a moment, I doubted the evidence of my senses, and
I thought that I had misheard, that perhaps it was Sylvia
who had spoken. But then Kassandra said, "Excuse me?" and
Shaye, slumping further down in her seat, repeated, "He
wants a war. He knows that if you find out that the Sangre
Sagrada have a rogue wolf that they can't put down, you'll
step in to clean up the mess – and likely try to take over the
den in the process."

Shaye's jaw tightened, her mouth contorting as if she
had just tasted something disgusting. "He's been amassing
followers – denless wolves and dissatisfied members from
other dens, even yours. If you move against Doña Sangre, it
gives him the excuse he needs to fight back and take over."

It was as if she was speaking in tongues --the words
were garbled, and uttered in an unsettling, unnatural tone.
I shook my head. Shaye shouldn't be able to even guess at
such a thing. I leaned forward in my chair, my eyes darting

"Why should we?" scoffed Sylvia, stepping forward in front of Kassandra as if to shield her.

"Why would I lie about this?" Shaye's hands clenched into shaking fists at her sides. She looked around the room as if at a loss. "Any of this? You think I'm having a good time? You think this has been fucking fun for me? People have tried to kill me."

Kassandra rose from her seat. She redid the button on her suit jacket, letting out a long breath through her nose. Then, when she had composed herself, she crossed the room at a gentle amble, shaking her head. "Okay. I'm going to ask this one more time..." She came to a stop just in front of Shaye, dragging her eyes up her body as she spoke. "How do you know? How do you know what Cabral is planning? How do you know about the sacrament, but not what it is? How do you know–"

Shaye backed away, bumping against the glass before she screwed her eyes shut and shouted, "I–I saw it, okay!"

Kassandra tilted her head to one side. "Well, what the hell does that mean?"

Much more quietly, Shaye continued, rubbing at her left arm and staring at the floor. "Sometimes...when I dream...I see things. Things that...haven't happened yet."

My brow furrowed slowly as I took in her meaning, my mouth falling open. I scooted forward to the edge of my seat. "Um...what?"

"Like..." Caleb shook his head, his brow furrowed. "...you're psychic or something?"

Shaye brought her hand up to her forehead, rubbing her skull hard. "Something, I guess." She jerked her head up, looking into Kassandra's face. "I know it sounds crazy, but-"

"Honey, you're standing in a room full of werewolves," said Sylvia, perching herself on the arm of the chair previously occupied by Kassandra. "Our threshold for crazy is higher than the average joe."

I had lived a hundred years in a world where the majority of the people I knew transformed into wolf-like creatures every time the moon was full. In that kind of world, there had always been whispers of other kinds of miraculous occurrences – of things that humans might call magic, of supernatural and preternatural happenings. But I had never taken any of that talk very seriously.

Perhaps I should have.

I felt trapped in my seat, unable to move, almost unable to breathe. I stared at Shaye, at the woman I thought I had begun to know, and realized, slowly and with a sickening lurch, that I really didn't know her at all.

"How long has this been happening?" I asked, speaking at last.

Shaye still didn't look at me. She bobbed her head from side to side, gritting her teeth. "My whole life?"

"Your parents." Kassandra hadn't moved from the spot in front of Shaye. She lifted her brow. "Did you also see that in a dream?"

Shaye's face, already drawn and haggard, turned a sickly shade of green. Her next words came out in a strangled croak. "How...how do you know about that?"

"What are you talking about, Kassandra?" I demanded, shooting up onto my feet at last.

The older wolf waved me off, her eyes never leaving Shaye's face. "She knows what I'm talking about."

The two women stared at each other, each one seemingly unwilling to look away and equally unwilling to speak. Finally, Kassandra broke the contest, rolling her eyes and crossing to the desk at the far side of the room, over which various papers and notepads were strewn. She held aloft a thin, innocuous looking file folder.

It had Shaye's name on it.

"I may not be psychic, but I'm not sloppy either. I do my homework." Kassandra flipped open the thin folder and trailed her finger along the top page, reading out the information. "Shaye Cassidy, twenty-nine years old – born in Los Angeles County California, married to Jordan Yates–" Glancing away from the dossier, Kassandra nodded in Shaye's direction. "He did divorce you, by the way, in case you were curious. Paperwork went through about three years back."

Shaye didn't move. She merely made a small sound in the back of her throat. "I'm...surprised it took him so long."

Kassandra shrugged. "Courts can be a bitch, especially when half the equation drops off the face of the earth." She returned her attention to the folder, shaking her head. "No children. Parents were killed in an electrical fire at their home in Chino Hills." Tapping her pointer finger against the folder, she straightened up, rolling her shoulders back. "There's a note here about the fire – arson suspected but ruled out for lack of corroborating evidence."

Shaye didn't immediately respond to the allegation, unspoken but clear, hanging in the air like smoke. She dropped her head low, her chin touching her chest. She flexed her fingers, curling her hands in and out of fists.

When she did speak, her voice was hollow, quiet and empty, like it was coming from far away and long ago. "I told them to go. Take a vacation. Sell the house. Move away." As I watched, Shaye struggled to swallow. The next words came out choked, thick with effort. "But they wouldn't listen. They said I was being paranoid. Ridiculous. But I..."

She began crying, her chest hiccupping as she forced herself not to sob out loud. I wanted to go to her then, to hold her, but I couldn't move. I was frozen to the spot, horror holding me as firmly as silver chains.

"I saw them burn. I heard them screaming." She closed her eyes, lifting her head, tears winding freely down her cheeks. "I smelt..."

I didn't so much sit back down in my seat as collapse into it, my legs no longer strong enough to keep me upright. As I watched, Shaye lifted her shaking hands to her face, digging her fingers into her flesh as she dragged them down her cheeks.

"I knew it was going to happen, I just didn't know when or why." Her head wobbled from side to side. "I even told Jordan about my dreams. He was the first – the only person I'd ever told. He said they were just dreams. I almost believed him. I wanted to believe him."

Shaye's voice gained strength as she turned away, a forced lightness that felt somehow sadder than everything that had come before it. "Turns out he just didn't believe me. After. He thought I had...that I had..." She stopped and shook her head. "Well, I can't say that I blame him. It made more sense. I came into a lot of money when my parents died."

I could imagine how it all went down. How it would appear to the average individual, the run of the mill cop. But I still felt a swell of anger well up in me on Shaye's behalf, anger that anyone would think her capable of something so unforgivable.

"So," said Sylvia, the first one brazen enough to break the heavy silence. "You came to the big bad city for a fresh start?"

"I came to Los Angeles to disappear," said Shaye, her gaze fixed on the city outside the suite's window, her hand falling to her side. "And I did. Just not quite the way I thought I would."

There are all kinds of reasons people become homeless, she had said to me. *None of them are good.*

I sunk low into my chair, my hand covering my face, my stomach heaving. I had never imagined anything like this. It was like something out of a Greek tragedy, too dismal to be real. And she hadn't told me any of it. Well, why would she? It's not like she trusted me – that much was obvious.

I had risked everything, lost everything, for a woman who didn't trust me enough to tell me the truth.

Someone cleared their throat. I peeked through my fingers to see Kassandra cracking her neck, tongue probing the inside of her cheek.

"Okay," she said. "Okay. Cabral wants a war." Kassandra sat down in the chair behind the desk, steepling her fingers in front of her face. "Then that's exactly what we won't give him."

"What?" I said, feeling at a complete loss.

"What do we know?" Kassandra lifted her hand, ticking off her points as she spoke. "We know Sangre Sagrada has a rogue wolf problem. We know this rogue wolf is Lazlo Cabral. We know that Cabral wants us to move against the den to give him an excuse to depose Doña Sangre." She spread her hands wide in front of herself, smiling tightly. "So, we don't give him that excuse." Standing, she began to pace the area behind the desk, rubbing the back of her neck. "We... We will go ahead with the meeting tomorrow night. We will convince Sangre Sagrada that we think that they have everything under control." She tossed her hand in my direction without looking at me. "Hell, we can even make you the hero, Vazquez."

I scoffed aloud. "And how are you going to manage that?"

"We'll say that you came to us, convinced us that everything was being handled, and that there was nothing to worry about," said Kassandra, her eyes growing bright with excitement.

Shaking my head, I avoided looking at Shaye as I insisted, "But I already told Emilia–"

Kassandra cut me off with a shake of her head. "It doesn't matter. She'll be so relieved that we're not moving in on her territory, she'll take the win without fully understanding why. Lazlo on the other hand..." Kassandra grinned. "He'll be frustrated. Angry. And when that happens, he'll get sloppy again."

"He'll do something bigger," said Caleb, nimbly jumping onboard Kassandra's train of thought. "More reckless to get your attention. Try to force you to act."

Nodding, Kassandra clapped her hands together. "All you have to do is catch him at it, and catch him in such a way that you can prove to Doña Sangre, beyond a shadow of a doubt, that he's been behind everything and–"

"–you're all golden," finished Sylvia, smiling broadly.

My head swimming, my stomach a sucking pit of dread, I felt anything but golden. I numbly nodded my assent, never having felt less in control of my life than I did at that moment.

~ 17 ~

CHAPTER 17

Shaye

The moment I had been dreading had come and gone. My secret was out in the open. Now, I had to deal with the fallout.

Everyone had taken the news pretty well, considering. I guess what Sylvia had said made some sense: in a world where people regularly turned into gigantic, man-eating beasts every month because of the phases of the moon, a person who had visions of the future seemed a little less far-fetched.

I thought I'd feel relieved, for once having been believed. Not being treated like a freak, or like I was out of my mind. And it was nice, a pleasant change. But it wasn't all sunshine and warm breezes.

Standing a few feet away from the sliding glass door which led to the suite's balcony, I watched Andy. Sitting outside on a metal bench, staring out at the sunrise, he had been avoiding being alone with me ever since they'd decided to go ahead with the meeting with Sangre Sagrada.

I owed him an explanation. An apology even. And if there was one thing I hated more than anything else, it was admitting I screwed up.

Taking a deep breath, I stepped outside. Andy must have known I was there because he didn't even look up, just continued watching the skyline, elbows on his knees, hands clasped between his legs.

"Can I join you?" I said, gesturing to the empty space on the bench beside him.

No answer.

I sat down next to him, mimicking his stance. "The silent treatment is getting really old, Andy."

With a slow exhalation of breath, he straightened in his seat, the tip of his tongue clenched between his teeth. He remained facing forward, and for a moment I thought he was going to stand up and walk away, but then he spoke, glancing at me from the corner of his eye.

"Were you ever going to tell me?" he said.

"Maybe." I winced at the half-truth and then shook my head. "Honestly? I don't know. It's not the kind of thing you just blurt out. 'Oh, by the way, I see the future sometimes'."

He ran his tongue along his teeth, but the smile I was hoping for failed to appear. "Fair." His brow fell in a hard line over his eyes, and he turned to face me fully, grimacing. "So, what, you were just going to wait until it came up in conversation?"

I rubbed at the bridge of my nose, not daring myself to look at him. "I was hoping it wasn't going to come up at all."

Shaking his head, Andy clicked his tongue off the back of his teeth, disgust clear in his posture. I dropped my hand into my lap with a smack, gritting my teeth. "Look, I hadn't had an episode...a vision...whatever the hell you want to call it, I hadn't had one in ten years. I thought I was done." Glancing away from him to study the pattern in the tiles, I muttered, "Should've known I wasn't that lucky."

We sat in silence for a minute, and then another. I let the time pass, feeling no need to interrupt the quiet, feeling the least I owed Andy was the space to come to terms with what he had learned about me in whatever way he needed. Still, I found I couldn't sit still, picking at the hem of the shorts I was wearing until I loosened a thread enough to pull and begin to unravel the stitching.

He wasn't angry with me. I could tell that much. I wished that he were. Anger I could deal with. But this? Disappointment? Hurt? I didn't know what to do with that. Didn't know what to do with the fact that I actually cared that I had caused him pain by trying to protect myself.

With a quiet groan, Andy stood up and turned to face me, letting out a huff of air through his mouth. "So. This vision about Cabral – that was the first one you've had in ten years?"

I hated how much I didn't want to lie to him. I hated it almost as much as how easily he could read my silence. Shaking his head, Andy closed his eyes, his hand coming up to rub at his forehead. "Tell me."

"The night Jason died," I admitted haltingly. "I dreamed..." Swallowing down the words, I shook my head, avoiding looking at Andy's face. "I thought it was just a nightmare. But it didn't feel like a nightmare, so I went to check and that's when I saw what I saw."

"Mierda," he muttered under his breath, his eyes still screwed shut. "Shaye..."

I waited for the lecture that I was sure was coming. Waited for him to upbraid me for not telling him vital information, for potentially putting us all at risk after already costing him so much – to berate me for even thinking about withholding the truth for any longer.

After all, I was already doing all that to myself.

Andy sat down next to me and, with a touch so gentle it felt like he was afraid I might break, he caressed my cheek with his fingertips, coaxing my face up to look at him. In his eyes there was no pity, no disappointment, only a quiet affection that tore at my chest and made me want to weep.

"You should've told me," he said, his hand warm against my skin.

Closing my eyes, I leaned into his touch, even though I knew I shouldn't. Even though I knew it would only end badly. "Last time I told someone, it didn't go very well for me," I said, my voice barely above a whisper.

His hand fell from my face with an abruptness that was jarring. My eyes shot open, and I stared at him. His brows drawn up to a point, downturned lips parted, he looked as if I had just slapped him, and he drew in a sharp breath before standing, striding towards the balcony's edge.

"I'm not him," he shot back at me, the anger in his voice stinging like a whip.

I stood as well, but I didn't move to follow him, clasping my hands in front of my hips. "I– I didn't know that. How could I know that?"

It was the truth. But I could tell it didn't help any. I watched as he struggled to control his emotions, the muscles in his shoulders tensing and relaxing and tensing again, his hands strangling the railing.

"Andy, I'm sorry," I said, surprised to feel how deeply I meant it. "I didn't mean to hurt you."

Andy looked over his shoulder at me, his hickory brown eyes wide. "I didn't mean to let you."

My heart seized in my chest as I absorbed his words. But before I could marshal a response, before I could press him to explain if he meant what I thought he meant, he moved past me back into the suite.

"I'm going out. I'll be back in time to get ready for tonight."

I looked around the concrete balcony, at a loss. I couldn't follow him. Well, I could, but he clearly didn't want me to. He needed his space, he needed time – all because I hadn't been honest with him.

Spinning around to face the city, I leaned against the railing, gritting my teeth as I tried to will tears back behind my eyes. Why did I care? Why did it matter? Who the hell was Andy Vazquez to me anyway?

I spent the better part of two hours out there on the balcony, searching for the answer to those questions. In the end, I had to admit the truth – Andy Vazques was someone who had been kind to me, at great personal cost. He had risked life and limb for me, risked losing everything he'd ever known to keep me safe, and he did it all because he fucking *cared* about me. He saw me, saw things about me that nobody had seen in so long, things worth liking, worth...loving?

Well, who the hell asked him to do that?

"Damn it," I grunted, grinding the heel of my hand into my eye socket. "Damn it, damn it, *damn it.*"

What had I done to deserve this? To deserve kindness and care? I was a freak, a nobody, someone who hurt everyone who came near them...

But maybe it didn't have to be that way.

I blinked the saltwater out of my eyes. Yes – maybe this thing that I could do, this path it had taken me on – maybe it was all to lead me here.

To him.

After all, with him, I didn't feel like a freak. And now, he knew the truth and he still wanted to be near me.

Maybe it was time I started trusting more people again. Chief among them, myself. All my life, I'd hidden pieces of who I was from other people, never believing that all of me was worth loving. Never believing that all of me deserved to exist. Running from myself, I had nearly lost all of who I was in the day-to-day grind of survival.

Well, it was time to stop running.

My mind made up, I strode inside, moving down the hallway towards the master bedroom suite and pushing the door open without knocking. Sylvia and Kassandra stood in the center of the room, the latter buttoning up a pressed white blouse, while the former stood behind her, affixing small, bright gold flowers to the knots of her Dutch braid.

"I want to come tonight," I announced, my jaw set.

The two women stared at me as if I had just announced my intention to run naked down the walk of fame. One of the gold flowers slipped from between Sylvia's fingers, dropping to the floor with a tinkle. The sound seemed to reboot both of them, with Sylvia stepping back and stooping down to pick it up, and Kassandra starting towards me, shaking her head.

"That is not a good idea," she answered.

"I'm in this." I pointed at the floor, my hand shaking only a little. "My life is in danger because of this fucker. I want to watch him squirm." Looking from Kassandra to Syliva and back again, I lifted and dropped my shoulders. "So, that's it: I'm coming."

Kassandra opened her mouth to object but then shut it, seeing something in my face that made her reconsider. She cast a pleading glance at Sylvia, who stepped forward but gave a shrug as well, seemingly indicating that if anyone was going to stop me it was going to have to be Kassandra herself. The den leader let out a beleaguered sigh.

"How are we going to get her through the front door?" said Kassandra, looking me up and down as if I was a problematic piece of furniture she was trying to fit into a U-Haul.

Sylvia clicked her tongue off the roof of her mouth, her head falling to one side as she grinned. "I have an idea."

Thin heels clattering across the floor, she took a few steps towards the hallway. "Andy!"

My heart crawled up into my throat at the sound of his approaching footsteps. I had hoped to avoid telling him of my intentions until the last possible moment, but it looked like that wasn't going to happen. He turned the corner into the main room, fingers fiddling with the buttons on the cuffs of a crisp purple dress shirt that was halfway done up.

"Yeah?" said Andy as he entered, stopping in the archway as he saw me standing there.

I looked away from him quickly, not wanting to read his expression. I didn't want to know how he might be feeling about me. That would just lead me to thinking about how I was feeling about him and that was...complicated at the moment.

"You two are..." Sylvia made a sound in the back of her throat and then intertwined her pointer fingers around each other. "...together, right?"

I jerked my head up, all thoughts about not looking at Andy forgotten in a flash of embarrassed panic. Andy immediately took a step back from the three of us, his eyes widening as he stuttered, "Uh–I–ah–"

"That's a yes." Sylvia rocked back onto her heels, turning around to face Kassandra with a huge grin on her face. "There you go! Problem solved: he's claimed her."

"Oh, Dios ayúdame," groaned Andy, slapping his hand against his forehead. "Miss Laurent, I don't–"

"What the– claimed me?" I repeated, my voice dripping with disgust.

Sylvia ignored our reactions, her smile undimmed as she nodded. "See, if he's claimed you as his mate, it's no problem that you're coming along. It's no problem that you know about us, it's no problem with anything!" She rolled her eyes heavenward. "I am *such* a genius. You're welcome."

"Coming along?" Andy's blush began to fade, his jaw clenching as he moved towards me. "Shaye, you're coming with us tonight?"

"I've already told her it's not a good idea," said Kassandra, rolling her eyes.

"That's putting it mildly," he scoffed. "Shaye, you're going to be a human in a house full of werewolves. Does that sound like a place you want to be?"

Clenching my hands at my sides, I glared at him. "Uh, how exactly is that different from where I am now?" I held up my hand, silencing his rebuttal before he could utter a syllable. "Andy, I'm in this. You can't keep me out of it. You've tried, and you can't. I keep having visions about you, about your den, and I don't know why." Shrugging, I looked around at the ensemble of wolves, almost daring someone to disagree with me. "Maybe if I go tonight, I'll get some answers."

The trio swapped stares. Kassandra broke the silence, fanning her hand out flat against her chest. "It's a crazy enough idea, I think it just might work. Maybe it'll shake Lazlo up, make him even more prone to doing what we want."

I shook my head once, slicing my hand through the air as I frowned. "I don't want to be claimed by anyone though. And I'm certainly not a mate, no one is mating with me."

Andy held up his hands. "It's not – it's not quite like she's making it sound."

"It sounds pretty damn gross," I sputtered.

"It can just be for tonight," said Andy, rubbing the back of his neck as he winced. "But she's right – it will keep you safe." He stopped rubbing his neck, his gaze going blank as he stared at the floor. "Well, in theory."

Gritting my teeth, I shrugged. "I guess theory will have to do."

"Now, let's talk about *this*," interjected Sylvia, stepping between Andy and I and gesturing up and down at all of me, her lips pursed. "This will all have to change."

Face scrunching up in confusion, I turned to Kassandra, my mouth open, but she cut me off with a shake of her head. "You'll have to look like you belong."

"What do I look like now?"

"Like you've been living on the street for ten years." Sylvia waved her hands in the air and started to usher me out of the living room and down the hall. "Don't worry, this'll be easy. I'll make a few quick calls and we'll have you up to snuff in no time. You're about my size, so you can just use one of my dresses..."

The rest of the day was a blur of preparations, the likes of which I hadn't experienced since my prom night lifetimes ago. There were dresses to try on, nails to do, even a hair-stylist who arrived, looked at my head, and clucked at me sadly before settling in to work, gossiping with Sylvia all the while.

At the end of it all, I stood alone in an enormous master bathroom, staring at myself in a floor length mirror. I wobbled my head from side to side, playing with the asymmetrically long side of my blonde hair. I ran my light pink nails, kept short at my request, over the shorter side of my haircut, examining the way the strands had been cropped at the base of my neck. Frowning, I stepped back, looking at my reflection, trying and failing to be clinical as I watched the way the fabric of the strapless cocktail dress clung to my hips.

"Shaye?" I heard Andy's steps drawing closer. "You in here? We're ready to head–"

He stopped just inside the doorway. His eyes widened. I swear to God, I thought he was about to laugh. But instead, he just stood there, staring, his eyes running circuits over me.

"Do I look that stupid?" I asked, tucking the longer part of my hair back behind my ear, my gaze falling to the floor.

Jerking awake as if from a dream, he hummed, "Hm?"

We stared at each other in silence for a few moments before I gestured to myself, lifting a brow in question to prompt him again.

Andy shook his head, leaning towards me with wide eyes, panic oozing from him. "Stupid? What, no! No, no way!" Bringing his hand up to his forehead, he let out an obviously forced laugh. "Sorry, no, you don't look stupid. You..." He dropped his hand to his side. "You actually look beautiful, Shaye. Muy elegante."

The unexpected compliment made me flush, and I turned to face the mirror, readjusting the neckline of the ensemble with a grimace.

"You don't have to do this, you know," he said from behind me.

I looked at him in the mirror. "Yes, I do. I've spent all my life running scared, and it's only made things worse for the people I care about." I ran my hands down the shiny gold velvet folds at my abdomen. "I'm not running any more. I'm done letting people get hurt instead of me."

"No one expects you to be a martyr, Shaye."

"I know," I said, my voice growing quiet, my eyes unfocusing as my head dropped below my shoulders. "I just...don't want to be a coward." Staring at the top of my black heels, I heard the tremor in my voice and hated myself for it. "Andy, you should know – I really am sorry. You were right. I should've told you. I was scared and I–"

"Shaye."

I risked looking back in the mirror. Andy was watching me, a smile on his face, his brows drawn to a point. "It's okay. I get it." He shifted his weight onto his back foot, sliding one hand into his trouser pocket. "But from here on out, we tell each other the truth, okay? No matter what."

I nodded, swallowing hard. "Okay." I looked myself up and down and my lips twisted into a grimace. "You want the truth? I feel like I'm going to be sick."

"Well, that's not good," he said, lifting a hand up to my shoulder, but stopping just shy of touching me. "Are you going to be okay?"

As I watched my reflection, a tight, pained smile crawled across my lips. "It *is* stupid." I swallowed hard and shook my head, pulling myself up straight. "I– I haven't worn anything like this in years." My smile tipped to one side, turning again into a grimace. "It's just...bringing back some memories."

Andy let his head fall to one side. "Bad memories?"

"No. That's the problem." I rubbed at the back of my neck. "Good memories." I dropped my hand to my side, and my eyes looked past Andy as I turned around to face him at last. "But you can't go back, you know?"

"I do," said Andy, nodding earnestly. "I do, yeah. We can only go forward." He offered me his arm and gave me a small smile. "You ready?"

I wrapped my arm around his and nodded. "As I'll ever be."

~ 18 ~

CHAPTER 18

Andy

Stepping out of the back of the sleek black Escalade that had brought up the rear of our three-car convoy, I let out a deep breath through my nose, staring at the facade of the Bel Air headquarters of Sangre Sagrada.

This was the last place I should be.

"Andy?"

I looked back into the car. Shaye stared up at me from the back seat, one foot on the running board. "Everything okay?"

I nodded, offering her a hand to help her out of the car. It was the first time I'd ever lied to her. If this was the last place I should be, Shaye shouldn't even know it existed.

This was going to be an interesting night.

Kassandra had brought along a small handful of Nameless security staff, just in case things went as poorly as I suspected they might. They mustered in front of the first car, standing to attention as Kassandra exited.

"You all wait out here," said Kassandra. She looked over the assembled security personnel. "Remember – we are guests, and we are going to be gracious ones. Nobody does anything without running it by me or Sylvia first. Alright?"

A chorus of assent went up from the group, who then spread out along the drive and front of the house. Kassandra turned back around to face us, a grim sort of smile on her face, her hands palm up in front of her.

"Shall we?"

A nod was all I could manage. Kassandra offered her arm to Sylvia, who took it with a smile, and the pair started forward, leaving the rest of us to trail behind after them. Caleb and I took up flanking positions around Shaye, who walked slightly ahead of us, her chin held high, her eyes forward.

Sangre Sagrada security, not to mention half of the guests there for the evening's festivities, must have seen us coming. The front door was wide open, but that was just about the only thing warm about our welcome. The entryway was lined with menacing, grimacing wolves, hands clenched at their sides, and one of them, a man I recognized as the security head, Barros, stepped forward when we entered, lifting his hand.

"Bienvenida a Los Ángeles," he said, unsmiling. "My name is Barros. I'm afraid, Señora Arnaud, that some of your party members are not welcome in this house."

Kassandra stopped, unwinding herself from Sylvia as she spoke. "Let's leave that for Doña Sangre to decide, shall we?"

Barros gritted his teeth but shrugged his shoulders. By this point we had drawn quite a crowd into the entryway – seemingly all the wolves in California had gathered to gawk and whisper, dressed to kill and judging by the expressions on their faces, very much in the mood to do so with the unexpected appearance of Caleb, Shaye, and myself on their doorstep.

"You certainly know how to piss people off, don't you Vazquez?" muttered Kassandra from the side of her mouth, her rough tone in direct contradiction with the pleasant smile on her face. "I haven't felt this many daggers in my back in a long while."

"I told you this wasn't going to work," I hissed, leaning forward to speak over her shoulder, my eyes darting around the room, looking for exits I knew for a fact didn't exist. "We should–"

She gave a curt shake of her head. "Just relax and let me do the talking."

Glaring, a sharp retort was on the tip of my tongue, but I swallowed it down with a gulp when I saw Emilia moving through the crowd in front of us. She broke through the ring of people with Lazlo close behind her. She was dressed head to toe in a gorgeous red evening gown, her long black hair loose around her shoulders, a simple gold necklace hanging from her long neck.

"Kassandra Arnaud, Sylvia Laurent!" Doña Sangre opened her arms wide as she strode towards us, her smile dazzling. "Welcome to Los Angeles!"

"Thank you, Doña Sagrada," said Kassandra, coming to a stop in the entryway and offering her hand in greeting.

Emilia took Kassandra's hand lightly, shaking it once before releasing it. She nodded to Sylvia, her smile never dimming. "I certainly hope you'll enjoy yourselves this evening–"

Emilia stopped talking as soon as she laid eyes on me, standing behind Kassandra's left shoulder. She paled for a moment, her gaze flickering to Caleb, and then to Shaye. Eyes widening, color returned to her cheeks in a rush of angry red.

Kassandra made a big show of looking around us, her forehead wrinkled. "Is everything alright, Doña Sangre?"

Emilia stared at Kassandra through half-lidded eyes. "You bring two denless and a human to my house, and you ask me if everything is alright?" Drawing herself up to her full height, she clenched one hand at her side. "Explain yourself. Immediately."

The murmuring of the crowd intensified, growing louder and decidedly unfriendly. A blonde werewolf with short, cropped hair stepped forward from my left and, sneering, placed a restraining hand on my shoulder, jerking me backwards.

In an instant, the young wolf was on the ground, one of Kassandra's hands around his throat, the other wrapped tight around the wrist of the hand with which he had touched me. Crouched beside him on one knee, the muscles beneath her plain white shirt rippled and began to strain at the fabric, her claws lengthening to cut into the flesh of the offending wolf's neck.

"If you want a war with the Nameless," growled Kassandra, extra teeth crowding her mouth as she snarled. "That is a good way to start one."

Choking, the blonde man pulled uselessly at the hand at his throat, squirming against the floor.

"Explain," repeated Emilia, louder than before, the wolf clear in her voice as well. "Now."

Kassandra stood slowly, still glowering at the wolf on the ground. Tugging at the bottom of her suit jacket, she reluctantly tore her gaze away from the prone figure to address Emilia directly, the muscles in her tight jaw rippling. "Andy Vazquez and Caleb Beck *are* denless. But they are currently acting as consultants for us on several matters, some of which pertain to your den, some of which do not."

She looked back at Shaye. "Now, as for the human..." Clearing her throat, she tossed her hand out towards me. "She belongs to Vazquez. The Nameless are much more open about that sort of thing than your den, as I understand it."

A renewed ripple of murmurs greeted Kassandra's words. I felt even more eyes on me than before, if such a thing were possible. Some people near the edges of the entryway even pointed at Shaye, turning over their shoulders to whisper excitedly to those crowding in behind them. I took a step closer to her, my hand hovering over the small of her back.

Doña Sangre flushed red, her claws lengthening at her side. She looked from me to Shaye, her wide eyes almost bulging with rage, before returning her attention to Kassandra. "You would risk the exposure of our world?" hissed Emilia, stressing each word as she bristled with righteous indignation.

"I risk nothing." Kassandra looked down her nose at the smaller woman, sneering openly. "You, on the other hand, have a rogue wolf hunting openly in your city."

All the air left the room. A sucking, void-like silence took its place. Emilia stilled, like a rabbit that had just been spotted by a coyote and hoped to survive by blending into the surrounding scrub brush. After a moment, she released a deep breath, her gaze slowly sliding away from Kassandra and back to me.

I saw it in her eyes. My betrayal of her, of my family, was now complete.

There would be no going back now.

Lowering her voice, Kassandra took a small step forward, spreading her arms wide. "Now, do you want to do this here? Or would you rather we retire to a more private setting?"

Emilia's mouth snapped open, but before she could speak, Lazlo put a hand on her arm, leaning in to whisper into the shell of her ear. Some of the fire in her eyes died, her face relaxing ever so slightly as she listened to her advisor. After a moment she gave a curt nod in his direction and he stepped forward, indicating the larger room to our left with a broad sweep of his arm.

"Through here, please," he said, a sickly excuse for a smile on his face.

Doña Sangre had already begun to stride through the common room, heading for what I knew to be one of the small, private dining spaces near the back of the house. Kassandra gave a nod and an equally anemic smile to Lazlo and followed after her, Sylvia on her arm. Caleb fell in on the other side of Shaye and I, leaving Lazlo to bring up the rear. I felt his eyes digging into the back of my head as we walked, his and dozens of others, but I did my best to keep a neutral expression on my face, my shoulders loose, my grip on Shaye tight.

We moved through the large common room, down a high-ceilinged hallway, and stopped at a room with a beautiful ash door. Emilia, her hand on the doorknob, stared back at us, her jaw tight.

"The human bitch waits outside," said Emilia, the hatred clear in her words.

Kassandra gave a quick shake of her head. "The human goes where Vazquez goes, and Vazquez is going inside." She took a step closer to the shorter woman, leaning in and lowering her voice slightly. "No offense intended, Doña Sangre, but your den does still practice the Sacrament, does it not?"

Emilia gritted her teeth and for a moment I thought she would refuse to answer. But then, she inclined her head. "Certain members still do."

260 ~ ROBIN JEFFREY

Kassandra tilted her head to one side, giving a small smile. "Then you understand our hesitation to leave the human unattended."

"With respect," piped up Lazlo from the back of our little trope, moving to stand next to Emilia, "There's no full moon tonight."

Kassandra lifted her brows, her smile unwavering. "Still. We'd appreciate your kindness."

Lazlo and Emilia exchanged glances. With visible reluctance, Emilia opened the door and gestured for us all to enter.

The room was small, but not cramped. A round, thick wooden table sat in the center, its surface polished to an almost blinding shine. High-backed wooden chairs with velvet cushions were placed around the table, and around the walls of the room hung portraits of Sangre Sagrada's former leaders, stately and somber.

"She will not sit at the table with us," pronounced Emilia, pulling out a chair with one hand, pointedly not looking at the person about whom she was talking.

Kassandra waved her hand at Shaye, indicating a place for her to stand along the wall. "Acceptable."

Shaye stood to the left of the seat Kassandra took, clasping her hands behind her back. While everyone settled into the chairs, a young male wolf entered the room with an open bottle of wine and a handful of glasses. He moved around the table once, placing the empty glasses in front of each of us, before starting the circuit again, stopping at each person's side to pour a generous portion of red liquid into the crystal receptacles. Kassandra put her hand over the top of her glass, shaking her head.

"You won't drink?" pressed Emilia, all warmth from her voice now conspicuously absent.

"No, thank you," said Kassandra, smiling politely.

Sylvia stopped the server with a wave of her hand, her eyes going comically wide. "Is that a Sine Qua Non Patine Syrah?" She leaned back from the table, indicating her wine glass eagerly. "Oh, yes, please. I'll take as much as you're willing to give me."

Emilia waited in silence as everyone was served, her gaze fixed on me. I did my best not to squirm under her examination, but I also couldn't bring myself to meet her eyes for more than a few seconds.

When everyone had their beverages, her eyes at last slid off me and refocused on the woman now sitting across from her. "I'm not sure what Mr. Vazquez has told you about our...situation, but–"

"He's told us enough." Kassandra folded her hands on top of the table, shifting forward in her seat and looking straight at Emilia. "Enough that I want to assuage any fears you may have about the Nameless."

Emilia lifted a sculpted brow and reached for her glass of wine. "Oh?"

"I know that we've gained a certain reputation as of late for..." Kassandra looked up at the ceiling as she rolled her shoulders back, tongue probing the inside of her cheek. "...let's call it aggressive expansion." She shook her head, her high blonde braid swinging behind her. "But we only engage in such behavior when our involvement in other dens' affairs would be of mutual benefit. It's clear to us that no such involvement from the Nameless is needed when it comes to Sangre Sagrada's affairs."

I watched Lazlo as Kassandra spoke, searching for any hint that might confirm what Shaye had seen in her dreams. When Kassandra announced that the Nameless would not be taking a hand in Sangre Sagrada's affairs, his eyes widened, the careful, tight smile he had kept on his face disappearing slowly, like the tide receding from the beach. Lips pursing, he shifted in his seat, gaze flickering between the two den leaders.

For her part, Emilia swirled her wine around her glass, staring at Kassandra from beneath a furrowed brow. Lips parted, she gave a cough of disbelief and said, "¿Realmente? You expect me to believe that you have no interest in taking over my territory?"

"None," insisted Kassandra. "Furthest thing from our minds, in fact. We don't want to do anything to jeopardize our mutual monetary interests in this region, and those are largely built upon your infrastructure."

Shaking her head, Emilia rested her arms against the smooth black tablecloth. "I'm sorry – I don't think I understand."

"You have a rogue wolf on your hands." Kassandra shrugged. She pulled back from the table, crossing her legs. "It's unfortunate, but it does happen. Vazquez here assures us, however, that you have the matter well under control."

Lazlo's face clouded, his hands involuntarily flexing into fists, which he promptly slid off the table and into his lap. Emilia stared at me in shock, her lips parted. "I– Andoni, you– you said this?"

A curt nod was my response. Emilia drew herself up in her chair, taking a deep breath as if she were about to shout, but she was cut off by Kassandra, who leaned across the table, brows raised.

"Is that not the case?" asked Kassandra, her tone prompting.

Snapping back to the moment at hand, Emilia straightened in her seat, turning back to the head of the Nameless and adopting an imperious air as she replied. "It is. Of course. Yes."

The blonde wolf gave a cheery nod, smiling wide. "Wonderful. We're very glad to hear it." She relaxed back into her chair, folding her hands on top of her knee. "In that case, our business here can hopefully be conducted quickly and without incident."

Lazlo leaned in across the table towards Emilia, turning in his seat so he was only half facing the rest of us. "Doña Sangre, I think–"

"What about the human?" said Emilia, waving away Lazlo with a flick of her wrist.

Lazlo's jaw clenched, but he receded without another word. I smiled at him, even though doing so caused me physical pain.

"What about her?" repeated Kassandra, the bridge of her nose wrinkled in confusion.

"She..." Emilia struggled to put on a cavalier smile. "Well, I've been led to believe that she witnessed one of the rogue wolf's attacks. That she claims to know the identity of this wolf."

"Really?" Kassandra lifted her brows and threw her arm over the back of her chair, twisting around to face the human in question. "Shaye? Do you think you could identify the rogue wolf?"

I tensed in my chair. I had been dreading this moment. The truth was I didn't know how Shaye was going to react to being put on the spot. I didn't know how she would hold up under the pressure of being in the same room as the man who had not just murdered, but eaten, someone close to her.

It was a lot to ask of anyone.

The back of my chair vibrated, and I looked up over my shoulder to see Shaye standing there, her hand gripping the high back. She didn't look at me, but instead focused on Emilia. The corners of her mouth pulled down in a frown, she nodded, lifting her chin a little as she spoke. "I did see a werewolf kill someone. Jason. He was just a kid – my friend." Her brown eyes slid over to Lazlo. My breath stilled.

Then she smiled. It was a sickly, strained, laughable smile, but it was there, nonetheless. Head tilted to one side, she dropped her hand to her side. "But it all happened so fast. And it was dark." Her voice flat and emotionless, Shaye stared unblinking at Lazlo, her obviously fake smile unchanging. "No, I don't think I could say who it was."

"Well!" Kassandra lifted her hand in the air and smiled, a far more natural and convincing expression than the smear still lingering across Shaye's lips. "There you have it." Her expression sobered for a moment. "As for her witnessing the attack, that is most unfortunate. But since Vazquez has elected to take her as his mate – well, that solves that problem, doesn't it?"

"Yes." Emilia swallowed and looked down at her hands, flexing them a bit as she did so. "Yes, I suppose it does." Shaking her head, she looked up after a moment, a smile that didn't reach her eyes. "You received our proposed schedule for the rest of our discussions? Is it acceptable to you?"

"Yes, absolutely."

Emilia pushed back from the table and stood, gesturing to the door. "Good. Then in that case, I suggest we go and enjoy the party."

"We'd love to," replied Kassandra, mirroring our host and offering her arm to Sylvia as she rose.

We all started to follow her from the dining room, with Shaye and I bringing up the rear. I touched her gently on the elbow and was unsurprised to feel her shaking.

"You okay?" I whispered to her.

Her face was an unreadable mask, her jaw clenched hard enough to hammer in nails. "Yeah," she muttered through gritted teeth. "Yeah, I'm okay." She glanced at me from the corner of her eyes, and her facade broke slightly, a flicker of warmth in her sepia orbs. "Thanks."

Music grew louder and soon we were back in the main part of the house, walking through the parting crowd of wolves to the center of the house with Emilia in the lead.

The room buzzed and hummed, but the talking dropped to a low murmur when our group reentered the space, all eyes on us.

Kassandra smiled broadly, turning to face Emilia as she said, "It's very kind of you to welcome us in such grand style."

"It's the least we can do for our friends," Emilia said, managing the sentiment without a hint of an ironic sneer. She reached out to shake Kassandra's hand, gesturing to the room at large before backing away. "Enjoy yourselves, won't you?"

~ 19 ~

CHAPTER 19

Shaye

The hairs on the back of my neck refused to go down. Goosebumps prickled across my bare skin, and despite the warmth of the crowded room, I had to concentrate on not shivering.

Everywhere I looked people were watching me. I felt like an exotic fish in a crowded tank of sharks. I just hoped no one was feeling hungry.

Kassandra and Sylvia had people they needed to talk with, connections to make and old alliances to solidify. I soon grew bored with following them around the party, and asked Andy and Caleb if we could take a breather at the far side of the large common room, close to the foot of a large staircase. They were attentive and obliging escorts and we quickly cut through the crowd to a quiet spot by an enormous potted cactus.

"Phew," I said aloud, trying to mask some of my nerves with nonchalance. "Is there always this many people here?"

"No," said Caleb, tugging at his chin as he surveyed the crowd rolling out in front of us. "Looks like a lot of the wolves in Southern California turned up for the occasion." His eyes lit up as someone called his name. He lifted his hand in a wave and shot a quick, "I'll be right back" at us before moving off into the horde.

Andy stepped out from our alcove to waylay a passing server with a tray of drinks, taking one in each hand before twisting on his heel and heading back towards me.

"Here," said Andy, offering me a glass of champagne and pivoting to stand beside me.

"Thanks." I took the glass in one hand, bringing it up to my lips to hide my grimace as I turned towards him, pitching my voice at a rough whisper. "I feel like everyone is staring at me."

"Don't kid yourself," he said, a tight, small smile on his face. "They are." He nodded to a werewolf who walked past us, ogling us openly. "I don't think a human has ever stepped foot in this place."

Swallowing down a small sip of expensive alcohol, I shook my head. "I don't get it." I gestured to myself, eyes jumping around the room. "There's more of us than you. Surely you all must work with humans from time to time."

"Yeah," Andy admitted, rolling his shoulders back. "But they're just that: workers. Underlings. They don't get to come here. To meet Doña Sangre? That never happens."

"That's wild." I shifted my weight from foot to foot, my gaze still wandering. My eyes widened and I tapped Andy on the shoulder. "Uh oh, speak of the devil."

Andy whipped around, his cheeks losing some color as he saw Doña Sangre approaching us through the crowd, stopping here and there to shake hands and exchange pleasantries with other guests, but her attention clearly focused on us.

"Mierda."

The slight, muscular woman stopped in front of us, jutting her hip out to one side as she surveyed us with the same air as a person looking at a particularly nasty car accident.

"So," said Doña Sangre, tossing her long hair behind her shoulder with one hand. "You're going to bind yourself to a human, Andoni?"

"Emilia, I–" Andy started, but was quickly cut off by the woman herself, who turned away from him, her eyes burrowing into my face.

"And you," she barreled on, pulling her upper lip away from her teeth in a sneer. "You want to be a part of this world? You want this life?"

I met her intrusive stare evenly. I lifted my flute of champagne to my lips, took a slow sip and swallowed before answering. "When the alternative is a violent and painful death, wanting doesn't exactly come into it," I said. I lifted my brow and tilted my head to one side. "Does it?"

Doña Sangre looked down her nose at me and smiled with all her teeth. She gave a loud harrumph, before nodding in seeming approval. "Smart." She returned her attention to Andy, her eyes half-hidden behind her eye-shadowed lids. "Smarter than your last one, at least, Andoni."

I watched as her barb landed on Andy like a punch to the gut, the wind leaving him in a gasp. He stared at her, wide eyed and unable to move. But she didn't stay to relish her hit, leaning forward, words of congratulations working through her gritted teeth like a curse. "Blessings on you both," she hissed, stalking off into the crowd.

I watched Doña Sangre walk away, waiting until I was sure she was out of ear shot before turning to Andy, my nose wrinkling as I asked, "Smarter than your last one? What the fuck did she mean by that?"

Andy drained his drink and shook his head before he answered. "It doesn't matter. Don't worry about it."

There was a wall in his words that I supposed I deserved, but it still stung to crash into it. I looked away from him, focusing instead on the top of my shoes.

"Okay," I said. I straightened, but forced myself not to look at him, instead taking a drink of my champagne as I surveyed the milling crowd of partygoers in front of us. "Sure, yeah – whatever."

We stood in silence. I glanced at him from the corner of my eye and caught him doing the same. I looked away quickly, clearing my throat.

Sighing, he turned towards me fully, lowering his voice. "Look, I... I fucked up. Before this. About a year ago." Gesturing to me with his empty glass, he avoided my gaze. "Humans..." He struggled with the right words, shifting his weight from foot to foot and grimacing. "Bottom line is, you aren't supposed to know about us, and I did something really stupid and told someone, a human, who I–" Swallowing, he looked down at the carpet, eyes closing. "–what I was. It didn't end well. For anyone."

I swiveled to look up at his downturned face, my arms crossed over my chest. "Well, why'd you tell them?"

He looked at me askance once more. "What?"

I shook my head. "You know the rules. Why'd you tell them the big secret?"

Swallowing hard, his Adam's apple bobbing, Andy shifted his weight from foot to foot. "I guess I thought we were in love." Eyes opening, he turned away from me to place his glass on a passing waitstaff's tray. "I was wrong, turns out."

Frozen in place, I stared openly at him. He looked back at me, his expression blank, yet somehow still expectant. I forced myself to blink and stuttered, "I–uh–wow–I–oh. O-kay."

Snorting out a mirthless laugh, Andy shoved his hands in his trouser pockets, slouching as he turned away from me and back towards the living room. "Like I said, it doesn't really matter." He rolled his head around his neck. "But it caused a whole lot of trouble for the den. I didn't help, I got in the way, and–"

"You're on people's shit list," I finished for him, nodding. "Or you already were, and now you're even deeper in the shit."

That got a smile from him, weak and perfunctory as it was. "Pretty much, yeah."

I thoughtfully swished a mouthful of liquor. Swallowing it after a long moment, I fixed him with a pointed stare, lifting my brow. "So...you have a thing for humans, huh?"

Grimacing, Andy shuddered theatrically. "Oh no, don't – don't make it sound like *that*."

Smirking, I pivoted to face him, bringing my head closer to his shoulder. "What, like what?"

"Like a–a fetish or something." His volume dropping, his hand came up to slice through the air. "It is *not* like that."

"It's not?" I teased. "What's it like then?"

"I've been in relationships with other wolves before too, you know," he shot back, his shoulders stiff, his posture defensive.

"So, you swing both ways," I nodded, bringing the fingers of my free hand up to stroke my chin. "Interesting, interesting..."

Andy groaned, throwing his head back as he screwed his eyes shut. I grinned at this reaction, delighting in my ability to needle him. I was about to continue when a more serious thought struck me and I sobered enough to ask, "Hey... why didn't Doña Sangre kick you out after that first time? Why'd she let you stay in the den?"

"First offense?" he offered, shrugging his shoulders. "I don't know. But she stood up for me – vouched for me." He pushed his hand back through his hair, his jaw tight. "That's why I owe it to her to try and protect the den now."

I thought of the way Doña Sangre had looked at me. The venom in her gaze. The hurt. I looked back at Andy. If I had been so close to him, if he had been my soldier... well, I certainly wouldn't have been able to resist the hope that he might one day view me as something more than a superior.

Oh.

She had stood up for him, protected him, and he had repaid her by sleeping with another woman.

Ouch.

"What?" he said sharply.

Realizing that I had been staring at him for several long moments, I lifted my brows and turned away, rolling my lips under my teeth. "Oh, uh, nothing," I said.

"It's clearly not nothing," he parried, eyes narrowing.

"I just..." I wiggled my raised brows at him, grinning awkwardly. "Come on. You know, right? She *likes* you."

He blinked, frowning as he looked down at me. "Why'd you say it like that?"

"She likes you," I repeated, this time in a sing-song voice, swinging my hips from side to side. Reaching up, I poked Andy in the chest. "She's just dying to make little puppies with you."

Rolling his eyes, he brought his hands up to his tie, fiddling with the knot. "Jesus, what are you, five?" he sneered, before quickly adding: "Anyway, she is not."

I opened my mouth to goad him further, but quickly lost my train of thought when I spied the flush of blood underneath the collar of his fancy shirt. My eyes went wide, and my mouth fell into an 'o'.

breath, he let it out in a huff. "But not for a long, long time. I have my own place now."

But I was only half listening to his meandering explanation of his living situation. My attention was fixed on the floor to ceiling windows, through which the slightest glimmer of the city below was shining. "I bet you get a killer view of the city from here."

His eyes lit up. He smiled broadly. "Want to see?"

~ 20 ~

CHAPTER 20

Andy

Doing my best to keep us unobserved, I led Shaye up the house's main staircase to where the bedroom suites were located. I knew exactly which room to show her and, as luck would have it, whoever was currently living there had left the door unlocked.

Holding her hand, we walked through the room, and I drew back the curtains which led to the sliding glass door. She gasped aloud and I smiled. The door let out onto a small, round balcony from which you could see the entirety of Los Angeles laid out like a jumbled, sprawling collection of precious jewels.

Opening the door, Shaye rushed out ahead of me, a broad smile cutting across her face.

"Holy shit," exclaimed Shaye, her upper body stretched over the balcony railing, the slight breeze blowing the hair out of her wide eyes.

"This wasn't my room when I lived here," I clarified, standing back from her, enjoying her enjoyment more than I had any right to. "But I always wished it was."

She laughed, nodding as she took in the sight of the glittering metropolis below. "Well, yeah! I can see why! Wow..." Letting out a deep breath, she relaxed against the rail, folding her arms on top of each other, toying with the gold bracelet on her right wrist. "Would you just...look at it? Who knew? Los Angeles is actually really beautiful."

"Yeah," I looked over the city, slipping my hands into my trouser pockets. "Most things are from a distance."

The night was warm, with a pleasant breeze blowing through the hills, and for a few minutes we fell into an entirely comfortable silence. It was astonishing to me how easy it was to be with Shaye, even when things were really the most complicated they'd ever been in my life. I wandered to the far edge of the balcony, past the pool-style lounge chair that sat near the door and propped my foot up on the bottom railing. I looked up into the night sky, my gaze focusing on the waning moon above us.

When Shaye cleared her throat, I didn't immediately turn to face her. It wasn't until she spoke that she had my full attention once more.

"So. Did you and Doña Sangre ever...you know...get together?"

I started a little at her insinuation, whipping around to stare at her with wide eyes. "What? No!"

Shaye didn't turn to look at me, keeping her gaze straight ahead even as her eyes narrowed. "Come on. Don't say it like that – like it's so unthinkable. She's a gorgeous woman. Wolf. Whatever."

"I don't–" I pushed my hand through my hair, grimacing. "No, absolutely not. We grew up together. It'd be...wrong."

Shaye gave a derisive snort, scowling and dropping her gaze to the railing in front of her. She picked at a piece of dirt that had landed on the wrought iron, flicking it away as she grunted, "Well, she clearly doesn't think so."

As I watched her, the realization of what she was asking and why struck me like a baseball bat to the side of the head. Blinking rapidly, I stared at Shaye's back, seeing her and not seeing her at the same time.

There was no way, right?

"Well, I can't help what she thinks," I murmured. Drawing my hand down my jaw, I smirked, looking Shaye up and down appraisingly. "You're not...are...are you jealous?"

Shaye's shoulders tensed instantly, but she didn't turn around to look at me as she shot out a gruff, "Fuck you."

My heart leapt in my chest. I held the tip of my tongue between my teeth, struggling not to laugh, knowing that that would be the absolute worst thing I could do under these circumstances. Still, just knowing that Shaye was jealous...that she didn't like the thought of me with another woman...that she even cared about me that way...

It was intoxicating.

I ran my tongue along my teeth and took a breath, trying and failing to compose myself. "That's not a 'no', princesa," I said at last, stepping in close behind her. I rested my hands softly on her shoulders and leaned forward, my lips a hairsbreadth from her ear. "Do you know how beautiful you look tonight?"

Shaye coughed out a laugh. "Please. I look–"

I shook my head, spinning her around before she could resist me. "If the next words out of your mouth are in any way self-deprecating, I promise you, you'll regret it."

There was a flash of defiance in her eyes and for a moment I thought she might have misconstrued my threat. But, when I reached up to stroke the column of her throat with the tips of my fingers, her gaze softened.

"Oh," she said quietly, leaning into my touch. "Well..." Shaye swallowed, her eyes darting towards the downstairs floor of the retreat, where we could still hear muffled music playing, before returning to my face.

"Yes?" I said, prompting, trailing my hand down her arm.

She smiled wickedly, her hand reaching out to grasp mine. "What can I say? I do like pissing you off."

Biting my bottom lip in excitement, I let out a laugh. "Yes," I said, moving us backwards until my legs hit the side of the lounge chair. "You do."

I sat down perpendicular to the recline of the chair and continued pulling Shaye forward, forcing her to hike up the skirt of her already short dress and straddle me, bringing her knees up on either side of my thighs as she climbed on top of the lounge chair, settling into my lap with a laugh.

"Andy, what–?"

"I've wanted to do this since I saw you in this dress," I answered, placing my hands on either side of her head and guiding her lips down to mine.

Her mouth was soft and warm. I drew her bottom lip between my teeth, sucking and flicking at the soft pout that seemed ever present on her face. She groaned and squirmed in my lap, the movement making my cock stiff and aching even faster than I anticipated. Answering back in kind, the tip of her tongue trailed along the top of my mouth, tickling the sensitive flesh there and making me shiver.

After a few long moments of this, I released her lips to focus some of my attention on her chest, at least the parts of it that were exposed and available to me. Shaye straightened to allow me access, hands petting the back of my neck as she cooed in pleasure.

I nipped and licked at the top of her breasts, and she leaned down to kiss the top of my head even before asking, "Should we get back to the party? People might–"

Moving up, I littered kisses across her exposed collarbone, shaking my head. "No one's going to miss us, trust me."

Her fingers dug into my shoulders with a possessiveness I would not have expected from her. "Not even your precious la Doña?"

Growling, I ground myself up into her center, relishing in the all too brief friction against my hard cock. "Does this feel like I'm thinking about her right now?" I rested my forehead against the side of her neck. "I've got one thing on my mind right now..."

I felt her lean back a little from me, the excitement in her voice palpable as she queried, "And what's that?"

Smiling, I lifted my head just enough to capture her earlobe in my teeth. "Get down on your knees and I'll show you."

"Ha!" Shaye pulled away to look me in the eye. I was delighted to see a wide grin across her face, even as she teased, "That's a little presumptuous, don't you think?"

"You said you wanted me in your mouth," I responded, shrugging a little. "No time like the present."

"I did say that didn't I," she said, squeezing her bottom lip between her teeth. "Well, I wouldn't want to be called a liar..."

Getting down on her knees on the bamboo mat laid out on the balcony, I wondered briefly if I should pass her a pillow or something more comfortable to rest on. But all coherent thoughts quickly left my head when she began rubbing at my stiff cock through my trousers, the tip of her tongue coming out to wet her lips.

She glanced up at me, smirking. "You going to help a girl out? Or do I have to do all the work around here?"

I immediately fumbled my belt loose and unfastened the button cinching the waist band of my trousers closed. I couldn't smother a sigh as I pulled the zipper down, the relief of pressure immediate and sweet. But the sigh turned into a strangled gasp when Shaye reached forward, sliding her hand into my boxer/briefs and pulling my cock out into the open.

"You really are...impressive, Andy," she said appreciatively, stroking me gently as her eyes moved over me.

"No te burles, querida," I whined, inching closer to the edge of the lounge chair.

Shaye smiled, shaking her head. "Oh, alright. Work, work, work..."

Slowly, almost reverently, her lips parted, and she took me into her mouth, her own eyes flickering shut as she got her first taste of me. My breath stuck in my throat as her fingers wrapped around the base of my shaft and she began to stroke what she couldn't fit in her mouth.

"Mierda," I grunted.

Shaye moaned around my cock, moving her hands as she sank down lower around me, wrapping her tongue around my shaft as she sucked at my head. Her fingers dug into my still clothed thighs, the soft pink nail polish she wore standing out against my black trousers.

I rested on my arms splayed out behind me, taking in deep, heaving breaths, my head thrown back, my eyes screwed shut. "Oh, I should've known you'd be good at this, princesa, with that mouth of yours..."

With excruciating slowness, she pushed me further and further inside her mouth, almost taking me down to the root before she smoothly drew back, lapping at my head with the tip of my tongue before starting all over again. It felt incredible, too much and not enough all at the same time. My mind hazy with pleasure, I was at first only vaguely aware of lifting my hand to thread my fingers through her hair, resting my palm against the back of her head. Before I could stop myself, I began fucking into her mouth in slow, languid thrusts, stopping only when I felt the resistance at the back of her throat.

When I felt Shaye's grip tighten on my legs I almost stopped, worried I was pushing her too far too fast. But when she began sucking enthusiastically at my cock every time I drew back, groaning at every push forward, I knew I was doing something right. She confirmed this for me when her right hand slid off my thigh and into my boxer/briefs, fondling and squeezing my balls as if to encourage me further.

"Si, princesa, touch me *there...*" I murmured, lifting my head up so I could watch her as we moved together.

The sight of Shaye in her beautiful dress on her knees, my hand in her silky blonde hair, her soft pink lips wrapped tight around my cock – I almost came right then and there. And that was before I realized what she was doing with her other hand.

My eyes widened, my lips parting as I panted out, "Dios, Shaye, are you...?"

Her hand buried between her legs, pleasuring herself, Shaye's sepia-toned eyes flickered up to meet mine.

Overwhelmed by the realization of what was happening, my arms began to shake, my head rolling back on my neck as I moaned. "¡Carajo! Princesa! Oh Shaye, fuck, you're going to make me come, you're going to make me–!"

Warm California air hit me, and I shuddered, the sharp realization that I was no longer in Shaye's mouth making me lurch forward, my eyes flickering open in time to come face to face with the woman herself, who kissed me open mouthed as she stepped out of her underwear, tossing them carelessly to one side.

When she finally released my lips, it was only so that she could more easily climb on top of me, her knees on either side of my hips as I stuttered out, "What–why–?" my brain fuzzy, understanding just beyond my reach, even as her intentions were perfectly clear.

"I need you," she said simply, panting a little with the effort of what we had been doing.

My hands came up around her waist automatically to steady her as she swayed above me. I was powerless to stop the shout that erupted from me when she buried my cock inside her soaking wet pussy.

For a few moments we didn't speak. We were past words, past anything but the sensations we were sharing, and they were as vast and impossible to capture as the true nature of a starry night over a desert vista.

I looked up at Shaye, riding me, and I almost had to look away. "Shaye, you're so beautiful." I held onto her tight, more tightly than I'd ever held on to anyone before, wishing I could feel her skin under my hands, frustrated with the fabric that separated us. "You really are so fucking beautiful."

Rising and falling over me, fucking me in a strong, steady rhythm, Shaye dragged her hands down my back, her head

288 ~ ROBIN JEFFREY

So why did I feel so goddamn happy?

"Andy?"

I gave a hum in response, opening my eyes and twisting around to see Shaye walking out of the bathroom on wobbly legs, a damp washcloth in her hand. She gestured to me with it once before tossing it in my direction.

Catching it one handed, I began to clean up as best as I could, smiling to myself.

"Do you think anybody downstairs heard us?" said Shaye, attempting to repair her disheveled ensemble.

I wiggled my head from side to side as I stood from the lounge chair, doing up my trousers and walking to the inner edge of the balcony. "Not if we're lucky." I indicated the downstairs part of the house with a nod of my head. "The music is pretty loud down there."

She lifted a disbelieving brow at me, smirking. "We weren't exactly quiet up here."

"And whose fault is that?" I responded, smiling in turn.

"Oh no," she laughed, shaking her finger at me. "No, no, you're not blaming this on me." She closed the distance between us in a few quick strides, pointing at me in an accusatory fashion. "You're the one who looked at me with those great big brown doe eyes of yours–"

"They are not big!" I exclaimed, hands fluttering up to my face.

"And practically begged me to go down on you," she finished, finger into my pectoral as she grinned.

"Ah, ah," I chided, grabbing her wrist and pulling her a step closer. "Who got on top of whom?"

"Your fault again," she responded readily, slipping her free arm around my waist and holding me against her. "For getting me so turned on."

Laughing, I nodded. "Bien, bien," I said, internally thrilled by this new, easy intimacy between us. "I'll take the fall for this one." Reaching up, I flicked the tip of her nose with my finger. "On one condition."

"What's that?" she asked, still glowing from our intimate encounter.

"Stay with me." I heard the words in my own voice, but I still couldn't quite believe that I'd had the courage to say them.

She drew back from me, her head falling to one side, but she didn't let go of me entirely, which I took to be a good sign. "What? What are you talking about?"

"After all this is over." I ran my hands up and down her arms, leaning back and smiling. "Stay with me. I don't have much, but, you know, we could...share it."

A flurry of emotions passed over her face. Her mouth dropped open in shock, but her eyes sparkled with excitement. Her grip on me tightened and she started to pull me close, but then her brow furrowed, her chest rising and falling in a sigh. She stopped herself, releasing me with a reluctance that almost broke my heart.

"Andy..."

I shook my head, spreading my hands wide in front of myself. "I'm not getting down on one knee or anything. Don't get me wrong. I just–" I bit off the next few words that wanted to rush out of my mouth in panic and swal-

290 ~ ROBIN JEFFREY

lowed them down, wincing a little with the effort. I shifted my weight from foot to foot. "I think it could be fun. Good. For both of us."

I wanted to tell her then. That I loved her. That I'd fallen in love with her, with her abrasive independence, with her damn, wicked smile, with everything about her, even though I knew there was so much more to learn. And that couldn't be a bad thing.

But if it wasn't a bad thing, why did she look so sad?

I slid my finger under her chin and gently lifted her head so I could look into her eyes. "Could you just...maybe...think about it?"

Much to my relief, a small smile returned to Shaye's face. She nodded. "Okay. I'll think about it."

"Promise?" I asked, only half teasing, trying to keep the hope out of my voice.

"Promise." She ran a hand through her hair, shaking it out before looking towards the bedroom door. "We better get back downstairs before Caleb or Kassandra comes looking for us. Caleb's already pissed at you – you wouldn't want to make it worse."

I waved off her concern but started towards the door all the same. "He's not pissed, he's just..." Pausing with my hand on the doorknob, I looked back at Shaye and shrugged. "Well, yeah, he's pretty pissed. But he'll get over it."

Shaye laughed and walked through the door in front of me, shaking her head. "We need to get him a girlfriend," she said, stopping in the hallway to wait for me to close the door behind us. "Or a boyfriend, whatever his preference."

"What makes you think he doesn't have one?"

"A woman can always tell." We started down the hallway back towards the main part of the house, the sounds of music and talking growing louder as we walked. "He's been on his own too long. He's all...prickly. Needs his edges sanded off."

"I'll be sure to let him know," I said in mock seriousness as we took the first few steps down the main staircase and back into the thick of the party.

~ 21 ~

CHAPTER 21

Shaye

We hadn't made it halfway down the staircase before we heard someone calling our names. Caleb was waiting at the base of the stairs, a disapproving frown scarring his otherwise handsome face.

"Christ, there you two are," he said, his foot on the bottom step as if he had just been heading up to search us out. "Andy, Kassandra's been looking for you."

Andy lifted his brows, stopping on the step above where Caleb was perched. "Oh?"

Caleb nodded, his grimace softening. "Seems like she's serious about putting you to work as a consultant. She wants your perspective on some of the mutual Nameless/Sangra Sagrada business holdings before the next round of talks tomorrow."

Andy unwound my arm from around his own. "This is a party. Can't she just enjoy herself?"

"You don't know Kassandra," retorted Caleb, slipping his hand into his trouser pocket and rolling his eyes. "This *is* how she enjoys herself."

Shaking his head, Andy stepped down off the staircase. I followed, stopping to stand next to Caleb. Andy looked back at me, his brow crooked upward. "You going to be okay?"

Caleb stepped closer to me, ghosting an arm around my shoulders. "Don't worry about Shaye - I'll keep an eye on her."

"Thanks," he said, nodding. Then, with a final smile in my direction, he disappeared into the crowd in search of the head of the Nameless.

I watched him go, smiling. Then, with a lurch, I realized that Caleb was staring at me, his eyes wide. I glanced up at him from the corner of my eyes, shaking out the bottom of my dress. "What?"

Caleb gave a light, judgmental sniff and shook his head, peering down his nose at me. "I can't leave you two alone for five minutes, can I?"

I felt a flush of heat travel from my cheeks to the tips of my ears. "Excuse me?"

Caleb rolled his eyes, but I swear I saw a smile, quick as a lightning strike, flash across his face before he turned away, saying. "Forget it." He waved for me to follow him as he headed towards one of the large doors that led out onto the lawn. "Come on - I need some air."

We walked out onto the lawn, the luscious green grass collapsing beneath our feet, and even in the dark, the grounds of the estate were stunning. The shrinking moon was reflected in the still water of the pool, which itself was illuminated from within by halogen lights. Steam hung over the heated body of water, and I allowed myself to fantasize briefly about stripping off my expensive dress and taking a dip, with nothing between me and the open air but skin. Breathing deep, I caught the scent of hyacinths from somewhere on the property.

It really was a lovely night.

"So," I drawled, swinging my hips from side to side as we stood there. "How are you holding up, Caleb?"

"Me?" he sounded genuinely surprised. I nodded and he frowned in consideration before shrugging and answering, "Fine. I guess. Can't say I care too much about all this political bullshit."

I wrinkled my nose and tilted my head to one side, studying him for a moment. "Why aren't you a member of a den anyway?"

Caleb shook his head. "Never really saw the point. I do alright on my own."

"Isn't it, you know, kind of...lonely?"

His face clouded and he shot a look at me that I was hard pressed to interpret. I had clearly hit a sore spot, but how or why I wasn't sure. "Isn't it?" I pressed.

He took a moment before answering. Finally, shaking his head, he said, "You know, there are worse things than being alone." Swallowing, he took a step back, jerking his thumb towards the buffet table inside. "I'm, uh, going to grab something to eat – you want something?"

Nodding with enthusiasm, I rubbed my belly. "Yeah, whatever you're having."

"Don't move," he cautioned as he walked backwards towards the inside of the house, his brows low over his eyes.

I held up a swearing hand. "I won't wander."

Hands falling to my sides, I craned my head back towards the sky, taking several deep breaths as I thought back over what Andy had said to me upstairs.

Stay with him?

That was crazy.

But he actually wanted that. He wanted me to stay. With him. After everything, he still wanted to be around me. Even when I couldn't offer him anything but my companionship – that was enough for him.

I was enough.

My vision swam and I felt like if I took a step I would stumble. I wanted to laugh out loud and cry at the same time, feeling the same kind of joyous terror a person experiences their first time on a roller coaster. It couldn't happen, not like this. Was this how I'd be saved? Was this my redemption?

In the midst of these thoughts, I felt someone walk up and stand beside me. I turned towards them with a heady smile, ready to find out what aperitifs Caleb had managed to snag from inside.

Lazlo nodded at me with a polite smile. "Evening."

I jerked my head back to face front. Beyond that I didn't move an inch. I didn't dare.

"Enjoying yourself?" he asked, standing beside me as if we were nothing more or less than casual acquaintances.

"I always appreciate a good party," I managed without inflection, my skin prickling at having him so close.

He made a noise of assent, taking a sip of champagne from a nearly empty glass. Then, as if it were an afterthought, he leaned over to me. "You know, now that I see you–" He indicated my body with a lift of his crystal flute. "–I don't know if I blame our Andy. You certainly are...tempting."

In a beat, he reached forward, long fingers brushing my sheaf of hair behind my ear, his face drawing close to mine, close enough that I could smell his cologne, spicy and strong. "I know what you smell like, mamacita," he murmured, the tips of his fingers trailing along the shell of my ear, his breath warm and moist against my cheek. "But I wonder what you taste like."

My mind, dizzy with joy before, went hazy with rage. I took one large step to the side, sliding out from under him. Twisting sharply on my heel, I turned to face him, smiling with all my teeth.

"Touch me again," I said, leaning forward at the waist. "And you'll find out what your balls taste like, motherfucker."

His face reddened, and even in the dim light coming through the open doors, I could see his entire body tense.

"People don't talk to me like that," he said, every word clanging like steel.

"Fuck you," I spat back brightly, flipping him off before turning away, staring resolutely out over the lawn.

I felt him step closer to me and it took every bit of my self-control not to run or whip around and punch him. Instead, I stayed stock still as he stepped in front of me, coming close enough that the sleeve of his suit brushed against my arm.

Standing in front of me, his eyes burning like two lumps of coal in the darkness, he started, "I don't know what you think you've accomplished here tonight, Miss Cassidy, but–"

"I've screwed you," I interrupted, sneering openly as I shook my head from side to side. "All your little plans have gone to shit now, haven't they? The Nameless aren't going to play your game, Cabral. And without them, you've got no war. No war, no casualties, no way to get Doña Sangre out of the way, no way to swoop in and take power." The top of my lip pulled away from my teeth, my eyes flickering over him once more before I looked past him, fixing my gaze out over the lawn. "You're stuck being a glorified secretary, Cabral. Get used to it."

Lazlo took a step forward, bringing his face within inches of mine. "You understand *nothing*."

"I understand that you want to be king of shithill mountain and you don't care who you have to kill to get up there." I reached out and dug my pointer finger into the center of his chest, grinding hard enough to leave a bruise on a normal human. "You will *never* be the head of this den, Cabral. I will *never* let that happen."

He looked down at my hand as if he very much wanted to snap it off with his teeth. Running his tongue across his lips, he took a deep breath before speaking again, glaring up at me from under his brow. "You seem to be under the misconception that you and I are enemies, Miss Cassidy. We're not. For us to be enemies, you'd have to be a player in this game. You're nothing more than a loose end that needs to be snipped."

I threw my head back and laughed, crossing my arms over my chest. "It won't matter if you kill me. You've already lost. The Nameless aren't going to take your bait. The best you can hope for is a dignified retreat. And it's more than you deserve, asshole."

He blinked, jerking back like I had flicked water in his face. Then, he smiled. "Oh. I see. You think you have nothing to lose."

I gave a derisive snort. "I know I don't."

He opened his eyes, his head falling to one side. "Even Andy?"

It was like he had punched through my ribcage and squeezed my heart in his fist. Fear, hot and painful, like a heated brand to flesh, seared through me. I gasped aloud. Biting down on the end of my tongue, I tasted blood.

That was the downside of giving yourself to someone. They could always be taken away.

I swallowed once and then again. "You–"

"You honestly think I wouldn't?" Lazlo began to circle around me. "You think his life matters to me any more than that piece of filth in the parking garage? Than any of you humans?" He came to a stop in front of me once more, sneering. "I'll do what I have to do. *Whatever* I have to do."

My parents. Jason. Andy. How many people were going to die because of me?

Lazlo shifted his weight onto his back foot, spreading his arms wide in front of him. "Let me tell you what's going to happen. I am going to kill Doña Sangre. A silver bullet to the heart. You, and by extension your Nameless backers, are going to take the blame. Sadly, you will have been spirited out of the country before I can bring you to justice."

I heard him, but it was like hearing someone shouting from the other end of the long tunnel. It wasn't until he stepped forward, grabbing me by the elbow and jerking me towards him, that I fully comprehended his meaning, his voice a low growl in my face. "Do you understand? You are going to disappear. Tonight."

Looking past him, unable to meet his gaze, I stared into the bright depths of the pool, my mind going in a thousand directions at once.

I had disappeared before. I knew how to do it. To leave in the dead of night or the quiet of early morning, to slink away and never look back, to forget what you were to people and what they were to you – it wasn't easy, but it wasn't nearly as hard as people might think. It was nothing more and nothing less than cutting your heart out of your chest and leaving it where it fell.

Could I do that again? If it meant keeping Andy safe?

I knew the answer before my mind finished asking the question.

For him? I would do anything.

"And just where am I off to?" I said, my voice hollow.

"Do you think I care?" he sneered, looking down his nose at me. "I just want you gone. A conveniently absent patsy. It'll be the first useful thing you've ever done in your life."

Swallowing down the lump in my throat, I lifted my chin, working hard to keep it from shaking. "And if I say no?"

He released me with a rough toss, flicking my arm away like he was throwing a stone across the water. "What I did to your little friend will look like a kiss goodnight compared to what would happen to Andy." Sliding his hands into his trouser pockets, he smiled, his teeth white and shiny in the reflected light from behind us. "I've been alive a long time, chica. I've seen a lot of wolves meet grisly ends. I'll make sure he suffers."

***

The rest of the night passed by in a feverish blur. The only thing in focus for me was Andy – when he was next to me, when he stepped away to talk to Kassandra, or Sylvia, when he returned. I was hyper aware of him, of the way he stood, of the patter of his speech when he switched into Spanish, of the way he fiddled with the buttons on his sleeves without even thinking about it.

All the things I would never experience again.

When he wasn't at my side, I planned my exit from his world, from his life, from Los Angeles. I didn't have any

302 ~ ROBIN JEFFREY

money, any cash, but I didn't see why that should stop me. I was confident that I could hitch my way out of town, maybe even as far as Vegas. Then I'd have to see how far my bad luck would get me.

Before I knew it, the party was breaking up. Andy and I were alone in the third Nameless convoy car, and his presence was like a sliver of ice against the back of my neck, delicious and painful at the same time. I kept my attention fixed out the window.

The perfectly manicured streets of Bel Air wound by outside. Andy and I didn't speak, the only sound in the car was the muffled sound of the radio and the gentle woosh of air conditioning cycling through the cab. If he found my reticence odd or concerning, Andy made no indication, seemingly content to sit back and enjoy the ride back to Caleb's place. He was probably just relieved that no one had died tonight.

My stomach churned and I grimaced at my own reflection. What did I care if Doña Sangre met a bloody end? What did I care about any of them? They had nothing to do with me. I had to take care of what was important to me, the only way I knew how. There was no other option.

Right?

"Andy?"

He made a noise of assent in the back of his throat. I turned away from the tinted window, but I couldn't look him in the face, settling instead for staring at the tops of his shoes. "Why did you say...what you said before?"

He didn't answer immediately, and I risked a glance at him. The bridge of his nose wrinkled, and he shifted in his seat to look at me more directly. "When?"

I blinked once, slowly, before answering. "Upstairs. About us."

Andy flushed, casting a glance up at the silhouetted driver. His voice dropped, but there was still a ghost of a nervous smile on his face as he asked, "You want to talk about that now?"

Drawing in a deep breath through my nose, I shook my head. "It's important. I need to know."

Something in my tone must have conveyed the gravity of the situation because his smile vanished. He leaned back into his seat, his eyes roaming over my face for a moment before he spoke. "I said it because...Her... her name was Melanie Harper."

I stared at him in confusion.

He took a deep breath and let it out slowly. "She was the woman who I told – the girl I fell in love with." He edged across the seat closer to me, his eyes never leaving mine. "You need to understand – I couldn't protect her. Not from me, not from what I am, not from my world. I failed her. She died. My family killed her."

I couldn't stop myself – I reached out and grabbed his hand, my heart throbbing as if it had been stabbed. "Andy–"

His hand fell heavy over mine and he shook his head from side to side, still watching my face with all the intentness of a gambler watching the final seconds of a race. "I told myself I was never going to let that happen again. You

"We're right behind you," said Caleb at length, his tone strident. "Andy, don't do anything stupid – wait for–"

"Just hurry!" I shouted, before hanging up and shoving the phone back in my pocket.

"Andy," said Shaye, watching me from the opposite corner of the backseat, her arms outstretched to keep her upright. "What's our plan here?"

"*Our* plan?" I shook my head. "*You're* going to stay in the car. *I'm* going to head into the house and let security know what's going on, and then hopefully they can track down Cabral before it's too late."

"And if it is too late?" she pressed, her wide eyes earnest.

It was something I couldn't allow myself to imagine. Emilia was family. Lazlo had been a father to me. What would I do if she died at his hand?

Something of the conflict in me must have shown on my face because Shaye's expression hardened. She gave a sharp nod. "I'm coming with you."

"Shaye, por el amor de Dios, I don't have time to argue with you right now–" I started, but she interrupted me with a growl.

"Then you better not argue with me, huh?" She reached out to me and grabbed my arm tightly. "I'm coming with you. If that woman gets hurt, it's my fault. I'm not going to let that happen. No one is going to get hurt because of me ever again."

The Escalade tore up the drive, skidding to a halt in front of the darkened den house, still and silent except for a handful of clean up staff milling about the outside, packing up catering vans and carrying out bags of trash. The car slowed, but I didn't wait for it to stop, throwing open the back door and hitting the ground at speed.

"Stay behind me," I shouted back, running for the still-open front door.

As we sprinted inside, I was immediately struck by how utterly empty the building felt and my spirits began to sink.

"Where the fuck is everyone?" whispered Shaye, her voice still echoing off the cavernous ceilings.

I shook my head. "This must be Cabral's doing. Shit. We have to move."

It looked like we were on our own for now. I thought briefly of Caleb's entreaty to wait to make a move until he and the Nameless arrived as we tore through the main common room towards the staircase. When a phalanx of security guards stepped out of the darkness from either side of Shaye and myself, clearly intent on stopping us from going any further, I realized that I had made a mistake by not listening to my older and wiser friend.

One of the guards lunged for me, and although I did my best to avoid him, he grappled me, wrapping his arms around mine and holding my hands tight behind my back. "¡No entiendes!" I shouted, pulling and fighting against the guard. "¡Doña Sangre – ella está en peligro! Tienes que–"

"Get your fucking hands off me, you stupid piece of shit!" Shaye struggled to free herself from the grip of a second guard, who was holding her by the arm, but she might as well have been trying to wriggle her way out of handcuffs.

"I suppose your pet told you my plan," he said once he got some of his breath back.

I nodded.

He sniffed hard, trying to draw some blood back into his nose. "She... she was supposed to disappear."

"She's not going anywhere."

Lazlo gritted his teeth. "Fine," he spat out the word, rolling his shoulders back as he drew himself up. "It doesn't matter. Maybe it's better this way. They'll find her here, with Emilia, and they'll know that what I say is true. That Shaye killed our beloved la Doña with the help of the Nameless before I could stop her."

"Walk away, Lazlo," I demanded. "It's over."

"You know... it doesn't have to go like this," said Lazlo between ragged breaths. He wiped sweat from his brow, the saltwater soaking into the white linen sleeve of his jacket, mixing with the blood. "We - we could help each other, Andy."

"Why would I help you?" I said, my upper lip pulling away from my teeth in a disgusted sneer.

"You want to protect the den - your family." He knocked his fist against his chest, puffing himself up. "I want the same thing."

The woman on the floor shifted, letting out a low moan as she struggled to return to consciousness. My eyes darted between her and Lazlo, settling finally on the barrel of the gun in his hand. "Starting a war?" I demanded, clenching my fists at my sides. "How exactly does that keep us safe?"

Lazlo scoffed, and as he turned to face me, the barrel of the gun lowered ever so slightly. "Please, Andy. You know as well as anyone that Sangre Sagrada is weak. It has been for years, ever since Emilia took over from her father. We can't let the old ways die, we can't abandon who and what we are." He waved his free hand between us, scoffing, "We're werewolves, damn it. We don't obey the laws of nature, let alone human beings. The Sacrament is part of our culture. If we turn away from it, if we try to tame the beasts within, we will only grow weaker."

"You'd tear everything down around our heads for the Sacrament?" I stared at him in disbelief.

"To keep us strong? I'd set the world on fire." He met my gaze evenly. "Help me, Andy. Once I'm head of Sangre Sagrada, I see no reason why you shouldn't be welcomed back into the den with open–"

As he was ranting, Lazlo lowered the gun a little more, the barrel now aimed just past the toe of his shoe.

This was my shot – it might be my only shot.

"¡Jódete!", I growled as I charged Lazlo, my shoulder aimed at the center of his chest. I heard the gun clatter to the floor, but my attention was fixed wholly on Lazlo, who had wrapped his arms around my shoulders as we stumbled back. We spun in a tight circle, Lazlo's claws ripping into the back of my jacket while I jerked up, catching him hard under the chin in an attempt to break his grip on me. I felt his jaw crack, and he lurched away from me with a pained growl, but not without first digging his claws into my skin, leaving long bloody streaks across my ribcage.

~ 23 ~

CHAPTER 23

Shaye

Skirt of my dress pulled up to my knees, I sat with my legs plunged into the warm water of the heated pool. I kicked my feet slowly back and forth, watching the ripples spread out from me, and was only partially aware of the hubbub of activity going on inside the Bel Air house and out in the drive in front. Additional Sangre Sagrada security had been called in from elsewhere in the city to deal with the traitors at the house, those that were still alive, of course. Everyone seemed to have a job to do, whether it was cleaning up the grounds or patching up the fighters or securing the defectors.

I didn't have a job. I didn't want one.

Andy had stayed with Doña Sangre even after medical personnel arrived to tend to her wounds. They talked qui-

326 ~ ROBIN JEFFREY

arm and pulled me tight against his side. "No. Not without Shaye."

I stared up at him in utter confusion. His den, his family, meant everything to Andy. Had meant everything to Andy. Being ostracized, disowned, had nearly destroyed him. This was his way back in, and he was refusing it – because he wanted to be with me?

Andy glanced down at me and smiled shyly, his beautiful dark eyes bright in the dim early morning light.

Oh. He...he was in love with me. Me.

I was grinning before I knew how to hide, smiling like a child, and it wasn't until Doña Sangre spoke that I remembered we weren't standing there alone.

"Of course. If she wants this life, that is."

My smile dimmed. I looked at Doña Sangre. "Do I...have a choice?"

The den leader nodded. "You *can* walk away," assured Emilia gently. "After what you've done for us tonight, we won't chase you. You could be free."

Free. There was a time when I thought that freedom was the only thing that would keep me safe. When I thought that freedom was the only thing that would keep the people that I loved safe from me. But independence had turned into isolation and freedom had swallowed me whole.

Maybe it was time to try belonging to something for a change. Like a family. Like a den.

"I think..." A manic trill of laughter escaped from me, and I swallowed it down before it went on for too long, flushing a little at the sensation of so many eyes on me. "I think this might actually be where I belong."

I didn't believe in happily ever afters. After all, I lived in Los Angeles – I knew better than most that happily ever afters were paper thin, made on dirty back lots with filmy gauze over unforgiving lenses. But there, in that moment, with Andy looking at me with undisguised adoration, with having gained something like a family for the first time in over a decade, with having beat the bad guy and saved the day – it all felt like the closest thing to real life movie magic I'd ever experienced. If I hadn't known better, I'd have said I was drunk – but the truth was I was head over heels in love.

A thought occurred to me, and my feet touched ground again with a rapidity that made my head spin. "I *really* don't want to be a werewolf though," I said quickly, slicing my hand through the air. "I have enough trouble shaving as it is."

Doña Sangre shook her head, her lips pulled down into an exaggerated frown. "Not a requirement."

I cocked my head to one side. "Shaving? Or the werewolf thing?"

She shrugged, her frown flipping into a smile. "Either."

Andy leaned towards me as if he were about to kiss me, but stopped halfway, his eyes widening as he turned his attention once more to Emilia. "Ah, there is one thing you should know, Emilia..."

He looked back at me and lifted an eyebrow, gesturing towards Emilia as if prompting me.

"Oh, yeah!" I said, starting when I realized what it was Andy wanted me to say. "I, uh, I see the future from time to time. Would that–that be useful? At all?"

Emilia stared at me, her face blank. Then, slowly, a grin spread across her lips. "Oh, extremely."

READ ON FOR A PEEK AT BOOK 3 OF THE NIGHT SERIES

LONELY IS THE NIGHT

CHAPTER 1

Vi

Like most people who lived and worked in Las Vegas, it wasn't at all unusual for me to wake up from a sound sleep at around three in the afternoon to start my "day". The last night of the change was always rough for me, so it wasn't unusual for me to wake up the next day after a full moon feeling like the floor of a party bus. It wasn't even unusual for me to wake up with a stranger in the bed beside me.

The gun pressed against the side of my head, though? That was different. That was cause for some concern.

I knew it was a gun before I opened my eyes, familiar with the sensation of a gun barrel kissing my temple. Even if I hadn't been, the click of the chamber being primed would've clued me into exactly what was happening on the other side of my lids.

"Where is it?"

I took a deep breath in through my nose. The person kneeling on the mattress beside me shifted and pressed the gun more firmly against my skull. "Don't try anything cute. Just tell me where it is."

"And what?" I said. "You won't shoot me?" I eased my eyes open and looked askance at the male werewolf who had somehow gotten through all my security. "Please."

Hidden behind sunglasses and a balaclava, I could see nothing of the man's expression. He was tall, lean, and under different circumstances he might have been my type. As it was, though, I didn't appreciate the way he dragged the barrel of the gun down my neck, across my collar bone, and, pulling down the rumpled top of my negligee, rested the mouth of the gun against the top of my left breast, just above my heart.

"I can shoot you now," he said, the hint of an eastern seaboard accent thickening his vowels. "Or you can buy yourself a few minutes and give me what I want."

Rolling my eyes, I let loose with a deep sigh. I wasn't in the mood for this. "How about I give you this instead, asshole?" I countered, pulling one of my hands out from under the pillow where it had been resting, revealing the flashing panic button I had pressed some minutes ago when I had first smelled him in the room.

His attention snapped to the panic button, and he let out a curse in a language I didn't recognize, recoiling from me. Before I had a chance to take advantage of his distraction, though, he had regrouped, bringing the butt of the gun down hard into my forehead.

Crying out in pain, my vision went black for a split second. I dropped the panic button and gripped my head instinctively, only vaguely aware of the crashing sound of the door to my suite being kicked in.

The weight of a body on my mattress vanished abruptly. My vision returned to me just in time to watch the intruder force open the venetian style windows with his shoulder, shattering one of the panes of glass as he stumbled out onto my balcony. His gloved hand rested against the balustrade just long enough for him to vault over the railing and disappear into the blinding afternoon sun. But it was all the time Saint, my head of security, needed to aim and fire their gun, missing the back of his appendage by mere millimeters, taking out a chunk of marble instead.

Gun still at the ready, Saint rushed through my room, wisps of blonde hair flying away from their sharp, scowling face. They leaned over the balcony, let off another couple of rounds, and then, face screwing up, shouted, "Damn it!"

Hurrying back into my bedroom, they pressed the comm device on their belt, speaking quickly into the microphone/ receiver that rested by their ear. "Everyone! Runner, balaclava, desert camo, heading across the roof next door – someone try to cut him off!"

"They won't get him," I hissed, more out of pain than anger, one hand still pressed to my forehead, blood seeping between my fingers and dripping onto my expensive silk sheets. "He's good enough to get in here, he's good enough to get away."

Spinning around, Saint took quick stock of my physical state and, seeing that I was mostly unharmed, relaxed out of their fighting stance and into angered annoyance, striding away from the window with a growl.

"Goddamnit, If I've said it once, I've said it a hundred times," fumed Saint, settling onto the mattress at my side, sliding their weapon back into their shoulder holster. "You need another werewolf as your bodyguard, not me. A wolf could've followed–"

I scoffed, pulling my hand away from the gash in my head and examining the amount of blood on it with a frown. "And if I've said it once, I've said it a thousand times," I said, shaking my head. "I trust *you*, Saint. Find me a wolf that knows half as much as you and won't sell me out and I'll hire them. But until then, you're stuck with me."

Frowning deeply, I was surprised to see their blue eyes begin to shine with barely controlled tears. They let out a heavy sigh, tongue probing the inside of their cheek, but stayed sitting there on the edge of my bed, staring at me. "Sometimes I wonder if you have a death wish, Vi. Or do you just really not realize what you getting hurt would do to me?"

Their concern sobered me, for once. "I don't have a death wish," I snapped, hiding my other hand under my pillow, hoping Saint wouldn't notice how badly it was shaking. "And nobody is ever going to hurt me again."

Their head fell to one side. They blinked slowly and then, perhaps sensing that this was a subject not to be pushed at this time, forced a sickly smile onto their thin lips. Scooting across the bed, they took up the corner of my gray sheets and wiped some of the blood away from my forehead. "This gash says different," they said, lifting their brows pointedly.

I didn't pull away, but tsked all the same as they dabbed at the edges of the wound with the bedsheet. "Oh, come on. Don't fuss – it'll heal up in a few hours. No harm done."

"This time." Saint fixed me with a worried stare, their brows drawing up to a point. "Boss, I don't know how long we can keep this up."

I took a deep breath and let it out slowly. "Yeah. Yeah, I know." My gaze fell to the floor. "My luck is going to run out eventually."

The truth was, I'd been winning pots with a fistful of bad cards through sheer bluff alone for a while now. If luck had a way of balancing the scales, I was due for a run of some dangerously bad karma any day now.

"Any word from Hayes?" I asked hopefully.

They shook their head. "Not yet."

Tossing the bedsheets off me with a growl, I launched myself out of bed. "Christ! It's a simple yes or no question. What the hell is taking him so long?"

"If he lets you do this–" They started, but I cut them off with a roll of my eyes and a wave of my hand.

"Come on, he will. He totally will." I hurried into the ostentatious bathroom that sprawled off one side of the suite, running a soft blue hand towel under some warm water before pressing it to my head wound. "The Aces have a cash flow problem. This would solve that."

Saint pressed on, rising to their feet and standing in the doorway of the washroom. "*If* he lets you do this, it's going to ruffle a lot of feathers. There's going to be questions, accusations of disloyalty–"

I grimaced, only partially from the sting of water in my wound. "Hey, since when have we ever cared about shit like that?"

They gave a derisive snort, crossing their arms over their chest. "Since when have *you* ever cared about shit like that? Never. The den, though? They've always been concerned about the politics of it all." Saint took on a professorial tone, and the irony of a human explaining the intricacies of den politics to me was not lost. "The Aces are a small, relatively new family. They've accrued a lot of power and influence in a short amount of time. There are certain other dens that would love to see us disappear."

Saint was right of course. The danger wasn't just from den outsiders looking to get their hands on what I had – it was from within as much as without, from the other lieutenants who saw me as a threat, as a boat rocker, as a ladder climber.

They were right to be worried. I was all those things. And I had no intention of staying where I was, of knowing my place. I was a child of Las Vegas and Las Vegas never did anything half-way. Never went for mere showboating when spectacle was right there within reach. Bigger, louder, glitzier – excess was the name of the game, getting so big that nothing could bring you down, that touching the ground was unthinkable. That was Vegas.

"The meadows in the middle of the desert," I muttered, half to Saint and half to myself. "We're not supposed to exist. But here we are." Staring at my face in the mirror, I wiped the gash on my head dry and dropped the towel into the sink, smirking. "An affront to God herself."

"Didn't know you believed in God," muttered Saint, their eyes fixed on the back of my head.

"I don't," I lied, my smile widening as I turned from the mirror and headed for the door. "Cheer up, Saint," I chirped, patting them on the shoulder as I moved past them and back into my suite. "Things will roll our way soon. I can feel it."

ABOUT THE AUTHOR

Robin Jeffrey was born in Cheyenne, Wyoming to a psychologist and a librarian, giving her a love of literature and a consuming interest in the inner workings of people's minds, which have served her well as she pursues a career in creative writing. She holds a BA in English from the University of Washington and as MS in Library Science from the University of Kentucky. She has been published in various journals around the world as well as on websites like *The Mary Sue* and *Introvert, Dear*. She currently resides in Bremerton, Washington. More of her work can be found on her website, RobinJeffreyAuthor.com

Robin would like to thank her amazing readers – the long term, rabid fans, and the brand-new devotees who have found their way to her with this book. She writes to connect with each and every one of you. If she's managed to bring a little joy into *your* life, then *her* life has gotten a little richer. Thank you, thank you, thank you.

*Reviews are the lifeblood of authors everywhere. If you enjoyed reading **Bloody is the Night (The Night, Book 2)**, please consider taking a few moments to leave a review on Amazon, Goodreads, or wherever you'd like to share your thoughts! You can also sign up for Robin's newsletter or follow her on social media – she'd love to stay in touch!*

Milton Keynes UK
Ingram Content Group UK Ltd.
UKHW030757121124
451094UK00014B/1133

9 798218 504205